BURY HER BONES

A GRIPPING SERIAL KILLER THRILLER

DANIEL PADAVONA

GET A FREE BOOK!

I'm a pretty nice guy once you look past the grisly images in my head. Most of all, I love connecting with awesome readers like you.

Join my VIP Reader Group and get a FREE serial killer thriller for your Kindle.

Get My Free Book

www.danpadavona.com/thriller-readers-vip-group/

1

Monsters are real. We see them on the evening news —murderers, rapists, child predators. Though we construct walls and moats around our families to keep them safe, the danger always finds a way past the barricades.

Darcy Gellar, former profiler with the FBI's Behavioral Analysis Unit, must keep her children safe, for the monsters are coming for them again. They're here in Scarlet River, Georgia, and it's only a matter of time before they rear their ugly faces.

It's the fourth day of December. Darcy and her fourteen-year-old daughter, Jennifer, walk the aisles of a small southern-based grocery store with dirty, scuffed floors that haven't seen a mop in days. With her long brunette hair pulled into a ponytail, Jennifer is the spitting image of Darcy as a teenager. Her daughter's demeanor can shift from jovial to furious without warning, a growing issue as Jennifer closes in on her fifteenth birthday. Darcy can't blame Jennifer. She'd uprooted her family for the second time in half a year, and her daughter had just made friends in their new village when the Full Moon Killer invaded their lives and forced them to flee.

Two weeks have passed since serial killer Richard Chaney abducted Jennifer in Genoa Cove, North Carolina, or Darkwater Cove as the locals refer to it because of the black shadowed waters below the cliffs. Two weeks since Darcy and her old FBI partner, Eric Hensel, shot and killed Chaney. Jennifer won't talk about it, won't even acknowledge the nightmare happened, but Darcy can see the fear in the slump of the girl's shoulders, as though she cowers from a shadow coming up behind her. Her nails, usually garish and manicured, are gnawed to the quick, pink and angry. The teenager seems muted and suppressed as she reaches for organic oatmeal and places it in the cart.

A scrawny, thirty-something woman pushes a cart spilling over with processed food and snacks. The woman steals a glance at Darcy and Jennifer when they aren't looking, but Darcy spies the woman from the corner of her eye and shifts a step closer to Jennifer. Darcy and her family are outsiders, strangers. This is cousin Laurie's town. Darcy and her family should still be in Genoa Cove, cobbling together the pieces of their shattered autumn, but fate calls them to Scarlet River.

When Laurie told Darcy about the man stalking her, Darcy urged her cousin to go to the police. Then Laurie discovered the smiley face, the signature of the Full Moon Killer, painted in bleeding reds on the back of her house, just as Darcy and Amy Yang found on the backs of their houses before the Darkwater Cove murders tore apart the village. The nightmare had begun again.

Except Michael Rivers, the legendary murderer Darcy shot and captured three years ago, is in prison outside of Buffalo, New York, and couldn't have painted the symbol on Laurie's house. Just as Rivers paid Richard Chaney and Bronson Severson out of his unlimited funds to butcher Darcy and her family in North Carolina, he's contracted another killer to terrorize Laurie. Rivers vowed to destroy Darcy and everyone close to her. He means to keep his promise.

Jennifer never hides her disdain for being in Georgia. As they wheel the shopping cart through the store, Jennifer keeps hissing at Darcy as though there's a leak in the heating vents.

"You'll have high blood pressure before you're twenty," Darcy says, grabbing a head of lettuce off the shelf.

"Whatever. Why did we come here? If Laurie is in trouble, she should call the police."

"We're family, and family supports each other. Besides, there are no police out here. Only the county sheriff, and he's way up the road in a town called Millport."

"Sounds more like a disgusting whole grain bread than a real town."

Not that it matters if the authorities don't take the danger seriously. Had the Genoa Cove PD reacted sooner, Amy Yang would still be alive, and Hunter and Jennifer wouldn't have experienced a night of horror, courtesy of the Full Moon Killer's henchmen. She pictures Amy's body strewn on the shore of Darkwater Cove, her throat sliced open by the murderer's knife and the smiley face branded on her neck.

When Darcy turns the cart down the beverages aisle, she catches a reflection in the glass. Painted ghost-like over the beer containers is a large, bearded man with his belly rolling out of his red flannel shirt and over his jeans. A fine line exists between paranoia and awareness of her surroundings, and Darcy has learned to detect people following her. Jennifer, unaware of the man, slides the glass door open. A cool breath of wintry air puffs out as Jennifer grabs a six pack of bottled soda. When she bends over and slides the soda into the bottom of the cart, the man leers at Jennifer from behind and makes a hungry sound in his throat.

"Let's go," Darcy says, wishing Agent Hensel and her son,

Hunter, weren't across town at the outdoor and camping store. She appreciates Hensel taking a week of annual leave from the FBI to watch her family's back in Scarlet River but doesn't understand why the FBI won't send a team here.

"What's the matter?" Jennifer asks as Darcy locks elbows with her daughter and nudges her forward.

Darcy wants to tell Jennifer not to turn around. It's too late. A six pack of beer dangling from his hand, the man follows them around the corner into another aisle like a hungry dog trailing a cart of raw meat.

Jennifer spins around and picks up her pace, Darcy relieved her daughter doesn't fire a scathing remark at the man. After they turn down the bread aisle, the man appears behind the display case of hamburger buns. Darcy snatches a loaf of oat bread off the shelf and tosses it into the cart. The wheels squeak and wobble as Darcy pushes faster.

The man materializes in the canned goods aisle while Darcy loads the cart with soups.

"Who's the creep?" Jennifer asks a little too loudly.

Darcy cranes her head and searches for a store manager.

"Don't look at him. He won't hurt us inside the store. And keep your voice down."

Darcy worries what will happen after they pay for their groceries and wheel the cart into the parking lot. Passing the customer service desk, she searches for a friendly face behind the counter and instead finds a sullen woman stacking returns in a disorganized pile.

Shooting a look over her shoulder, Darcy grabs her phone. When she finds Hensel's number, the man blends into the crowd until it swallows him. The cashier, a boy with a pink and red landscape of acne across his forehead, rings them up and stuffs their food into brittle paper bags that will rip before Darcy gets them inside Laurie's farmhouse. The boy's face colors when he glances at Jennifer, and he avoids eye contact while he fumbles with the bags and wrestles them into the cart.

Outside, Darcy dodges a muscle car of teens speeding through the parking lot. The Prius blinks its lights when she presses the key fob. Unlocking the trunk, she helps Jennifer load the bags inside. But as Darcy rounds the car and opens her door, she sees the man staring at them through the windshield of a red SUV.

Before she slides inside, the man climbs out of the SUV. He's walking toward the Prius, and there can be no mistake in his arrow-straight trajectory that he's coming at Darcy. A young worker pushing a train of shopping carts blocks Darcy from fleeing. Jennifer, who spies the man in the mirror, swivels on the seat and urges her mother to get in the car.

To the man's surprise, Darcy walks right at him. With a van between Darcy and the Prius, Jennifer can't see what her mother intends. And Darcy wants it this way.

"You got a problem, lady?"

Darcy glares bullets into the man. He stands two heads taller than her, his chest barrel-thick.

"I don't like it when a grown man follows my underage daughter."

He steps closer. She smells the sour perfume of beer and fast food on his breath.

"No harm in looking."

His grin displays a jaw full of crooked teeth pockmarked by decay.

"Sir, I don't want any trouble. She's only fourteen. Leave my daughter alone and walk away. Please."

Is it Darcy's imagination, or does he smack his lips when she mentions her daughter's age? He nods at the license plate on the Prius.

"North Carolina. That where you're from? Because you talk like a New Yorker."

"Where I'm from is hardly your business."

"She don't look like no fourteen-year-old I know. They make all the girls that sweet up north?"

He's on top of her now, his work boots brushing against the toes of her sneakers. She searches for an ally in the parking lot, someone to diffuse the situation if it spins out of control. The boy pushing the carts vanishes inside the store, while an elderly woman struggles with a grocery bag on the far side of the lot.

"I'm leaving now. Stay away from my daughter."

When Darcy spins around, the man snatches her by the arm.

"You fucking bitch—"

His mouth hangs open when she pulls the gun. It's a Glock-22, the same model she carried with the FBI, and the muzzle points at his ample belly.

"Don't touch me."

His arm drops to his side as he takes a step backward. There's fear in his eyes, but something primordial lurks behind the sneer. This is a man who wouldn't think twice about raping Darcy and burying her in a deep, dark hole nobody would come across.

"No need to start a war. Put the gun away before you hurt yourself, lady. Someone like you is more likely to shoot a hole in her foot than defend herself."

"I know what I'm doing. Now walk back to your vehicle like we just finished a nice conversation, and we won't have any trouble."

His body tenses, and for a terrifying moment she's sure he'll call her bluff and lunge at Darcy. Beat her to death in the parking lot and leave her for the vultures to pick at.

Then he walks backward, his eyes fixed on her.

"I'll be seeing you around."

He flashes his wicked grin and climbs into the SUV.

Darcy's body trembles as she hurries back to the car, praying Jennifer didn't see the altercation. She holsters the gun and conceals it beneath her jacket before opening the door. In the cold silence of the car, Jennifer stares at Darcy.

"What did he say? He didn't hurt you, did he?"

"Don't worry about him. There wasn't any trouble. He'll leave us alone now."

Jennifer begins to ask another question, but Darcy's white-knuckle grasp of the steering wheel dissuades her daughter from prying. Darcy cuts across the lot and heads toward Main Street, one eye on the mirror until she's sure the red SUV isn't trailing them.

Scarlet River looks like a hundred different small southern villages. A white-pillared mansion with a steep staircase holds the advisory council for historic preservation. A Baptist church, also white, juts its steeple above the trees at the corner of Main and Standish.

"Hunter and Mr. Hensel finished at the store and are heading to Laurie's," Jennifer says after checking her messages. "Should I tell them something about that man?"

Darcy casts a worried glance at the mirrors and doesn't see anyone following.

"No need to worry everyone. He's gone now."

"He was a creep."

Darcy nods. If the man had ogled her from across the store, she would have brushed it off and ignored him. But threats against her daughter push Darcy to a higher level of anxiety.

Turning down Main Street, Darcy studies the ma and pa hardware, clothing, and office supply stores. Scarlet River appears locked in a time warp. Even the hairstyles and clothes look thirty years out of date, the little town clinging to the past. An old-fashioned ice cream parlor gleams on the corner. Darcy pulls into the lot and nestles the Prius between two 4x4 trucks. Jennifer gives her mother a cockeyed glance.

"Ice cream for lunch?"

"Why not?" Darcy says with a shrug. "You aren't going vegan on me, are you?"

"Mom, it's the twenty-first century. They make vegan ice cream these days."

Darcy narrows her eyes at the sea-blue storefront.

"Fat chance you'll find vegan ice cream in this town."

Inside the parlor, Darcy stands in line behind a mother with two young boys clinging to each hand. Jennifer wanders to the wall and reads the posters. All the local bands advertising upcoming shows seem to be flavors of country or western. Ted is selling his Subaru for two thousand dollars, and there's an apartment for rent on Harrington Avenue. Jennifer stops on one poster, fastened at the top and bottom by tacks. She removes the bottom tack and angles the poster toward the window light. It's a photograph of a missing girl. Jennifer pulls the picture off the wall.

"Leave it there," Darcy says.

Jennifer scowls and refastens the tack.

They sit at the rear of the parlor under a rotating fan that blows the sweet scents around the room. Darcy digs into a banana split sundae while Jennifer nurses a dripping waffle cone of pumpkin praline. Before she eats too much, Jennifer snaps a photograph of the ice cream cone.

"Nice picture, but don't think about uploading that to Instagram."

Jennifer tosses the phone on the table.

"I might as well not have a phone. It's not like you let me use it for anything. Just take it."

"If you insist."

Darcy reaches for the phone. Jennifer snatches it away and stuffs it into her pocket.

"This is ridiculous. Why can't I talk to my friends?"

"We've been over this."

Darcy's rules are ironclad. No social media posting, and no phone calls or texts outside of family.

"*You've* been over this. *We* haven't discussed anything, because nobody has a say but you."

Darcy switches the subject before Jennifer erupts. She's already drawn eyes from the customers waiting on their orders. The ice cream works its magic. Jennifer can't stay angry.

Darcy brought Jennifer here to talk, but she's content to leave well enough alone while her daughter indulges in this rare treat. When was the last time the family went out for dinner or did something spontaneous and grabbed dessert? As far as Darcy can tell, Jennifer didn't see her pull the gun and has no idea how close she'd come to a violent confrontation. For several minutes, Darcy watches the entryway, convinced the bearded man will shove the front door open and block their escape. But he doesn't come.

The mother of the two boys sits cross-legged at the next table, checking her phone while her children lick chocolate ice cream cones. An elderly couple with two straws share a raspberry milkshake. The other customers take their orders to go.

The tension rolls off Jennifer's shoulders by the time they finish their ice cream, and when the conversation percolates, she doesn't complain about the friends she misses back in North Carolina or why they're in a backwoods town with spotty cell service and no shoe outlets. Jennifer never knew Tyler, the father who died when she was a year old, and she's shouldered the burden of having a mother whose morbid claim to fame is surviving a stab wound from the most feared serial killer of the last decade. Like Hunter, Jennifer raised herself when Mom struggled with anti-anxiety pill addiction and developed a paralyzing fear of the dark. Jennifer is a fighter, a survivor. A little rough around the edges, but Darcy is damn proud of her daughter.

Darcy avoids the real reason they're here, but the truth sits in the corner like a corpse gathering flies. The stalker. She prays she's wrong, that Laurie's stalker is a shy guy who can't bring himself to ask for her phone number, and the painting on the house is an elaborate prank by someone who reads too many Internet news sites and craves attention. Not likely.

After they finish eating, Jennifer drops a dollar in the tip jar and eyes the picture of the missing girl again. Orange and yellow leaves drop from the trees and bury lawns as they drive through the town's residential area. The houses become stunted and ramshackle, and soon the population thins and the pine forest leans over the road from both sides like giants massing for war.

Laurie's house sits five miles outside of town in a grassy meadow, flanked by forest for as far as the eye can see. Humpbacked, tree-smothered hills tower toward a gray, low hanging sky that threatens rain. Despite the calendar, the eastern United States is under the grip of an early winter. A blizzard cripples New England, and Virginia has a three-inch coating of snow and ice. Clutching her jacket shut against the chill, it isn't difficult for Darcy to imagine flurries on the horizon. But what most unsettles Darcy is the isolation. There's a difference between Genoa Cove and the outskirts of Scarlet River. Back home, people heard if you screamed.

Inside the vale, a perpetual wind sets the tall grass in motion. To Darcy, the meadow appears to laugh at her as she stops the car in the dirt driveway and opens the trunk. The fresh coat of white against the back of the house seems out-of-place amid the faded, chipping paint. Darcy can't decide if the smiley face is bleeding through the new paint or her subconscious fills in the details.

Laurie, thirty and carrying a few extra pounds on her hips from when Darcy last saw her, shields her face from the wind and pulls blonde curls behind her ear. Darcy's cousin is an unsolvable puzzle. Though high cheekbones and curves in all the right places made her popular during high school, she's a loner, a recluse, the product of her parents' messy divorce. That unwelcome surprise blew up in Laurie's face when she was twelve and forever altered the trajectory of her life.

Laurie works for a small accounting firm in Scarlet River, a creative use of her theater arts degree, but she lives where the closest neighbor is a half-mile up the road. One look at the little house in the meadow and Darcy might assume Laurie is a survivalist living off the land, waiting for the apocalypse to hit. But she's the furthest thing from a survivalist. Instead of chopping wood from the acres of forest, she has a man deliver firewood for the stove every November, and a jumbled cord of unstacked pieces grows out of the earth. Mother Nature rained on the wood the last two weeks, and if Darcy doesn't help Laurie stack the wood soon, the elements will dump a few inches of snow on the pile by New Year's.

"I have food in the house, you know?" Laurie says, gazing at the bags.

"Not enough to feed two teenagers."

The bag of canned goods rips on the stairs, and Darcy sets the groceries on the kitchen table a second before the paper shreds.

The familiar scents of ash and coals waft off the walls, ingrained in the furniture and rugs. A small fire in the stove blankets the chill as the rained-on fuel pops and snarls.

A car horn announces Agent Hensel and Hunter. Darcy's

relationship with her former FBI partner is complex and tangled. While he's intent on protecting Darcy and her kids, he's hypercritical of Darcy's dependency on the anti-anxiety medication. Having Hensel under the same roof will feel like living with an overbearing parent, an experience the forty-one-year-old Darcy doesn't wish to revisit, but having a law enforcement agent watching their backs is a luxury she appreciates.

Darcy peeks out the door window and watches Hunter carry two shopping bags while Hensel wields a pair of hunting rifles over his shoulder. Darcy doesn't like to see Hunter near a weapon, but circumstances require the kids learn to handle guns.

The wind rattles the panes and whistles over the roof. Scarlet River celebrated an elongated summer until Thanksgiving, but the chill of winter's approach has followed the Gellar family from North Carolina.

Hunter shivers and blows on his hands inside the kitchen. Though he turned eighteen a week before Halloween, the wiry, blonde teen wears a child's face as though he's regressing. Unlike Jennifer, Hunter has no qualms over leaving North Carolina. He never fit with the elite, entitled students of Genoa Cove High School, though he left his girlfriend, Bethany, behind. He misses Bethany, and Darcy suspects Hunter calls and texts her. Long-distance relationships rarely work, especially among teenagers, and Darcy fears it's a matter of time before Bethany meets someone new and breaks Hunter's heart.

"How was the store?" Darcy asks Hunter as he sets the bags down.

"Wicked cool. They had stuff you'd never see in Genoa Cove. Agent Hensel says maybe we can go camping next summer."

Hensel suppresses a grin when Darcy looks at him from the corner of her eye. Hunter hasn't had a father figure in his life since Tyler's fatal aneurysm, but as much as a camping trip would please her, they won't be taking any trips as long as Michael Rivers is alive. When Darcy doesn't voice her approval, Hunter shares a look with Jennifer and drops his shoulders. Both kids' consternations grow each day Darcy forbids them to use social media. Too many people watch Darcy's every move, and some of those people have bad intentions. She follows a website dedicated to serial killers, and though the admins delete the threads, new posts update site visitors with the locations of Darcy and her children. Some are wrong and the result of hearsay and conjecture. Others are frighteningly accurate.

Jennifer isn't happy when Hensel ushers the kids outside. Surrounded by open land, Hensel can teach Hunter and Jennifer to fire a rifle without leaving Laurie's property. As Darcy stocks the cupboards, she watches through the window. She winces when Jennifer, under Hensel's watchful eye, bumbles the rifle in shaking hands and aims the muzzle at the sky.

"Take the kids back to North Carolina," Laurie says, standing on tiptoes to shove the pasta onto the top shelf of the pantry.

"Genoa Cove isn't our home anymore. I already put the house on the market."

"That was fast."

Darcy shrugs.

"There's nothing for us in Genoa Cove except bad memories."

"What about school?"

"The kids won't fall behind in their studies. I'm home-schooling them until we find another town."

Laurie sets the tomato paste down and levels her eyes with Darcy's.

"Don't kid yourself. How long do you plan to stay once you find a new town? Weeks, months? I don't understand why you keep running. The killer is dead, Darcy."

Darcy tilts her head at the new coat of paint outside the dining-room window.

"It's a practical joke," Laurie says, rolling her eyes. "Some idiot figured out I'm related to you and drew a stupid face on my house. The sheriff isn't worried."

"Your sheriff wasn't in North Carolina to investigate the Darkwater Cove murders, so his opinion means squat. And anyway, Sheriff Tipton won't take my calls."

Stubborn, the women work in silence until the first gunshot explodes in the backyard. Darcy sets her work aside and expects Hunter to be the one holding the rifle. But it's Jennifer. The girl's mouth gapes open in an *oh-my-God-did-I-do-that* expression. She grins, shocked but a little proud. Then when reality sets in, her face twists in abject terror, and she holds the rifle at arm's length as though the muzzle grew teeth.

"Not bad," Laurie says over Darcy's shoulder. "She shoots better than her cousin."

Despite Laurie's flightiness, she's an experienced shooter. Before the divorce, Laurie's father took her hunting and taught his daughter how to shoot with an old Remington, which she stores in a gun safe in her bedroom.

"I'm not convinced that's true," Darcy says, but the corner of her mouth quirks up when Jennifer bounces in excited anticipation for Hunter to shoot. Her kids survived their father's death and escaped a serial killer. They're warriors like Darcy. And though Hunter and Jennifer couldn't be less alike, they're forever bonded and stick up for each other.

As Darcy returns to the kitchen, she unpacks the last of the groceries and studies the downstairs. The front door is steel and secured by double bolts. The back door is a wooden relic that clatters when the wind blows. A swift kick will snap the lock set and buckle the wood. Hiding from prying eyes and easily breached, the back door is the most likely point of entry for an intruder. The kitchen wall holds two casement windows, too small and cumbersome to bother with. But the living room picture window and the double-hung windows are weak points. As it has since the moment Darcy walked inside Laurie's house, her mind acts out her reactions to emergency situations. Which rooms offer the best hiding spots in the event of a break-in, and will Laurie have time to hustle the kids outside if Hensel and Darcy can't hold off their attackers?

Reading Darcy's thoughts, Laurie shakes her head.

"You're seeing ghosts, cousin."

"I don't want to frighten you," Darcy says, slamming the pantry door closed. "But there wasn't one killer in North Carolina. Michael Rivers had two people working for him, and like a communicative disease, those two thugs brought more people into the fold. Kids no older than mine. You can ignore the danger, but I won't. Agent Hensel isn't here for his health. He's concerned and doesn't want us alone."

Together at the window, Darcy and Laurie watch Hunter aim the rifle at a tin can on a tree stump. Jennifer bends over with both hands clutched to her ears as Hensel corrects Hunter's stance and takes a step away. The shot misses the can, but not by much. Hunter wobbles from the kickback but maintains his stance. A natural shooter. Rookie police officers shooting handguns struggle more on their initial shots than Hunter had with a rifle.

"Tell me about your stalker," Darcy says.

"Again? There isn't much to add."

"Humor me. Don't leave anything out, no matter how unimportant."

Laurie glances down and picks an invisible piece of lint off her sweatshirt. Darcy knows her cousin is more frightened than she's letting on.

"A few weeks ago I went for a walk through Cass Park. It's a walking trail on the edge of town. People take their dogs, and it's busy all year. I saw a guy about a hundred feet behind me. He was alone, no kid, no pet, but what the hell? I was alone, so who am I to judge? I walked the entire loop. Sometimes I looked back and saw him, other times I didn't and figured he'd called it a day. But then he appeared again, and I started to get this idea in my head that this was a game for him. Like he wanted to scare me. Yeah, pretty stupid."

"Not stupid at all. Did you get a good look at the man?"

Laurie chews a nail.

"He never got close enough. The man was tall, and he wore a black coat that fell to his knees."

"Like a trench coat."

"Yes, a trench coat. As I came around the backside of the park, I kept worrying I'd turn my head and he'd be right behind me, smiling because he knew he'd caught me. Then I didn't see him again until the next day when I left work."

"Are you sure it was the same guy?"

"Definitely. He hung out down the block so I couldn't see his face, and when I walked toward him, he turned the corner. That was the last I saw of the guy. Darcy, it's been two weeks. If the man is a stalker, why no contact since?"

The repeated sightings remind Darcy of Amy Yang, the girl Michael Rivers attempted to abduct four years ago. Amy complained of a stalker in Smith Town, North Carolina, and after a quiet period during which Amy didn't see her stalker, Richard Chaney murdered the girl and left her body on the shores of Darkwater Cove.

"He made contact, Laurie. The painting on your house." Laurie turns her head away and rubs her hands. "When is the last time you fired the rifle? It wouldn't hurt to have Eric work with you before he heads back to Quantico. Hell, I'll show you."

"I can't remember the last time I cleaned the Remington."

Darcy bites her lip. She doesn't want to be overcritical and treat Laurie like a child, but what is she thinking living five miles outside of town with no way to protect herself?

"Then we'll pull the Remington out after dinner and ensure it's in working order."

Laurie fills a glass of water at the sink and offers it to Darcy. When Darcy declines, Laurie sips from the glass and warms her hands beside the wood stove.

"How's Jennifer doing after the kidnapping?"

Darcy sinks into the couch cushions and rests her chin on her hand. A chill seeps through the ancient windows and crawls across the floor.

"She's terrified. Jennifer puts on a nonchalant act, but it shook her up."

"All the more reason to go back to North Carolina. She needs therapy, Darcy, not a week's vacation in the boondocks."

"Who says it will only be a week? Eric needs to go back to work, but I'm staying until we're sure you're safe."

And until Laurie takes the threat seriously, Darcy thinks.

Shaking off the cold, Hensel gestures for Darcy beside the entryway while Jennifer and Hunter climb the stairs. His face twists with concern.

"Jennifer talked to me. What's this about a man harassing you?"

Interesting that Jennifer won't express her feelings to Darcy, but she's fine confiding in a man she barely knows. Darcy tells Hensel about the burly man trailing Jennifer through the store and the ensuing encounter in the parking lot.

"I shouldn't have pulled a gun."

"He threatened you, but if he presses charges, it's your word against his. He didn't follow you out of town, did he?"

"The guy drove a red Escalade, hard to miss in the mirror. If he followed us, I would have noticed."

Hensel gives an unconvinced grunt and pulls the curtain back on the window.

"How did they do?" Darcy asks, changing the subject.

"The kids did good for their first time. You sure you haven't taught Jennifer to shoot?"

Darcy laughs.

"My gun club in North Carolina wouldn't have been amused if I walked in with my teenage daughter."

"She handled the weapon once she got past the initial fears, and Hunter looks like he's been shooting his entire life."

"That's good to hear. Thank you for teaching them."

When night falls, Hensel sleeps on the couch with his Glock beside him, while Darcy, Jennifer, and Hunter share the guest bedroom upstairs at the rear of the house. Laurie's room sits at the top of the stairs, and she'll be the first in the line of fire if an attacker makes it past Hensel. A trellis runs outside the guest bedroom. It won't support their weights during an emergency escape, but a small roof covers the back door. Jumping from the window to the roof is risky, but the option is viable.

The night begins with Darcy focused on Jennifer, but it's Hunter who draws her worry. He isn't talking. The doctor warned Darcy Hunter would be groggy. He sustained two concussions after Aaron Torres and his friends attacked him. Hunter needs physical therapy and a good neurologist, and Darcy will find neither in Scarlet River. Sharing the bed with Jennifer, Hunter thumbs through his phone while his sister snores beneath the covers. The screen throws black shadows against the wall. Hunter misses his girlfriend. Despite being Aaron Torres' sister, Bethany is a positive in Hunter's life. She draws him out of his shell and makes the boy smile, something he rarely does in Darcy's presence. But they can't return to North

Carolina. Too many skeletons in the closet, too many people who refuse to accept Hunter's innocence in the Darkwater Cove murders.

Hunter rolls over and goes to sleep, and oily darkness rolls over the room. Darcy thrashes inside the sleeping bag, the floor murder on her back. Sleep comes unexpectedly.

2

The county sheriff's office sits on the east end of Millport, fifteen miles north of Scarlet River, in a long modular building with brown siding. Five windows display a sparsity of activity inside. Darcy's car is the sole vehicle in the lot besides two black and red cruisers.

Six feet tall, Sheriff Harley Tipton sports a gray handlebar mustache above his upper lip. The dull yellowish brown of his buttoned khaki is the color of fescue in winter, and the brown hat atop his head tilts forward like it has something to hide. The office is too small to swing your arms without toppling the coat rack or putting a fist through the window. Multiple stacks of paper droop over on the sheriff's desk. The scowl on his face suggests he's ready to sweep the mess into the garbage.

Tipton rests his booted legs on the desk and assesses Darcy and Hensel.

"I read about you," Tipton says, tapping a finger on his desk when his eyes rest on Darcy. "You caught that serial killer in the Carolinas a few years back, and then you shot another one last month."

Darcy fidgets in her chair.

"How long ago did you leave the FBI?" Tipton asks, squinting.

"Three years."

"And this gun you used to kill the last killer. Did you bring it to my county?"

He knows she did. The deputy out front required Darcy to check her firearm.

"I did. And I brought my permit, if you need to see."

"That won't be necessary." Tipton drops his boots to the floor and leans forward on his elbows. "But you'll take care not to cause problems in my county, and I better not hear you're running around Scarlet River like a half-assed vigilante. Tell me again about your cousin's stalker."

Tipton's face remains unreadable while Darcy repeats the story, drawing parallels with the North Carolina murders. She wants to tell him about the moon phases, how Richard Chaney copied Michael Rivers' insane calendar, murdering during the ten days surrounding the full moon. Darcy feels certain the sheriff's eyes will glaze over if she recites the lunar calendar or theorizes the first murder will occur in the next few days.

"Don't take this the wrong way, Ms. Gellar, but two sightings of a man who never harmed or harassed your cousin doesn't convince me she's in danger." The next argument is on Darcy's lips when Tipton raises his hand to stop her. "But my sister had a stalker while she was at the University of Georgia, and I empathize with any woman who believes she's in danger. And that's the rub. Laurie Seagers says she's not in danger, that she hasn't seen the guy since he followed her in the park, and she doesn't think the face painted on the wall is related. Now, I'm willing to have a deputy check on her over the coming week, but there isn't much more I can do until Ms. Seagers tells me someone is stalking her."

Learning Laurie already spoke to the sheriff irritates Darcy.

"How much evidence do you need? You know what happened in Genoa Cove."

"The spray paint could be a sick prank. People read the Internet and get bad ideas stuck in their heads." Tipton swivels his chair toward Hensel. "You've been mighty quiet, Agent Hensel. What are your thoughts?"

Hensel chews on his words for a heartbeat.

"I'm concerned enough that I accompanied Darcy and her family to Scarlet River. As you state, this could all be a coincidence, but I'd rather exercise caution after what happened in North Carolina."

"But you're here unofficially, and the FBI isn't involved. I reckon you think that's a mistake."

Hensel gives a noncommittal shrug.

"All the FBI has to go on is one painting. In Genoa Cove, we had multiple murders and rapes."

"You've seen pictures of the painting on Ms. Seager's house. In your expert opinion, is it the same art the Full Moon Killer branded his victims with?"

"Not a perfect rendition, but it's similar, yes."

"And you believe Michael Rivers financed Richard Chaney because he wanted Ms. Gellar murdered."

"Either Chaney was the Full Moon Killer's hired hand, or he was a crazed fan who wanted to please Rivers. Either way, Rivers threatened to murder Darcy's family as a way of striking back at her."

Tipton rubs the day-old stubble on his cheeks.

"We haven't had any murders in this area, not for a long time."

"If another killer is loose in Scarlet River, you'll find the bodies soon."

Sheriff Tipton isn't burying his head in the sand, yet he resists the possibility that the devil is at his doorstep. Satisfied a deputy will check on Laurie, Darcy accepts the small victory, though she'd hoped for more.

She asks Tipton to recommend a good place to grab a sandwich, and he directs them to a bar and grill called Nicky's a quarter-mile from the interstate. The inside of Nicky's is dark. A dozen stools gird a polished bar where a blonde man with a tired face serves drinks and burgers to the patrons. A leggy waitress with an overbite invites Darcy and Hensel to sit at any of the tables along the wall. From the back, a jukebox pumps out a Kenny Chesney song about rum and tropical islands.

The waitress takes their orders—Hensel gets a medium-rare hamburger with a side of fries, while Darcy opts for the grouper sandwich. Despite the gloomy interior, the drone of the crowd's chatter and music make Darcy feel safe for the first time since before the Darkwater Cove murders.

"What did you think of Tipton?" Hensel asks as he wipes ketchup off the corner of his mouth.

Darcy gives Hensel a reserved tilt of the head and sips her Pepsi.

"He didn't dismiss our concerns outright. That's a plus. But he isn't taking the danger seriously."

Darcy's words trail off when a skinny woman with her hair tied back in a blue kerchief scurries from one stool to the next. Her shirt is red flannel, blue jeans three sizes too large and drooping off the woman's hips. She shoves a photocopy in front of each customer at the bar and glares at them imploringly. Most shake their heads. One man rocks back as if he's afraid he'll catch something contagious. With a groan, the barkeep sets his cleaning rag down and rounds the bar to cut her off. Too late. She's scurrying between two women in business attire toward Darcy and Hensel.

"Please, ma'am. Have you seen my daughter?"

The woman slaps a picture of a preteen girl with sandy hair, close-set eyes, and braces in front of Darcy and stabs her finger at the photo. Her hip brushes the table and spills soda.

"That's enough, Cherise," the barkeep says with an apologetic roll of his eyes as he prods the woman away from their table. "Go home before I call the sheriff."

"You look at that picture, ma'am. My baby's back. Nina's alive. You call me if you see her."

The door opens to a cool breeze and the scrape of dead leaves crawling down the sidewalk. When it swings shut, Darcy hears Cherise begging sidewalk shoppers to look at the photo.

"I'm sorry, folks," the barkeep says, toweling up the spill. "I hope she didn't ruin your meal. Let me get you another drink."

"It's not necessary," Darcy says, tilting the photograph until the light from the bar pulls out the details. She squints at the text. "I saw one of these yesterday."

"Not surprised. Cherise wallpapered half the county with them."

"Is this right? It says Nina disappeared ten years ago. She'd be twenty-two now."

His face sags, somber and pitying. Lowering his voice, he leans down so his eyes are even with Darcy and Hensel.

"Ten years ago, we had a rash of child abductions between Millport and Scarlet River. Cherise Steyer's daughter was one of the girls who went missing."

Hensel sets his napkin aside and swivels the paper toward him.

"I'm familiar with the cases, though it's been a long time since I read the notes. Four girls abducted over a twelve-month period. Didn't they find the bodies?"

"Three of them, yes. All but Cherise's girl, and that's why she believes Nina is still alive. Tragic. It's like Cherise lost her girl ten years ago and again on every day since. She was getting better until a month ago. Then some trucker in Scarlet River swore an older girl who looked like Nina asked him for a ride out of town."

Darcy shifts her chair toward the barkeep.

"We're staying in Scarlet River. Where did the trucker see the girl?"

"There's a diner on route 32 called Maury's. This guy claims the girl walked into the diner and stared at Cherise's poster. Then she sat down, ordered breakfast, and asked if he'd let her hitch."

"That's all? Did she say where she wanted to go?"

"Funny thing. The trucker claims she just wanted to get out of town. Didn't matter where he took her. But when he returned from the restroom, she was gone."

Darcy meets Hensel's eyes as the barkeep continues.

"What Cherise needs is closure, but after all these years..." He presses his lips together and shakes his head. "They'll never find Nina. It's been too long, and they can't excavate the entire county."

After the man returns to the bar, Hensel slides the photograph back to Darcy, who folds the paper and slips it into her bag. Hensel cocks an eyebrow.

"Taking up the case?"

"I feel bad for Cherise," Darcy says.

"You heard what the barkeep said. It's been ten years. Kidnapped girls don't walk into diners after a decade and ask for a ride. Who's to say what Nina Steyer looks like as an adult?"

The ride into Scarlet River takes them through a patchwork quilt of forest and farmland before it empties into the downtrodden neighborhoods at the town's outskirts. This community never thrived, but it clung to a lifeline a decade ago when the pharmaceutical manufacturing plant set up shop on the edge of town and brought good paying jobs to Scarlet River. Then came the flood of 2010 when the river reclaimed the south wall of the plant and dragged it downstream, taking the Scarlet River's fleeting prosperity and dreams with it. Thirty people lost their homes in the great flood, and what the water didn't take in property and commerce, it stole in morale. The village seems cursed.

Preoccupied, Hensel stares at the scenery whipping past the window.

"Something is on your mind," Darcy says, passing a tractor.

"Just thinking. The BAU wants me back at Quantico in six days, and they could call me to a case at any moment. You'll be on your own, and I'm not comfortable with that. It's not good here, Darcy. I don't trust the town."

"Neither do I."

"Then leave. Put Laurie and the kids in your car and go back to North Carolina. At least you'll have a police presence in the village."

"Laurie won't go, Eric. I begged her to leave, but she's dead set on staying. Besides, I can't put Hunter through that again. Half the neighborhood thinks he's Michael Rivers' progeny."

"I don't want to upset you, but eventually you must choose between Laurie's safety and your family's, and you can't defend the house with Laurie and two teenagers."

Darcy knows he's right, but after failing Amy Yang, she can't turn her back on Laurie. Her bag lies open on the floor beside Hensel's feet. The folded white photocopy pokes through the opening. Hensel catches her eyeing the paper and folds his arms.

"Let it go, Darcy. Those cases couldn't be any colder."

"What if the same person who abducted those girls sought Michael Rivers?"

"And went from hunting preteen girls to stalking adult women? That profile change is a tough sell."

"Some killers hunt outside their target age ranges," Darcy

says. "Maybe his preferences changed over the years, or Rivers made it worth his while. Hell, this is just guesswork."

"Millport and Scarlet River are small towns, not enough room for multiple serial predators. I'll grant you that. But how do you explain the ten-year hiatus?"

Darcy drums her fingers on the steering wheel.

"Could be the killer did jail time, or he moved from the area and came back."

Hensel nods in thought.

"Just promise me you won't pigeon-hole Laurie's stalker into a child predator from a decade ago."

The windows are dark when Hensel pulls into Laurie's driveway. Darcy's heart flutters when she unlocks the door and finds the downstairs empty. Then the laundry room door swings open, and Laurie carries a stack of folded towels toward the staircase.

"You better check on the kids," Laurie says, nodding up the stairs. "They yelled at each other while you were gone."

Odd. Hunter and Jennifer rarely argue. In the bedroom, Jennifer curls on her side, facing away from Hunter, whose earbuds crank heavy metal. Darcy motions for Hunter to kill the music.

"What's the issue? It's not like the two of you to fight."

Before Hunter can speak, Jennifer turns over and yells.

"Why does Hunter get to talk to his friends on social media? If I try, you'll ground me from my phone."

"I wasn't on social media," Hunter says.

"Bullshit. You talked to Bethany for twenty minutes."

"That was FaceTime. It's not like I posted our location on Instagram."

Darcy crosses her arms.

"We talked about this, Hunter. No social media, no Internet chat."

"FaceTime is a private conversation, Mom. If it makes you happy, I didn't tell Bethany where we are."

"Like she can't figure it out," Jennifer says. "Two-thirds of the country has snow on the ground, and you're outside in a sweatshirt and jeans. That narrows it down to the south."

"I'd talk inside, but the signal in here sucks. Check this out," Hunter says, holding up his phone. "One bar. Oh, wait. Zero bars, wonderful."

"Jennifer, leave us alone for a minute," says Darcy, glaring at her son.

Jennifer huffs and tosses her legs over the edge of the bed. Darcy waits until her daughter stomps down the stairs before she closes and locks the door.

"That wasn't smart, Hunter."

"All I did is say hello. Isn't it bad enough we're stuck in the middle of nowhere?"

Darcy sits on the edge of the bed. It's not fair to imprison her children and take away their communication with the outside world, but every message, every phone call, every Internet post leaves a breadcrumb for the deranged to follow.

"It sucks it has to be this way, Hunter, but this isn't my fault."

"You sure? You shot Michael Rivers, but he's still alive. If you'd killed him, we wouldn't have to deal with this for the rest of our lives."

Hunter's words knock Darcy off balance. There's an air of truth to them. If Darcy's shot had killed Rivers instead of wounding him, the murdered teens of Genoa Cove would still be alive, and Darcy wouldn't have to glance over her shoulder and fear for her family every time darkness fell.

"This isn't just about you. When you make a phone call, you put all of us at risk, including Bethany. What if some psycho follows up on Hunter Gellar's girlfriend and pays her a visit?"

Hunter doesn't respond.

"All I'm saying is we need to be careful. Let me talk to Agent Hensel about FaceTime. If the technology specialist working with his team says the app is difficult to hack, I'll consider allowing it."

"Sure you will."

He pops the earbuds in and turns his head toward the window. Darcy wants to yank them out and finish their conversation, but this isn't a fight she can win. Better to let him cool off and revisit this in an hour.

Leaving the bedroom is like leaping from the frying pan into the fire. The tension is palpable, a whip ready to snap. Downstairs, Laurie drags Darcy aside before she walks into a fight with Jennifer.

"Get it together, cousin. Put too many restrictions on kids and they rebel."

"I'm well aware of that."

"Hey, get your daughter out of the house before she goes stir crazy. There's a path at the edge of the woods that connects with a beautiful trail. You'll hit the falls in an hour."

"I don't know if that's a good idea."

"It's not a good idea, it's a great idea. Exercise will put the color back in your cheeks."

Darcy touches her face. Is she that pale?

"I haven't been well. Probably caught a bug after all the sleepless nights."

Laurie glances around to ensure Jennifer is out of earshot and lowers her voice. When she turns to Darcy, there's a hard, no-nonsense look in Laurie's eyes.

"You're not fooling anyone, Darcy."

"Fooling anyone? What are you talking about?"

"You were never this argumentative. Since you arrived, you jump at every shadow, your skin tone is all wrong, and you're constantly irritable and bickering with the kids. So what is it? Barbiturates?"

"Oh, that's rich. I'm not an addict."

"Tell me what you're on."

Darcy huffs and turns toward the window.

"I'm on prescription anti-anxiety medication, okay? I have been for three years. Hate to break this to you, but getting stabbed in a dark house by a serial murderer messes with your brain. Excuse me if I need a little help."

"This isn't about needing help. You're stronger than anyone I know, Darcy. But look me in the eye and tell me you're following the prescription."

Darcy glances at the pot boiling on the stove.

"One isn't always enough."

"How often?"

"Some days are worse than others."

"So you pop an extra pill, or do you take a few more? And what does the doctor say when you show up at his office asking for refills when the bottle should be half-full?"

"Jesus, Laurie."

"Darcy, this isn't a witch hunt. I'm here for you and always will be. But you need to promise me you'll follow the prescription. What good are you to the kids if you overdose?"

Darcy crosses her arms and stares at her sneakers.

"Okay, I promise."

"Did your doctor give you an official diagnosis?"

"You mean my shrink?"

"There's no shame in admitting you need help."

"It's Nyctophobia. An extreme fear of the dark."

Laurie scratches behind her ear.

"Yet I've seen you function after sunset. Does it not affect you all the time?"

"It's always there, like that sensation you get when someone creeps up behind you. But it's not always paralyzing. It helps to have people around and to be close to the house."

Reaching out, Laurie takes Darcy's hand in hers.

"You're doing great, Darcy, and I'll always be here for you. Don't depend on pills. Now, get your daughter out of the house. You both need clean air and a fresh perspective. Believe me, you'll feel better after a good walk. I'll talk to Hunter while you're gone."

Darcy hasn't exercised since Richard Chaney abducted Jennifer in the state park. She worries the trail might trigger bad memories for her daughter, but Laurie is right. A walk will do them good.

Sulking and dramatic, Jennifer agrees after Laurie lends her a new pair of hiking boots. The trek across the meadow loosens the stiff joints in Darcy's knees and gets her blood flowing. The feeble December sun splits the clouds and takes the bite out of the air, and it isn't long before Jennifer removes the hooded sweatshirt and ties the arms around her waist.

At the edge of the forest, Darcy searches for a break in the trees and finds the overgrown trail. Branches reach across the path and snag at their clothes, the thin and brittle pieces snapping and crackling as they struggle up the incline. Jennifer doesn't speak, but she hangs close to Darcy as if afraid she'll lose her mother if she falls behind. A fiery landscape of red, orange, and yellow leaves blankets the forest floor, the scent of leaf mold strong as animals dart for cover.

Jennifer sounds out of breath when the path bisects the state park trail. The footpath is wider here and maintained for hikers and bicyclists, though Darcy and Jennifer have the trail to themselves as they near the falls. The water's roar reaches their ears before they see it behind the trees. As the aroma of fresh water mingles with the dead leaves, Darcy imagines the fine mist awaiting them. Spurred by excitement when she sees the falls,

Jennifer passes Darcy. This invokes a good-natured race to the top. Darcy jogs to keep up with her daughter while Jennifer sprints to put distance between them.

When they round a bend flanked by oak and ash trees, the falls appear. Darcy pulls up, stunned by the magnitude of the waterfall. The cliff towers two hundred feet over a stream bed. Water rushes over the edge and cascades into the stream where it explodes and spreads mist down the creek. Jennifer's mouth hangs open. She leans on a rusted black railing and gapes at the power of the falls. Nervous over the rail's stability, Darcy wants to pull her daughter away from the ledge.

"Be careful, babe."

Jennifer shakes her head in wonder.

"Look at it. Who knew Georgia had waterfalls?"

Darcy can't pull her eyes off her daughter. For a frozen moment in time, Jennifer has forgotten the horrors of the past year. The infectious grin reminds Darcy of Jennifer as a child when she first saw a tiger at the zoo.

That's when Darcy spots the man watching them from the other cliff. There's no trail there, just untamed wilderness from the ridge to the valley below. A shiver rolls down Darcy's back. She can't make out the man's face, but he's staring at Jennifer.

3

Hazy sunshine filters through weathered windowpanes as Darcy stands in the hallway with Hensel. Inside the bedroom, Hunter and Jennifer slog through homework assignments, the door open a crack so she can monitor them.

"It was probably a hunter," Hensel says after Darcy tells him about the man at the falls.

"He didn't have a rifle. And what would he be hunting on top of a cliff, anyhow?"

"Let's assume he's Laurie's stalker. There's one path down that ridge, so we'll see him coming long before he gets here. Don't overreact."

Darcy leans against the wall and rubs her temples.

"This place is making me paranoid. A lot of good my security system did us in Genoa Cove, but I'd feel better if Laurie had something. At the very least, she needs to replace the back door. A child throwing a tantrum could kick his way inside."

A giggle from the bedroom tells Darcy the kids aren't taking the homework seriously. She emits a low growl.

"That's my cue to get out of your way," Hensel says. "I told Laurie I'd help her stack firewood in the garage."

"Might as well. She never parks her truck inside."

After Hensel descends the stairs to help Laurie, Darcy pushes the bedroom door open. The snickers die, then Hunter and Jennifer share a grin and return to their work. They've forgotten this morning's argument. Good.

Darcy picks an empty piece of floor between the dresser and window and slides into a sitting position. Jennifer looks up. One glare from Darcy convinces Jennifer to bury her head in her homework. In the silent room, Darcy is aware of the hiss of the furnace and the dusty heat it pushes off the wall, the jiggle of the windowpane every time the breeze picks up, and the filthy sunshine over the glass. It's an unnatural light. Secretive and sullied.

Pulling her eyes from the window places her at the mercy of her imagination. Michael Rivers is at the glass, eyes wild with bloodlust as he peers inside. Then he's in the hallway, tap, tap, tapping against the door with the wicked knife he used to butcher his victims. Every creak and groan inside the house is the Full Moon Killer creeping through the dark, the bloody bodies of Laurie and Hensel left in a heap outside.

With the kids focused on their studies, Darcy slides her laptop out of the case and enters her password. With the screen facing away from Hunter and Jennifer, Darcy loads the serial killer website and reads through the forums. While the site purports to be an academic study of famous serial killers, it's a fan site. The admins crack down on posters who glorify violence and ban repeat offenders, but she's discovered fiction which would make a fan of slasher movies blanch. Searching for her name, Darcy glances around the screen when she finds an entry. Neither Jennifer nor Hunter notice Darcy's hands tremble as she moves the mouse.

It's another speculative thread devoted to the whereabouts of Darcy and her family. Pulse pounding, she scans the text for Georgia and Scarlet River. One poster remains convinced Darcy never left Genoa Cove, while two others argue she returned to Virginia. Darcy's determination to keep her kids off social media paid off. The posters lost Darcy's trail.

Darcy is about to shut the browser down when curiosity tempts her to click on the names of banned forum members. She recognizes *FM-Kill-Her*, the Michael Rivers fan who fictionalized the gruesome murders of Darcy and Amy Yang in a short story. Then another member catches her eye. He wrote five posts before the admins blocked his access to the site. In his fifth and final post, he announced the Gellar family is in Georgia somewhere near Millport. The mouse jitters in her hand as she scans the message, written seven hours ago. Somebody knows she's here.

Pounding on the front door brings Darcy to her feet. Jennifer drops her notebook and stares at Darcy. The paralyzing moment lasts until the pounding starts again. The escape plans fly through her mind—out the window and onto the roof if they can't get out in time, defend the stairs at all costs until then. Nobody gets to her kids.

Where is Hensel? Still outside with Laurie? Hunter climbs off the bed when Darcy moves to the door. She wraps the holster around her hip, struggling with the clip as the pounding starts up again. Angry and insistent.

"Stay here with your sister. Lock the door behind me and don't open it for anyone." He protests, and she cuts him off. "No arguments. Do it."

Pulling her sweatshirt over the gun, she shuts the door and doesn't budge until Hunter turns the lock. Slashes of shadow and bloody light pour across the landing. Ten minutes ago, the clunk of wood tossed into a wheelbarrow echoed outside as

Hensel and Laurie worked. Now it's quiet, and she realizes too much time has passed since she last heard them.

She looks down the stairs and plays the scenarios through her head. Stay along the wall where the killer can't see her when he breaks inside. Shoot for the kneecaps. Disable and disarm. And if he reaches for his weapon, put the next bullet between his eyes. Be ready to dive into the kitchen if he gets the jump on her and hems her in with gunfire. But do not let him reach the staircase.

Edging the curtain back from the window, Darcy spots the sheriff cruiser in the driveway. She places her hand over her heart and closes her eyes. Thank goodness.

The deputy is ready to descend the front porch steps when Darcy opens the door. He spins and slides his hand along his holster.

"Ms. Seagers?"

The deputy's nameplate reads Filmore. A younger version of Tipton, Deputy Filmore towers above Darcy. Stubble covers his cheeks. Beneath the tilted hat, Filmore's eyes are deep set and acorn colored.

"No, I'm her cousin. Darcy Gellar."

Darcy gazes down the driveway. Light spills out of the garage, but she can't find Hensel or Laurie.

"Gellar," the deputy says, rolling the name around in his head. "You were at the office yesterday."

"That's right."

"Hello?"

Laurie's voice echoes from the driveway. Hensel pushes the wheelbarrow beside her.

"You Laurie Seagers?"

"Yes."

"And your name, sir?"

Hensel states his name and fishes the FBI badge from his pocket.

Deputy Filmore introduces himself. Though Darcy had told Laurie Sheriff Tipton planned to send a deputy by the house, she seems surprised and a touch embarrassed.

"This isn't necessary," Laurie says. "Nobody comes out this way, and if someone wanted to cause trouble, I'd hear them coming a mile away."

Arms folded and his forehead beaded with sweat, Hensel joins Darcy on the porch while Filmore and Laurie round the house. Laurie points at the wall where she painted over the face. Filmore aims the flashlight against the wall, then sweeps the beam along the windows. He gestures at the panes and Laurie nods, but Darcy can't hear them from the porch.

"Put the gun inside," Hensel says, flashing his eyes toward the holster concealed under Darcy's sweatshirt.

"Is it that obvious?"

"No, but don't give this guy an excuse. Some of these small county deputies have nervous streaks, and you look a little suspicious with all that worry pouring off your face."

Darcy tells Hensel about the website post. His jaw pulses as he considers the implications of someone in town watching them.

"I called you before, but you didn't answer," Darcy says, unhooking the holster.

"Neither of us heard the cruiser pull up. Laurie had the radio on while we stacked firewood." He touches his back and winces. "And I've done enough stacking for tonight."

Hensel follows Darcy inside, both relieved to escape the chill spilling off the ridges. Jennifer stands at the top of the stairs with her brother beside her.

"It's okay," Darcy says, calling up the stairs. "Just one of the county sheriff deputies stopping by. He might walk through the house and assess the security."

Darcy gives Jennifer a meaningful look. It takes a second for Darcy's suggestion to register, then Jennifer hurries to the bathroom to clear the feminine hygiene products off the sink.

With Laurie in tow, Deputy Filmore moves through the house, questioning Laurie about the stalker as he offers suggestions for beefing up security. Filmore tells her to install an alarm system, a recommendation Laurie balks at. Security systems are expensive and ineffective, she argues, though Darcy expects the cost is Laurie's only concern. Filmore is adamant Laurie replace the back door. Maybe now she'll listen to Darcy.

Satisfied no imminent threat exists, Deputy Filmore leaves his card and drives back to Millport. Exhaustion drags Hensel and Laurie into sleep. Darcy lies awake, watching the shadows move across the window.

~

FROST GLISTENS over the meadow when Darcy awakens the next morning. She can't see Hunter and Jennifer, both teens nestled beneath the covers. Her shoulders and hip ache from sleeping on the floor, and a deep cold pours through the drafty house, locking her joints while she pads on bare feet toward the bathroom. Hensel is sound asleep on the couch when Darcy creeps down the stairs. One squeal is all it takes for Hensel to pop his eyes open and reach for his gun.

"Don't shoot, cowboy," Darcy says as she stokes the coals in the wood stove. "How did you sleep?"

"Like a baby."

When Hensel reaches for his back again, Darcy doubts he's being truthful.

"In my experience, babies scream all night and mess their diapers. Coffee?"

"Sure."

Darcy starts a pot of water boiling and slips her sweatshirt on, clutching her elbows with a shiver.

"This place is like an icebox. If it gets any colder, I'll see my breath. I always figured Georgia was warmer than this."

Hensel half-shuffles, half-limps into the kitchen and looks out the window.

"You won't see much snow down this way, but mornings will take your breath away during the heart of winter. It shouldn't be this cold in early December, though."

"The news says it snowed again last night in Virginia. I've never seen it this cold so early."

Darcy drops a sliver of butter in the pan and pulls eggs out of the refrigerator, hoping the scent of breakfast will rouse Laurie and the kids.

"Why are you up so early?" Hensel asks, nodding his chin at Darcy.

"There's a home repair store a block from the grocery market. If they have steel doors, I'm replacing the back door. I can't sleep knowing someone could walk inside in the middle of the night. A new door will help with this damn draft too."

"Want company?"

"If you don't mind. An extra set of hands would be nice."

Laurie runs her hand through her hair and itches her forehead as she staggers bleary-eyed into the kitchen.

"You must really want to put a guilt trip on me. First you uproot your lives and take the world's worst vacation, and now you're cooking breakfast for me."

"Never said the eggs are for you," Darcy says with a wink. "Eric and I will drive into town after breakfast. Need us to pick up anything?"

"You're doing too much as is." When Hensel leaves the room, Laurie joins Darcy at the stove. "Hey, I don't want you to think I'm unappreciative. Yeah, I have doubts about this stalker thing, but after what Deputy Filmore said, you might be right. And if you are..."

Laurie shivers.

"I hope I'm wrong, Laurie. If I'm off base, there's no downside. We spent time together, and that's a good thing. When was the last time we spent more than a day together?"

"That's the problem with phones and everyone being online. We think we're connected, but we've never been farther apart. It's good to see you and the kids. But about this guy. The truth is I'm scared."

Darcy draws Laurie into a hug. When they part, Laurie reaches for the spatula and pushes the eggs around.

"Eric and I are replacing the back door." Laurie looks like she wants to argue, then she nods and reaches for her wallet. Darcy holds up her hand. "Hold on to your money."

"Oh, come on. I can pay for my own repairs."

"After. We won't know the cost until we get there. Besides, I know where to find you if you don't pay up."

Laurie giggles.

"Don't worry. I'm good for the money. Listen, while the two of you go into town, I'd like to take Hunter and Jennifer to the mall. It's an hour drive, but it's worth the trip. They have two hundred stores and a food court."

Letting the kids out of her sight sets Darcy on edge. Still, Hunter and Jennifer need to experience something besides miles of dead, wilted grass.

"That's fine. It might make them feel like normal teenagers for a few hours. Take the Prius. You'll get better mileage on the highway. We'll use your truck to load the new door."

By the time the five of them cycle through the shower, milky sunshine melts the frost and takes the chill out of the air. Jennifer rolls her eyes, and Hunter gives a disinterested shrug when Darcy cautions them to keep their eyes open while they're at the mall. Any stranger could be an enemy, even inside a shopping center holding a few thousand people.

"Feel like driving this morning?" Darcy asks Hensel. The BAU agent holds a thermos of coffee.

"No problem."

Darcy tosses the keys to Hensel, who slides behind the wheel. Darcy climbs into the cab, closing her eyes as she pinches the bridge of her nose.

"Stop worrying about Hunter and Jennifer," he says, setting the thermos between his knees. "Your cousin is a tough cookie. She won't let anything happen to the kids."

Darcy forces a wan smile, but she senses the distance from her kids grow as they pull away.

Steel doors at the Scarlet River hardware store run double what Darcy would expect to pay at a chain retailer, but the stock boy carries the door to the parking lot and wedges it into the rear of the truck. She'll sleep better knowing an intruder trying to break inside will have a fight on his hands.

Hensel turns the wrong way out of the parking lot and takes them down a street Darcy doesn't recognize. It isn't until he turns at the intersection, intending to reverse direction, that Darcy spots the marker for route 32 off the shoulder.

"Hey, the diner the barkeep mentioned is on this road," Darcy says, searching for the restaurant.

"Maury's."

"That's the one."

Hensel studies Darcy from the corner of his eye.

"I suppose you'll want to stop."

He answers the question for himself with a nod.

Maury's Diner appears cobbled together by two generations

of owners, the main building red brick with a blue awning over the front door. A white vinyl-sided expansion juts out to the right. The roar of a tractor trailer speeding behind the trees announces the highway, and two eighteen-wheelers park horizontally at the rear of the parking lot.

Opening the front door unleashes the scents of fried burgers and fresh baked pies. The clatter of utensils against plates sing of organized chaos as patrons come and go. Though she finished breakfast two hours ago, Darcy's eyes wander to the menu on the wall.

"Table for two?"

The leggy waitress wears a coral shirt and skirt. A pencil sticks out from behind her ear. Tall and muscular with auburn curls past her shoulders, the woman was once a cheerleader or sports star during school. Her makeup doesn't conceal the hint of crow's feet. The name tag reads Margaret.

Darcy glances at Hensel, who shrugs.

"I could go for a slice of pie," Hensel says.

"So just dessert?"

"Sure," Darcy says as the waitress grabs two dessert menus. "And if you have a moment to speak with us after, we'd be obliged."

Margaret's jaw drops when Hensel displays his FBI badge. She glances toward the kitchen as if worried one of the cooks is a wanted man.

He raises his hand and says, "We only want to ask a few questions about the trucker who came through here a month ago. The guy who claims he saw the girl on the poster out front."

Margaret touches her heart and exhales.

"Nina Steyer. Sure, I was here that day. Let me show you to your table, and I'll get your orders going. My shift ends at the top of the hour, if you want to talk."

The waitress walks Darcy and Hensel to a table in the new

addition. The room is empty except for a heavyset man with a stack of blueberry pancakes in front of him.

"Here are your menus," Margaret says, anxiously glancing at Hensel. "I'll be right back with waters."

When Margaret is out of earshot, Darcy gives Hensel a conspiratorial smile.

"So this is official FBI business?"

"Just greasing the wheels," Hensel says, reading the back of an artificial sweetener packet. "This stuff will kill you."

Each chooses a slice of blackberry pie. By the time they finish eating, Margaret's shift ends. When she returns to their table, she's wearing a pair of blue jeans which appear painted on. A black T-shirt shows off the arms of a woman who is no stranger to the gym. A colorful tattoo, something floral, curls from her shoulder to her elbow. Margaret stands back with her hands clasped until the waitress who took over her shift drops the bill in front of Hensel.

"Please," Darcy says, motioning for Margaret to sit beside her.

The waitress doesn't know what to do with her hands, which she shifts from the table to her lap and back again.

"The trucker who claims he saw the missing girl," Darcy says, removing the folded picture of Nina. "Do you know his name?"

Margaret shakes her head.

"We get truckers from all over Georgia. He wasn't someone I recognized, but Donna, she ran tables in the main room with me that morning, said his truck had Florida plates."

"What about this girl he bought breakfast for?" Hensel asks. "Did you see her?"

Margaret nods her head slowly.

"The trucker came in alone and ordered eggs and toast. I stopped by to make sure he had everything he needed, and then there was this girl sitting across from him. Straight, brownish hair down to about here." Margaret touches her neck just below the ear. "Pretty little thing, late teens or early twenties. I figured it was his daughter. Sometimes the long-haul truckers bring a family member along for the ride."

Darcy slides the picture in front of Margaret.

"Did she speak to you?"

"Well, I took her order. All she wanted was a bowl of plain oatmeal, no fruit or maple sugar or nothing. She was here ten or fifteen minutes, just long enough to eat."

"So she just walked out?"

"I guess. I didn't see her go, but when the man came back from the restroom, he kept asking people where she went. I got worried because I still thought she was his daughter and the girl had wandered off. But he was supposed to give her a ride out of town, so I figured she found somebody else to drive her, or maybe she got cold feet about hitching."

Hensel leans back and squints his eyes in thought.

"But the girl appeared to be around twenty. It's not like a toddler went missing."

Margaret's eyes dart around the room like bats in a cave.

"To me, she seemed like a little girl. She wasn't slow or nothing, more like she didn't know what to say or how to act. Like it was her first time in public. I had to kneel beside the girl to coax her into ordering."

Darcy taps her finger on the picture.

"Margaret, is this the girl you saw?"

A tear trickles out of Margaret's eye. She lifts the picture and stares for a long time. After she sets it down, she sniffles and dabs her nose with a tissue.

"I don't know. I mean it could have been her. It's so dark in that room, and she always had her head down like she didn't want nobody to look at her. Oh, God. What if it was Nina? She sat right in front of me, and I let her get away."

Margaret breaks down and cries into her hands. Darcy meets Hensel's eye, and he runs to the restroom for tissues. Lowering her voice, Darcy touches Margaret's shoulder.

"Besides the resemblance, is there anything the girl said or did that makes you think she could have been Nina?"

Margaret hitches and drops her hand to the table.

"I didn't see her come in, but the trucker said she stood in the doorway and stared at a poster, except there are a few dozen on the wall. No way any of us knew it was the missing person poster. It wasn't until the girl disappeared that the guy looked at the picture and noticed the resemblance. But why would a kidnapped girl walk into Maury's ten years later and ask for a ride out of town? That's what makes me think it wasn't her. A normal person would have wanted the sheriff or asked for a ride home."

Darcy thumbs through her wallet and removes a business card. On the back of the card, she scrawls her phone number.

"This is my mobile number," Darcy says, handing her the card. "If you see the girl or the trucker in town, call me."

Margaret inspects the card, turning it over between her fingers and biting her lower lip.

Darcy loses herself in her thoughts during the ride back to Laurie's. Scarlet River is a walking, breathing dichotomy. Small southern town values manifest themselves in the well-dressed families filing out of the Baptist church and the long line at the community bake sale to support the elementary school. Mothers with children crowd the park in the edge of town, the merry-go-round, slide, and swing set overflowing with laughing children. And yet a darkness pervades the town. It curls sleeping in the shadows and slithers out when no one is paying attention.

"It's hard to believe someone in this town would follow a

degenerate like Michael Rivers," Hensel says, nodding at the park. "Could be the painting was a prank like Tipton theorized."

Christmas garland and lights splash holiday colors through neighborhoods. Darcy lowers the window a crack. Someone is playing a Bing Crosby song.

"You don't believe that, and neither do I."

"Let's assume the same guy who kidnapped those girls ten years ago sought Michael Rivers. The abductions stopped. Where has this guy been?"

"Prison? If he did time in Buffalo, that would explain how he met Rivers."

"Sure, but what about the girl? Nina."

"If the trucker met Nina, the kidnapper couldn't have gone to prison. He kept her all this time."

"Then one day he let her go?" Hensel cocks an eyebrow.

Darcy doesn't have a good explanation. When she glances off to the side, she taps Hensel's arm and points.

"That's the guy that harassed us at the supermarket."

The predator stands outside a bar on the corner of Main and Church Street, hands buried in his pockets.

"The big guy?"

"Don't slow down. I don't want him to see us."

Hensel pulls into an open parking place in front of a drug store. The man's eyes swerve to the truck. Not good. He recognizes her through the windshield and marches across the sidewalk. It isn't until he spots Hensel in the driver seat that he pulls up short of the curb and stares bullets into the cab. His hands pop out of his pockets and curl into big meaty fists that would pummel both of them on a desolate roadway and bury their bodies in the forest. But this is downtown, not a lonely stretch of country road, and Hensel is armed and knows what he's doing. The predator stands and considers his options, one arm leaning against the lamp post as flies feasting inside a garbage can swarm out at his presence.

Hensel wears an amused grin, not acknowledging the threat. Perhaps because he wasn't at the grocery store parking lot to witness the encounter. This man has no boundaries. It's evident in the wild set of his eyes, the toothy grin. His gaze moves across the car to Darcy. He runs his tongue across his lips.

Hensel pulls the FBI badge from his pocket.

"Should I say something to him?"

"No, just drive."

The man steps off the curb and towers over the hood.

"You sure? He looks like he wants to talk."

"Get us out of here."

The man's eyes follow the truck as Hensel backs up and speeds down Main Street.

"That was kinda fun," Hensel says with a smirk.

"For you, not for me. Who knows what he would have done?"

"In broad daylight in front of half the town?"

"I doubt he cares." Darcy looks over her shoulder at the predator, still watching their progress as the truck moves from light to light. "Jennifer fits the kidnapper's target age, and that guy seemed awfully interested in my daughter."

Hensel slaps the steering wheel.

"Damn. We missed our chance to ask him where he disappeared to over the last ten years."

"Laugh it up, Eric. That guy isn't playing around."

Despite Hensel's reservations, Darcy convinces her former FBI partner to swing past the park before they leave town. The bustle continues, young children laughing and playing tag while mothers in sweatshirts and wool sweaters watch from benches. With Hensel trailing, Darcy removes the photograph of Nina Steyer and shows it to the women. Nobody has seen Nina, and worse yet, the women shrink from Darcy as if she carries the plague. They whisper among themselves when Darcy moves to the next group.

She spends twenty minutes strolling from one group to the next. By the time she converges on the last few women, they snatch their children and hustle out of the park before Darcy can question them. Word spreads ahead of her approach.

In the car, Darcy folds Nina's picture and stuffs it into her bag.

"Why are they afraid to talk?"

"The kidnappings caused this area a great deal of trauma," Hensel says, cutting down an unmarked street as he searches for the road back to Laurie's. "You're unearthing bad memories they buried years ago."

"But there's a good chance one girl is still alive. Nobody will ever find Nina if they bury their heads in the sand."

Darcy feels eyes watching them until they pull into Laurie's driveway, the car gone and the house empty. A twinge of anxiety pangs at Darcy before she remembers Laurie drove the kids to the mall. Inside, she tosses her keys on the kitchen table and rubs the cold off her arms. The fire burned out, but it shouldn't be this cold.

"You want to get started on the door?" Hensel asks.

"Good idea. It feels like someone left a window open, it's so drafty."

Hensel climbs onto the truck and hauls the steel door off the bed. With Hensel in front and Darcy in the back, they carry the door around the house and set it against the wall. Darcy's eyes halt on the old door.

It's wide open.

4

Hip-hop thumping out of a sneaker store overwhelms the monotonous Muzak playing over the mall sound system. Leaning against the rail on the shopping center's third level, Hunter and Jennifer people-watch, Jennifer sipping on a yogurt smoothie and Hunter nursing a Coke. It took a lot of persuading before Laurie allowed the teenagers to break off on their own. After a short debate, Laurie agreed, acknowledging the teenagers hadn't been out of their mother's watchful glare since the kidnapping in North Carolina. Hunter loves his mom, but ever since the Darkwater Cove murders and the altercation with Aaron Torres and his jock goons, she's given him the mother hen treatment, following him everywhere and binding him with rules. For all of Laurie's faults—she's better at recognizing everybody else's messes than cleaning her own—at least she gives Hunter and Jennifer space. They have an agreement to meet in the food court in an hour, and Hunter keeps one eye on the big clock outside Lord & Taylor's so they aren't late.

Jennifer swipes through her phone.

"Hey, you sent Mom into a shit-fit after I messaged Bethany,"

Hunter says, swinging his sneaker store bag against her leg. "Now you're cruising. What's the deal?"

"What Mom doesn't know won't hurt her. Besides, I'm not texting, just reading." She smiles at Hunter's dubious smirk. "And you wouldn't tell Mom, anyway, because you agree with me. These rules are bullshit. Nobody's watching every move we make. There's like security and stuff on our phones."

Hunter grunts in semi-agreement and slips his own phone out of his pocket.

"Holy shit!" Jennifer's exclamation draws a glare from a woman pushing a stroller. "Oh my God. This is why we should be able to use the Internet. You won't believe what went down back home."

"Genoa Cove?"

"The police just charged Aaron Torres and Sam Tatum with rape."

"But they were in jail."

"No, the Smith Town rapes. Remember?"

Hunter slides down and sits on the floor, leaning his back against the rail. The Smith Town rapes preceded the murders by a few months, and to this point, the police believed Richard Chaney went from raping girls to murdering them. Escalation, they called it. Hunter is surprised the police never charged him with the rapes after they attempted to pin the murder conviction on him. While playing on the football team with Aaron, Hunter realized Aaron and Sam were bad kids and bullies, though he never believed they would attack Hunter just because he dated Bethany. And he never suspected they raped Smith Town girls.

"I gotta talk to Bethany. She's taking the arrest hard, but she must be going crazy now. Damn. It couldn't happen to a better guy, though. Screw Aaron Torres and Sam Tatum."

"Truth. I hope they cut off their—"

"I don't think the police do that."

"Well, they deserve it."

Hunter opens his contacts and finds Bethany's number, indecision yanking him in opposite directions. Mom overreacts, and she's been paranoid since the Full Moon Killer attempted to murder her, but she's no fool. A group of miscreants search for Hunter and Jennifer on the Internet, and there's no telling how far the extremists will go. But a FaceTime session shouldn't pose a threat.

"Just call her," Jennifer says, reading his mind. "I won't tell Mom."

"You did last time."

"Because I was the only one following Mom's orders. But if we both break the rules..."

Jennifer's eyes sparkle. Hunter grins.

"That's my cue to test perfumes," Jennifer says, leaving Hunter to speak with Bethany. "No witnesses."

"Stay where I can see you," says Hunter, giving her a pointed look.

"Yes, boss."

Jennifer wanders into the department store and sets her bag down at the perfume counter. Two women stop to test perfumes, spraying the scents against their wrists.

Keeping Jennifer in sight, Hunter calls Bethany. A moment later, her face appears on the screen. Despite the red, sleepless eyes, Bethany Torres is more beautiful than he remembered. Dark locks curl down to her shoulder. A copper, tanned face forces a smile. He realizes with a jolt he'd begun to forget what she looked like.

"You heard," she says, swiping a tissue across her nose.

"Yeah, I just found out. Hey, Bethany. I'm sorry."

"Don't say you're sorry, Hunter, because we both know you're not. Shit. I don't even know if I'm sorry. My brother is a rapist. How can I look him in the eye again?"

"More like how can he look *you* in the eye."

Bethany sniffles.

"He's such an asshole, but he's my brother, you know? I can't turn my back on family, but I never want to see him again. Those girls...some of them were a few months out of middle school. And I don't understand any of it. You remember how popular Aaron was. He could have dated any girl at school. Why would he need to rape someone?"

Hunter shakes his head. He knows the answer, but sharing it won't help Bethany. Aaron is a sociopath, the rare teenager who gets his thrills from hurting others. Relationships are meaningless to boys like Aaron Torres and Sam Tatum. They get off on power and delusions of superiority. Neither feels remorse over the rapes, only that the police caught them.

"How are your parents dealing with this?"

"Not good. Mom hasn't slept in weeks, and Dad stopped talking to me like it's my fault. Like it was my responsibility to see this coming and stop Aaron before he did something stupid."

"What do you mean *your fault*?"

Bethany lowers her head. When her face reappears, her eyes are puffy, hair angled across her scalp as if she yanked it.

"Hey, Bethany. You're telling me everything, right?"

"Yeah," she says, glancing away.

"Your parents don't blame you, Bethany. This is just your folks trying to process Aaron's charges. Give them time."

Bethany coughs into her hands and wipes a tear from her eye.

"Yeah, I get it. It sucks, but I get it. But listen to me acting like I'm the only one in the world going through problems. You can't even tell me where you are, but I'll ask, anyway."

Hunter glances around the mall. It's beginning to clear out, the crowd thinning as they finish shopping and head home for dinner.

"You wouldn't believe me if I told you. We're in some Georgia town I've never heard of, staying with my cousin."

"Georgia, why?"

"I better not say. I'm not supposed to be talking to friends, not even you."

"That sucks. Is this about that crazy guy who tried to kill your mom?"

"Something like that," Hunter says as Jennifer sets her bags at his feet and sits beside him.

"What's that in the background? It looks like you're shopping."

"If I told you, I'd have to kill you."

"Not funny."

"Too soon? Okay. It's just some mall up the road from where we're staying. Well, I better sign off. I don't know if my mother checks data usage."

"Don't be a stranger, Hunter. I miss you."

"I promise I won't, and I miss you too."

"It's not fair of me to say, and you don't have control over any of this, but I really need you, Hunter."

She's hiding something. Whatever happened to Aaron, it's worse than she's letting on. Anxiousness surges through Hunter as he concocts plans to return to Genoa Cove so he can fix this.

"I'm coming back for you. Do you believe me?"

"Yeah."

"I promise."

When he closes the FaceTime app, his heart drops. He'll see Bethany again, he tells himself. Except Mom won't return to Genoa Cove except to load the moving truck, and even then she might hire somebody to clean out the house so she never has to set foot inside again.

"She still loves you?" Jennifer elbows him and giggles.

"Knock it off."

Hunter forces himself to grin before the hair on the back of his neck prickles. Shoving the phone into his pocket, he stands and lifts his bag, scanning the crowd.

"What's wrong?" Jennifer asks, climbing back to her feet.

"You know that feeling you get when someone is watching you?"

"It's not a real feeling. That's just a horror movie cliche. If you want to know the truth..."

Jennifer's words fade as Hunter moves his eyes over the crowd. A group of teens, the boys with their arms around the girls' shoulders, sneer as they pass by. Two girls make sarcastic jokes and playfully shove one another outside the video game store. Then Hunter sees the man in the long black jacket staring at them from a bench down the hall.

Hunter swats Jennifer on the arm, just enough to stop his sister's chatter and grab her attention. She gives him a quizzical look, and he lifts his chin at the man.

"Still think it's a cliche?"

The man stands and walks away, blending into the crowd until Hunter can't find him.

"It was just a guy. So what? Whatever you do, don't tell Laurie. And don't let Mom know. She'll never let us out of the house until we're in our fifties."

"That guy was watching us."

"So he's a creeper. Who cares? People stare all the time in malls. You scared him off, anyway."

Though Hunter wants to believe Jennifer is right, the voice whispering in his head warns of trouble. This wasn't some ordinary guy checking out his little sister.

He glared like he knew Jennifer. Like he knew Hunter too.

5

"Yes, I'm certain the door was closed and locked," Darcy says, running her finger along the jamb.

The ancient wood rises and falls with warps and rot. Drawing an exasperated sigh from Hensel, Darcy enters the house ahead of him. Wind shoves at her through the open doorway. Laurie's bills lie scattered on the kitchen floor.

At the staircase, Hensel grips her arm and purses his lips. She steps back and lets him take the lead, the FBI agent's gun drawn as they move up the stairs. It takes a few minutes to check each room and determine the house is clear. Nothing appears out of place or missing, but Darcy will tell Laurie and the kids to check their belongings after they return.

"Think we should call the sheriff?"

Hensel shakes his head.

"And tell him what? For all we know, the wind blew the door open, and based on the lack of damage, I believe that's what happened."

"It doesn't feel right."

Hensel slips his gun into his holster. He sits on the top step and runs a tired hand through his hair.

"I'm inclined to agree. It looks like someone forced the door open, but a gust of wind could have done the job. Let's install the door before your cousin returns. If she finds anything out of place, I'll call Tipton."

The wind cuts through Darcy's sweatshirt and touches her skin with cold fingers as they work outside. Standing on tiptoe, she unscrews the hinges on the old door while Hensel observes with his hands on his hips.

"What?"

Hensel exhales.

"This is no good. Look at the construction. The wood flakes off in my hand. All of it needs replacing."

"You're turning this into a full day's project."

"Sorry, but there isn't any point installing the new door if the jamb falls apart."

With no other choice, they drive back to Scarlet River, Darcy behind the wheel this time while Hensel answers work emails on his phone. As they pass through downtown, Darcy keeps an eye out for the man who harassed them.

By the time Hensel picks out the supplies and loads the truck, clouds swallow the sun and steal what little warmth remains. They race against the lengthening day, and Hensel is out of the cab before Darcy puts the truck in park. Laurie hasn't returned with the kids yet. Darcy wants to fire off a text, but she doesn't want to seem pushy or more of a worrier than she already is.

Behind the house, Darcy aids Hensel as he replaces the rotten wood. Then they lift the door and attach the hinges, both Darcy and Hensel blowing on their numbing hands as daylight fades. The final hinge in place, Hensel aims a flashlight so Darcy can twist the last screws home. Then the headlights of the Prius sweep across the yard. As if he'd sensed her anxiousness earlier, Hensel gives her an *I-told-you-not-to-worry* smirk.

Hensel admires their handiwork with a satisfied grin as Darcy forces herself to walk, not run to the driveway. Her heart slams until Jennifer and Hunter climb out of the car, Hunter holding a large bag from a sneaker store, no less than four bags tucked under Jennifer's arm.

"How was it?" Darcy hopes they didn't catch the jitter in her voice.

Jennifer talks faster than an auctioneer, listing all the cool stores they visited and how crowded the mall was with shoppers and teens their age. Hunter hangs back with a small upward tilt at the corner of his mouth. Typical Hunter. He hides his emotion and brushes off excitement as though he's seen and done everything too many times.

"Mom, it was freaking three levels," Jennifer says, swinging the largest bag over her opposite shoulder. "We didn't even see all of it. Can we go back, please?"

"First, thank your cousin for taking you, then we'll discuss future trips after I assess the damage you did to your wallet."

Laurie accepts a brief and awkward hug from Hunter. Bouncing on her feet, Jennifer plants a kiss on Laurie's cheek.

"They don't have to thank me," Laurie says, giving Jennifer a wink. "Now let's get inside before I turn into an ice cube."

In the kitchen, Jennifer and Hunter are too busy chattering to notice when Darcy pulls Laurie aside.

"Did you shut and lock the back door before you went to the mall?"

"I always lock my doors," Laurie says, cracking open a can of Ginger Ale. She takes a drink and wipes her lips with the back of her sleeve. "Don't tell me the wind blew it open again."

"We came back and found it wide open."

Laurie's teeth chatter.

"That explains why it's so cold. Thanks for loading the wood stove."

"Listen, we installed the new door and replaced the wood where the frame rotted. But check around the house and make sure nothing is missing."

"How did you finish so fast?"

"Teamwork. Do you want to see?"

"Hell, yeah."

Hensel stands on a chair and affixes weather stripping around the frame when Laurie follows Darcy to the back door.

"This is amazing," Laurie says, touching the door with a grin. "I can't thank you enough, but I'll start with my wallet."

"First," Darcy says, locking eyes with her cousin. "I'm serious about what I said. Check out the house so we're sure nobody broke in."

"The wind blew the door open, Darcy. That damn door was a thorn in my side since the day I moved in."

"Let's not take any chances."

Laurie glances at Hensel, who nods in agreement.

"Okay, but I don't own anything worth stealing."

Fire crackles inside the wood stove and spreads pleasing warmth through the old house, the steel door paying immediate dividends. Laurie investigates the downstairs, and with Darcy in tow, she ensures none of her belongings are missing on the second floor.

"All good?"

"Like I said, it was the wind."

A flash of light across the windows cuts Laurie off. Someone is in the driveway. Unspoken anxiety passes from Laurie to Darcy. Laurie doesn't get visitors, especially after dark.

When they clamber down the stairs, Hensel stands in the open door and looks over his shoulder at Darcy. Curious, Darcy peers around Hensel at the brights beaming through the entryway like hurtling meteors. She shields her eyes as the engine cuts off, killing the lights. A sheriff cruiser. But it's not

Filmore paying Laurie another visit. Sheriff Tipton steps down from the cruiser and clicks the door shut as one of his deputies exits out the passenger side. The sheriff stares at the three adults in the entryway before he adjusts his hat and strides on long legs to the front porch. The deputy, a rotund man with a boyish face, folds his arms beside Tipton.

"Sheriff," Hensel says in greeting.

The sheriff's eyes look different from when Darcy last saw them. They're piercing, accusatory. Visions of Genoa Cove flash through Darcy's memory, and she's tempted to slam the door shut and usher Hunter to safety so Tipton and his deputies can't lock him up for a crime he didn't commit. And someone has committed a crime. She's certain. Darcy reads the truth on Tipton's face as she spies the nearly full moon leering through a break in the clouds.

"Ms. Gellar and Mr. Hensel."

"Is there a problem?"

"Where were the two of you between the hours of three and five this afternoon," Tipton says, singling out Hensel and Darcy.

Hunter and Jennifer crowd behind Laurie. Darcy glances at her cousin, who nods and corrals Hunter and Jennifer into the kitchen.

"We were here," Hensel says. "Working on the house."

"Both of you?"

"Yes."

Tipton chews his lip and jots a note on his pad.

"Can anyone corroborate your whereabouts?"

Darcy glances at Hensel in confusion.

"No," Darcy says, folding her arms against the chill. "We spent the afternoon working on the house, and Laurie took my kids shopping out of town. They just returned. What's this about?"

"We misplaced one of our children," Tipton says, searching Darcy's face for a reaction.

"I don't understand."

"The two of you need to come with me."

Darcy looks back at Laurie, praying her kids hadn't heard Tipton. Too late. Hunter tries to push past Laurie, who braces her arms against the counter and refrigerator to keep him from getting around her.

"Are you placing us under arrest?"

"No. Not at this time. But this will go a lot easier if you come with me."

6

Darcy and Hensel sit at a wooden table inside a white room with one dark window she can't see beyond. They're inside an interrogation room. So much for Tipton claiming they weren't under arrest. Three strips of florescent lights hum overhead, one row flickering every several seconds.

Joined at the front door by Filmore, the overweight deputy led Darcy and Hensel inside the interrogation room a half-hour ago and promised them Tipton would come inside. Still no Tipton, though Darcy hears them speaking in low tones outside the door.

"This is bullshit. Tipton knows he can't hold us."

"Take a breath," Hensel says. "Whatever Tipton thinks he has on us, we've done nothing wrong. But blowing out of here will increase his suspicion that we have something to hide."

Darcy's mouth closes when the door opens. Tipton nods at the deputy in the hallway and shuts the door behind him. He rounds the table and pulls out the chair with the deliberate sluggishness of a dentist poking around a decayed molar. When he sits down, he sets his elbows on the table and leans toward them.

"You want to tell us what this is about?"

Hensel rests a hand on Darcy's forearm. The salve doesn't help. She's stir crazy with impatience, exactly what Tipton wants.

The sheriff reveals the folder in his lap as Darcy shares a look with Hensel. Tipton removes a photograph of a young teenage girl with light brown hair, round, thoughtful eyes, and braces that sparkle from a camera flash. The lush, phony landscape and idyllic blue sky in the background marks the photo as a school picture. Tipton slides the photograph between Darcy and Hensel.

"Sandy Young of twenty-six Church Street in Scarlet River. Age fourteen."

After divulging the girl's age, Tipton watches their faces as he had on Laurie's porch.

"What does this have to do with us?"

"She went missing this afternoon, last seen at Cass Park between three and five o'clock. Witnesses spotted the two of you in the park around this time."

Tipton removes a second photograph. It's a picture of Darcy and Hensel in the park approaching a group of women gathered around the swing set.

"You can't possibly think we kidnapped a teenage girl."

"The woman who took this picture says you approached Sandy Young. Frightened her enough that the girl ran off."

Darcy looks at Hensel, who shrugs.

"I don't remember this girl," Hensel says, squinting at the picture. "But we spoke to quite a few people."

"Yes, you asked questions about Nina Steyer, the last kidnapped girl from ten years ago. And we know you were at Maury's inquiring about Nina. An hour later, the first kidnapping in a decade occurred after dozens of people saw you speaking to Sandy Young. It makes me wonder why you're so interested in Nina and why you wanted to speak with Sandy."

"Like Agent Hensel said, we met many people in the park," says Darcy. "I don't recognize this girl, but we'll help you find her."

Tipton itches his stubble.

"What business did you have in town before you stopped at Maury's?"

"We purchased a replacement door for Laurie's house. I have the receipt." Darcy stands so she can dig the wallet out of her jeans. She hands the receipt to Tipton, who looks it over and hands it back. "Sheriff, we're trying to help. Margaret, the waitress who spoke with us at the diner, saw Nina."

"Our people already interviewed Margaret Polson. She saw a girl who *looked* like an older version of Nina Steyer, but who can say what Nina would look like if she was still alive today?"

"She's still alive. Her appearance and Sandy's abduction are related, Sheriff, and somehow they tie in with Michael Rivers and my cousin's stalker. This can't be the only kidnapping. Are you certain there are no other missing girls in the area?"

Tipton knots his fingers together.

"Not in my county. Not in over ten years."

Darcy's eyebrow arches.

"Not in your county? Is that a way of saying a kidnapping occurred outside your jurisdiction?"

Tipton shakes his head.

"Girl by the name of Emily Vogt went missing outside Atlanta, but that's nowhere near Millport."

"Age?"

Tipton swallows an angry reply and taps his fingers against the desk.

"Fourteen."

"Same age as Sandy Young?"

Tipton doesn't answer, only glares at her.

"If you want our help, we'll give you anything you need. But you can't hold us because some woman spotted us in the park. Either press charges or let us walk."

Darcy holds her breath, hoping she won this game of chicken. The truth is Sheriff Tipton can hold them overnight if he chooses, but Darcy doesn't believe his conviction is strong enough. Tipton glares at them, then he snatches the photographs and slides them inside the folder.

He keeps them inside the interrogation room for another half-hour, asking them mundane questions until he's written a novel based on their actions since three o'clock.

"No charges tonight," Tipton says, tossing down the pen. "Neither of you leaves my county until I say so. Do we have an understanding?"

Hensel, reserved to this point, shoves his chair back and stands.

"You know where to find us."

"Fine. I'll have Deputy Filmore drive you home."

Filmore doesn't speak during the ride. His eyes meet theirs in the mirror and dart back to the road. He radios back to the department when the cruiser turns down Laurie's driveway. Then he rounds the vehicle and opens the back door. Darcy shrugs her bag over her shoulder and waits for Hensel. Filmore locks eyes with her, and for a split-second she's certain the deputy wants to say something. Then he climbs into the cruiser and backs out.

Jennifer, Hunter, and Laurie await them on the porch. It's after ten, the long day hanging heavy on Darcy's bones as she climbs the steps. Laurie touches Darcy's shoulder.

"Well?"

"Go inside," Darcy tells Hunter and Jennifer. Jennifer opens her mouth, and Darcy shoots her a warning glare. "Do as I say. I'll be in soon."

Hunter's defiance earns him a pointed look from Darcy, and he marches into the house behind Jennifer. Laurie grasps Darcy's arms and searches her face.

"Why did Sheriff Tipton take you to the station?"

"A girl was kidnapped this afternoon. A teenager named Sandy Young."

"That's terrible, but what does that have to do with you?"

"We stopped at the park, and apparently Sandy was there, and a woman saw us talk to her."

Laurie puts a hand on her forehead.

"So the backwoods sheriff assumes the two strangers in town must be kidnappers, even though one is a federal agent and the other retired from the FBI three years ago. How's that for southern hospitality? Don't mess around. Get a lawyer, but nobody from this county. You can't trust anyone here."

"Laurie, we won't need a lawyer," Hensel says, sitting on the top step.

"Don't be so sure. What were you doing at Cass Park in the first place?"

"We stopped and showed Nina Steyer's picture around, hoping someone saw her," Darcy says.

"Wait, that's the abducted girl. I see the posters around town, but she disappeared ten years ago."

"Two people claim they saw her over the last month at Maury's. Tipton doesn't believe their stories, but it's possible the kidnapper is also your stalker."

Darcy holds back that many serial killers begin with petty crimes and graduate to kidnapping before they acquire a taste for murder.

"All right, stop. Just stop." Laurie holds up her hand. "I appreciate your concern, but if you throw wild theories around in this county, you'll end up in more trouble than you can imagine."

"I don't think so. Sheriff Tipton is a good man." Even Hensel glances at Darcy in disbelief. "He's desperate and grasping at straws. Put yourself in his position. Ten years ago, someone kidnapped four girls. Three bodies, one girl never found. The FBI failed to find the killer, but any lawman takes it personally when tragedy occurs on his watch. Tipton won't admit it, but the Nina talk has him rattled. Now he's staring at another abduction, and the public will have his head if he doesn't bring this girl back alive."

Laurie slumps against the railing and rubs a tension cramp out of her shoulder.

"Tipton shouldn't have blamed you. That's just ridiculous. I'm sorry you came here. I'm responsible for this mess."

"He didn't blame us," Darcy says, kneeling down beside Laurie.

"Well, he sorta did," Hensel says, giving her an unconvinced shrug over Laurie's shoulder.

"All that matters is we figure out who's kidnapping girls in Scarlet River, and that begins with tracking down Nina Steyer."

Hunter appears ready for war when Hensel and Laurie trail Darcy into the kitchen.

"It's happening again. Same as Genoa Cove."

"No, Hunter," Darcy says, running her hands under the water and wiping them on the towel. "It was a misunderstanding, Your mom isn't in trouble."

"Then why did he put you in the back of a sheriff's cruiser and drive you to the station? I heard what Laurie said about getting a lawyer. You should."

Darcy wonders what else Hunter heard.

"Agent Hensel and I aren't under arrest."

"Not yet," Jennifer says. Her eyes are red as she wipes a tear on her sleeve. "Wait until he comes back. We never should have come here."

Jennifer storms up the stairs before Darcy can reply.

"That one is on you," Darcy says, glaring at Hunter while she tilts her head toward the staircase. "I'll be up to talk with both of you soon. Right now, sit with your sister and keep her grounded."

Hunter lowers his head and climbs the stairs. When the door slams shut, Darcy sighs and taps her knuckles on the table.

"I'm sorry you needed to see that."

"They're worried," Laurie says. "Nothing you can blame them for."

Shifting from foot to foot, Hensel sips from a glass of water.

"I'll be out in the garage stacking firewood."

Darcy lets him go, sensing Hensel growing more uncomfortable. He accompanied Darcy and her family with a desire to help, and she's thrown him into a quagmire as thanks.

After Hensel closes the garage door, Darcy wanders outside to the porch. Wind shreds the clouds and hurls the remaining fragments toward the sea. The moon beams down on the farmhouse, turning the meadow silver and blue. From her pocket, Darcy removes the folded poster of Nina Steyer. She tilts the picture toward the moonlight and studies the girl's face, though she's committed it to memory. The child serial killer allowed Nina Steyer to live. But why?

The steady clonk of wood inside the garage settles Darcy's nerves as she listens to Hensel work. The sound makes her feel human again and reminds her there are other tasks in life besides tracking murderers. She pushes herself up and walks toward the garage, hoping Hensel will welcome the company, but her phone rings before she makes it to the door.

Darcy stops in the driveway and contemplates whether to

answer the unrecognized caller. Before she changes her mind, she answers the phone and cautiously says, "hello."

"It's been too long, Darcy."

She fumbles the phone upon hearing the voice of Michael Rivers. She changed her number after the Full Moon Killer called her in North Carolina, yet he's found her again.

"What the hell do you want, Michael?"

"To see your blood in the moonlight. You've been a busy woman, Darcy. I knew you'd come to Laurie's aid."

Darcy swings around and watches the meadow for movement. The moonlight drags black, monstrous shadows across the valley like blood spilling off the hills.

"Leave my cousin out of this. Your war is with me, not my family."

"My war is with everyone you care about, Darcy. You took my life away, and now I'm taking yours."

The garage door opens. Hensel stares at her, sensing something is wrong. Darcy points at the phone and mouths *Rivers*, and Hensel calls the FBI to begin a trace. It's futile. The FBI knows where Michael Rivers is: behind bars outside Buffalo, New York. Rivers is as intelligent as he is powerful. He's using a burner phone supplied to him by a corrupt guard or prison worker, someone Rivers bribed.

"You know about the kidnapping," Darcy says, realizing why Rivers called her after today's abduction. "Who took Sandy Young?"

A hoarse cackle travels through the phone.

"Don't you wish I'd tell you? He likes teenage girls, Darcy. They're like a drizzle of honey over ice cream. I bet he's enjoying himself right now."

Hensel winds his arm, a signal to keep Rivers talking.

"Let the girl go, Michael. She's not a part of this. Tell me who took her...hello? Don't hang up on me, Michael."

The line goes dead. Hensel's tight-lipped grimace tells Darcy the FBI didn't trace the call. Blocking the wind from reaching his ear with his free hand, Hensel finishes his conversation.

"What did he say?"

Darcy recounts Michael's words.

"He knew about Sandy Young, Eric."

"Did he say her name?"

She goes over the conversation in her head.

"I don't believe so."

"It could be a bluff, and he could have read about the abduction, but it's likely he's involved."

"Call the FBI back and get a team down here. This case is over Tipton's head."

Hensel opens and closes his mouth as if carrying on an internal argument.

"It won't fly. The case falls under local jurisdiction, Darcy. You know that. Unless Tipton requests FBI involvement, we're on the sidelines."

"That worked out well in North Carolina."

"Yeah, well. My hands were tied. If the Genoa Cove PD called us in sooner, we could have stepped in."

"Wait a minute," Darcy says, hands on hips. "Rivers called me from New York. Once a crime crosses state lines, it's the FBI's decision to step in."

"I like the way you're thinking, but we didn't trace the call."

"You don't need to trace the call. We already know where to find Rivers."

"Yeah, but we can't prove Rivers called you. If Warden Ellsworth presses him, Rivers can claim someone impersonated his voice. Don't shoot the messenger, but we need conclusive evidence to take the case."

"Unless Tipton invites you in."

"And you think that's likely?"

"Like I told you, Eric. Tipton feels scared, and he won't find Sandy Young without our help."

Hensel leans one arm against the garage door and grins.

"*Our* help?"

"If it means finding Nina Steyer and Sandy Young, I want to help."

Darcy's bravado is short lived, as fickle as autumn leaves caught in a gale. Hensel phones Tipton about Rivers, and Darcy can hear the unconvinced sheriff shouting through the receiver. When she returns to the house, Laurie is in bed and the kids are upstairs, hopefully doing homework and not cruising the Internet on their phones. She knows they break the rules and reach out to their friends. Thwarting their efforts lessens the chance someone will track them down.

The house feels cavernous. Footsteps above her head elicit groans from the bedroom floorboards, and Darcy imagines Hunter crossing the room to show Jennifer a funny meme. But the darkness at the window and the realization that Michael Rivers can reach out from behind his prison bars a thousand miles away and lay his cold, bloodless fingers on her neck sends a chill through her body. Even with two secure doors, every house has points of vulnerability. The windows. The attic. A skilled intruder can lift himself onto the porch roof and scale the wall by placing his feet on the window sill. Then it's a short climb to the attic where he can conceal himself for days and nights, silent as a ghost, until the house is asleep.

Shutting out her children's murmurs, Darcy pictures the attack. If she isn't wearing the Glock, she won't have time to obtain a weapon if the intruder breaks through the window. Darcy opens the kitchen drawers and assesses the potential weapons at her disposal. Laurie's cutlery tray overflows with knives. Mostly butter knives, but a handful of steak knives serve as weapons in a pinch. Knowing Laurie won't miss a few knives, she grabs three and patrols the living room, seeking hiding spots. She slides a knife below a thick encyclopedia with the hilt facing out. Leaning back in the recliner, savoring the waves of heat rolling off the wood stove, she imagines the window breaking and sits up. Reaching behind her, she snags the hilt between her fingers.

The intruder might have a gun. It won't matter. It's a short leap from the chair to the window. One stab to his arm when it gropes inside. The face and eyes are more vulnerable. She'll do whatever it takes to keep her family safe.

She repeats the process through the downstairs until she hides all three knives. After she finishes, Hensel returns from the garage, rubbing the cold off his hands.

"So I talked to headquarters," Hensel says, moving his hands in front of the wood stove.

"And?"

"They have a team on call and ready to deploy if Tipton gives the okay. In the meantime, the FBI contacted the warden about Rivers' phone call. It won't get us any farther than it did in North Carolina, but if they locate the phone, we can prove Rivers called you."

"Good start. I need to decide how best to approach Tipton, especially after he all but accused us of kidnapping Sandy Young. First thing in the morning, we'll drive to Millport."

"You're certain you want to confront the sheriff?"

"I'm not confronting him. I'll appeal to his sensibility. We both want the same thing: to rescue Sandy and find Nina."

"All right. Now, will you tell me what you were up to before I came inside?"

Hensel raises one eyebrow and awaits Darcy's response.

"The best defense is a good offense."

Darcy shows Hensel where she hid the knives. Hensel itches his head, his face torn between surprise and amusement.

"So you stole all the steak knives. Trying to convert your cousin to vegetarianism?"

"There are four more steak knives in the drawer. No worries."

Hensel collapses on the couch and touches the small of his back.

"Maybe we should trade places for a night or two," Darcy says.

"No, I'll be fine. Besides, Hunter and Jennifer don't want me sleeping in their room."

7

Dammit, when will she fall asleep?

Curled under the covers, Jennifer watches her mother through slitted eyes. She's good at feigning sleep, but she acknowledges her mother is better. Before the Darkwater Cove murders, Jennifer tried to sneak through the living room past her sleeping mother so she could meet up with Kaitlyn on a Saturday night. Except Mom hadn't been asleep, and to this day Jennifer suspects her mother figured out she broke curfew from time to time and set her up, baited her. It took a lot of pleading and arguing before Jennifer convinced her mother she was only going out to the car to grab her book bag, which she'd fortunately left in the backseat when her mother checked.

Beside Jennifer, Hunter mumbles something indiscernible under his breath and tugs the blankets over his shoulder. It's after midnight, the yard outside the window bathed in sharp moonlight. Checking the phone beneath the covers, Jennifer winces as the signal dances in and out. The last message she received from Kaitlyn mentioned juicy news about Aaron and Sam. Though Jennifer placed the phone in silent mode so she could read the texts without alerting her mother, the crappy signal inside the old house swallows Kaitlyn's replies.

When Jennifer feels sleep pulling her down and worries she'll miss the scheduled rendezvous, her mother closes the laptop and sets it aside. A yawn, then the room turns quiet. But is her mother asleep? Jennifer forces herself to count to one hundred before edging back the covers, one eye glued to her mother. No movement. She's out. Or she's set another trap for Jennifer.

Dressed in pajama bottoms and a heavy sweatshirt, a pair of sneakers in her hand, Jennifer touches her feet on the cold floorboards and stands. The floor moans, a soft, pitiful sound as if the farmhouse issues a dying breath. Jennifer freezes, ready to dive under the blankets if her mother awakens. She doesn't.

An antique clock ticks in the hallway as Jennifer slips out of the bedroom. Laurie snores down the hall. A shock travels through Jennifer's body when the fire snaps downstairs. Catching her breath, she descends the stairs and peeks around the wall. Agent Hensel sprawls on the couch, one arm hanging off, a leg dangled over the edge. Talk about taking a risk. Does she intend to sneak past an FBI agent?

But as she steps down the stairway, Agent Hensel never stirs. She's down the stairs and in full view if his eyes pop open, so she concocts a lie to cover herself if he catches her—she can't sleep and came downstairs for a glass of milk. It won't explain the sweatshirt and sneakers, but hopefully he won't ask questions.

For a second, Jennifer believes she forgot her phone in bed. Panicking, she touches her pockets until she finds the plastic shell inside her sweatshirt.

The cold is a living, breathing thing. Jennifer's breath catches in her throat as she steps outside. She clicks the door shut behind her, careful to leave the knob unlocked, and steps down the stairs. When her sneakers touch the soft grass, she spins back toward the house, expecting to see a disapproving face in the window.

But she's alone in the night. Free.

Excitement surges through her bones as she runs through the soft grass to the garage. Shit. Agent Hensel locked the garage door. She must brave the cold, a small price to pay for being a normal teenager for a few minutes. The phone rattles and hums inside her pocket as the messages pour in. They're all from Kaitlyn, too many to skim through.

To hell with it. If you're gonna live, might as well live on the edge.

She touches Kaitlyn's picture and listens as the phone rings. Hopping in excitement, she hopes her high school friend is still awake. Kaitlyn answers.

"Well, hello there, stranger," Kaitlyn says with a giggle. "Mama Bear let the cubs run wild tonight?"

"You don't know the half of it."

"Someone's gonna get in trouble." Kaitlyn draws out the last syllable.

"Like I care. Okay, I've been waiting all night. Give me the dirt on Aaron and Sam."

"You sure? I mean, you're not mature enough to talk on the phone without Mama Bear present. This could get you in so much trouble."

"Really? You go three weeks without hearing my voice, and the first thing you do is go mega-bitch on me?"

"Ha-ha. Okay, hold on to your hair, because this will blow your mind."

"Just tell me already. It's freezing as *fek* outside."

Kaitlyn snickers. Jennifer pictures her friend pacing the bedroom...the nice, warm, well-lit bedroom...phone clutched between her shoulder and cheek as she peeks into the backyard.

"All right, then. Since you had to sneak out of the den to hear my alluring voice, I'll tell you. So get this. Aaron and Sam didn't only rape Smith Town girls. They started in Genoa Cove."

Jennifer switches the phone to her other ear and glances around the garage. It's dark inside the farmhouse.

"Oh, my God. Are you serious?"

"Dead serious."

"Anyone we know?" Kaitlyn chomps on a piece of gum, a habit that turns Jennifer's stomach. "Hurry. I don't have all night."

"What would you say if I told you they started with Aaron's sister?"

Kaitlyn's reply doubles Jennifer over. She drops to one knee, unsure how she got there. No, there has to be a mistake. She can't mean Bethany.

"Who told you this?"

"It's the talk of the school, stranger. If you hadn't gone into hiding, you'd be in the loop."

"Give me the deets, or it didn't happen."

"Turns out it was Sam's idea. He came over to visit while Aaron was at the community house grabbing their mail. Bethany let him inside and told him to wait, but Sam followed Bethany to her bedroom."

Gray matter sits in the pit of Jennifer's stomach. She grabs her hair with her free hand and pulls, wanting to feel pain, wanting to experience anything besides the sickness gurgling through her body.

"Please tell me this is one of your jokes. Didn't Aaron help her?"

"Not exactly."

Jennifer doesn't recall the rest of the conversation. She can't be sure she didn't end the call before Kaitlyn stopped talking, yet she's haunted by Aaron Torres overpowering his sister and holding her down on the bed while Sam strips her clothes off.

Across the sky, the stars are sharp and uncaring as she sits in the dark and weeps. Hunter needs to know, but she can't tell him. No way. The truth will kill him, and God knows how far he will go to make it back to North Carolina. He might steal Mom's car or Laurie's truck.

Another shiver of nausea rolls through Jennifer. Kaitlyn treated the situation like it was a joke, something to laugh about over stolen bottles of beer. She's as artificial and caustic as the rest of the girls at Genoa Cove High School. And who leaked the story? Nobody should have learned the victims' names.

The bushes rattle in the meadow. Something moves through the brush, coming closer for a better look at the girl alone in the dark.

"Hunter, is that you?"

No answer comes.

Jennifer pockets the phone and runs for the house.

8

In the dingy morning light pouring through the bedroom window, Darcy narrows her eyebrows.

Hunter and Jennifer huddle under the blankets, eyes shut. Their sneakers lie jumbled at the foot of the bed, but a clump of grassy mud that wasn't there when Darcy fell asleep lies beside the door. She nudges the dirt with the toe of her sneaker. The mud crumbles at the edges.

She lifts her sneakers and checks each. Then she turns over both teenagers' sneakers and studies the treads. No mud, no grass.

Darcy sighs to herself and steps into the hallway, but as she shuts the door, she worries Hunter or Jennifer sneaked outside in the middle of the night. They wouldn't take that large a risk. Would they?

The smell of bacon wafts up the stairs. Entering the kitchen, she finds Hensel flipping bacon while Laurie starts a pot of coffee.

"Can I talk to you for a second?" Darcy asks, her brow creased as she waits beside the table.

Hensel reaches into the cupboard and removes the dinner plates.

"It's okay," Laurie says, taking the tongs from Hensel. "I'll take over from here."

While Laurie cracks an egg against the pan, Darcy pulls Hensel around the corner and into the living room.

"Did you hear anything in the middle of the night?"

"I slept straight through," Hensel says. "Why? Something make you think Laurie's stalker came back?"

"No, not that." Darcy sighs and rubs her temples. "It's probably nothing, but I found mud in the bedroom this morning and thought one of the kids sneaked out of the house last night."

"You sure the mud wasn't there last night?"

"Positive."

Hensel sits on the arm of the couch.

"I didn't see anyone come downstairs. Not to say someone didn't get past me. I was pretty out of it. Any idea why Hunter or Jennifer would have gone outside?"

"The cell coverage. None of us get a decent signal inside the house."

"And Hunter or Jennifer wanted to contact their friends without you knowing."

"That's the other reason. It scares the hell out of me they aren't taking the danger seriously."

"I'll try to stay awake later tonight. See if anyone shows their face after the lights go out."

"Don't lose sleep on my account. I'm just being paranoid."

Satisfied, Darcy follows Hensel into the kitchen.

"Did you call Quantico back?"

"They're waiting to hear from the warden," Hensel says, grabbing the orange juice from the refrigerator. "As of an hour ago, they hadn't recovered Rivers' phone."

Laurie's eyes shoot up at the mention of the serial killer.

"They won't," says Darcy, pushing the eggs around in the pan. "He paid someone well to keep his secrets safe. I'm surprised nobody opened the gates and let him walk out."

"What's on the docket for today?" Laurie asks as she plates their breakfasts.

"If he'll meet with me, I'll speak with Sheriff Tipton. Now that the FBI is looking into the Rivers phone call, he might view Sandy Young's kidnapping in a different light."

"You're not going anywhere until you eat," Laurie says, glaring at Darcy through the tops of her eyes. "If you lose another pound, you'll blow away before Christmas."

Eager to leave, Darcy rushes through breakfast. Hunter and Jennifer are still asleep when Darcy checks on them. His hair wet from the shower, Hensel throws on his jacket and tells Darcy to meet him at the door when she's ready. She doesn't get to the front door before her phone rings. A local number appears on the screen, and Darcy answers as she bounds down the stairs.

"Is this the woman from the FBI?"

The female's southern twang sounds familiar to Darcy, who holds up a finger when Hensel sends her a questioning stare.

"Yes, this is Darcy Gellar. Who's calling?"

"This is Margaret from Maury's Diner. You told me to call you if that girl came by again. Well, she's here right now."

"Wait, Nina Steyer is at the diner?"

"I'm not saying it's Nina, but it's damn sure the girl who asked the truck driver for a ride. She's talking to another trucker right now."

Darcy hurries into her jacket and grabs the keys off the counter.

Lowering the phone to her chest, Darcy asks, "Can you keep an eye on the kids this morning? We'll be back in a few hours."

"I've got it covered," Laurie says, standing aside as Darcy and Hensel rush out the door.

Hensel hustles ahead of her to the car where Darcy tosses him the keys and slides into the passenger seat. Darcy takes one last look at the house, shivering over the creeping sensation that the world has tilted off its axis as it did before the Darkwater Cove murders.

"Margaret, whatever you do, keep Nina at Maury's. Don't let her get in that truck, and don't lose sight of her. I'm calling the sheriff now."

In a cloud of dust, Hensel backs up and wheels the car around. As they speed toward town, Darcy reaches the County Sheriff's Office and convinces Deputy Filmore to put her through to Tipton. The sheriff isn't happy to hear from her, but his curiosity piques when she tells him Nina Steyer is at Maury's.

"I'll be there in twenty minutes," Tipton says after shouting instructions to his deputies. "Don't do anything until I arrive."

Every light in Scarlet River turns red at their approach, and Darcy bounces her legs as she curses the traffic signals. The Prius is the only vehicle at the intersection three blocks from the diner. Hensel glances in both directions.

"Should I run the light?"

Darcy chews a nail.

"Do it."

Hensel punches the gas and speeds from stop sign to stop sign until the diner materializes across the road. When they swerve into the parking lot, Margaret stands beside the door with her hands cupping her elbows. She shifts from foot to foot, the wind whipping hair across her face. Darcy knows Nina vanished again.

"Where is she?" Darcy asks, jogging toward Margaret.

"I tried to keep her here. I swear I did."

Margaret's chest hitches, and Darcy lays a hand on her shoulder.

"It's okay. Where did you last see her?"

Margaret shakes her head at Darcy and scrunches her nose.

"She didn't get in the truck. The guy noticed all the fuss and got cold feet over letting Nina hitch, then she disappeared. We were all watching her, all the wait staff and two of the cooks, but the commotion attracted a crowd. She must have blended in and escaped."

Hensel glances around the parking lot and spots an eighteen-wheeler parked parallel to the fence.

"The trucker is still here?" he asks.

"In the diner. He's seated at the counter."

"Okay, let's talk to this guy," Hensel says to Darcy as the sheriff's cruiser motors into the parking lot.

"Tipton looks pissed," Darcy says, eyeing the sheriff through the cruiser's windshield.

Hensel grimaces.

"Wait until he finds out it's another false alarm."

"Before you go inside," Margaret says as she reaches into her pocket. "I took her picture."

"A picture of Nina?" Darcy asks as Margaret cups her hand above the screen to block the glare.

Darcy squints at the photograph which catches the woman turning away as if she senses the camera. Her hair appears a touch lighter than the sandy browns in the posters, but hair color can change as a child matures into a woman. The eyes draw Darcy's attention. This woman looks like the aged phantom of Nina Steyer.

"Send a copy to my phone."

Margaret nods and swipes through her phone. Tipton's door slams. The onlookers crowded outside Maury's clear a path as the sheriff beelines toward Darcy and Hensel.

"Well, where's Nina?" Tipton places his hands on his hips. Darcy can see from the set of his jaw that Tipton itches for a confrontation. "Let me guess. Disappeared a moment before I arrived."

"She tried to hitch a ride out of town again," Darcy says.

"I suppose the trucker disappeared too?"

"He's inside the diner. We're about to interview him. You're welcome to join us unless you've already decided this is a wild goose chase. Would you at least look at the picture the waitress took of Nina?"

Darcy calls up the photograph and zooms in on the woman's face. Tipton groans. Then something flashes in his eyes. Anguish and desperation.

"The FBI doesn't have jurisdiction in Scarlet River," Tipton says, glaring at Hensel. He shifts his attention to Darcy. "And you're not an active agent. Stand aside. My county, my interview."

Tipton adjusts his hat and pulls the door open. The sea of customers splits as he struts toward the counter where a skinny man in blue jeans and a flannel shirt sits with his back to them. The man leans over a plate of pancakes and hash browns, unaware of the sheriff towering behind him. A female cook slides a cup of fruit in front of the customer. Her eyes go wide at the sight of the sheriff, and she swivels on her heel and escapes into the bustle of the busy kitchen, throwing harried looks over her shoulder.

Sensing the sheriff, the man drops his fork and turns.

"You the man who claims he saw Nina Steyer?"

The trucker touches a napkin to the corners of his mouth and clears his throat.

"A woman asked me if I'd drive her out of town, but I don't know any Nina Steyer."

"You got a name, son?"

"I'm Keith Boughton."

Boughton offers his hand, but Tipton ignores it.

"You in the habit of picking up hitchhikers?"

Boughton glances at Darcy and Hensel for help as he fumbles for a reply.

"I...I didn't mean any harm. Told her I was headed up Athens way, if that was okay, and I'd be happy to give her a ride. That's when I noticed everyone looking at the woman like they'd seen a ghost, and I thought maybe it wasn't such a good idea to let her inside my truck."

"So you left her alone in the parking lot?"

"No, she'd already gone. Hey, am I in trouble?"

Darcy removes the folded poster of Nina. Tipton snatches it from her hand and spreads it out on the counter, jabbing his index finger beside Nina's face.

"Is this the woman you saw?"

Lifting the poster, Boughton scrutinizes the photo. The truck driver tilts his head and furrows his brow.

"Well, I'll be."

"So it was her?"

"Couldn't have been. This was a woman, not a girl. But with God as my witness, this could be her little sister."

Tipton sighs and takes the poster from Boughton. Pointing at the text on the bottom, his finger follows each word.

"Went missing ten years ago."

Boughton sits back in his chair, the gravity of the situation pressing on him.

"Shoot...I didn't know. Ten years. You really think it could be her?"

Tipton wheels away from Boughton and moves among the intimidated wait staff and cooks, interviewing each as Darcy and Hensel trail behind. For a man convinced Nina never visited Maury's, Tipton appears dogged, relentless. Darcy glimpses anxiousness again.

While Tipton speaks with the staff, Darcy and Hensel split

up and move through the crowd. Using the poster of Nina pinned inside the entryway, Darcy shows the picture to each person. Most remain unconvinced, but a few point to Nina's photograph and nod, steadfast they saw an older version of Nina Steyer.

Tipton looks as if he's run a marathon at a full sprint when he meets Darcy and Hensel in the parking lot.

"I'll need a copy of the waitress's photograph," Tipton tells Darcy.

"Don't you think it's a good idea to put a BOLO out on this woman?"

"Already done," the sheriff says, removing his hat and wiping sweat off his forehead. "Except she's done nothing wrong, unless you want me to bring her in for hitchhiking. Shit. I can't deal with a ghost chase when I've got a missing girl to find."

Sandy Young went missing yesterday afternoon. Darcy knows the statistics. Few child abductions have happy endings after twenty-four hours pass, and the clock is ticking against them.

"You're already looking into known sex offenders in the area?"

"One step ahead of you, Ms. Gellar."

"I know one guy in town who likes girls Sandy Young's age."

Darcy recounts the story of the man following Jennifer through the store and the close encounter in town, doing her best to describe him.

"Gil Waggoner," Tipton says with a groan.

"You know him?"

"We've had our share of run-ins with Waggoner, mostly the drunk and disorderly kind. But two years ago he tried to pick up a fifteen-year-old girl hanging out with her friend behind a downtown pub. No place for two teenagers."

"Is he capable of abduction?"

Tipton ponders the idea as vehicles turn out of Maury's, the excitement dying down.

"It's not beyond the realm of possibility. I'll check on Waggoner." Tipton rubs his face. "This horse shit didn't happen around here twenty years ago. The whole area is going to hell. Serial killers. Kidnappers."

He spits *kidnappers* and looks toward the sky, seeking answers that don't exist.

"Sheriff, bring in my team," Hensel says.

Tipton's eyes narrow. Darcy can see him wrestling with the idea.

"A lot of good that did me ten years ago when we still had a chance to find Nina."

"You're dealing with a kidnapped girl and a stalker in league with Michael Rivers. Don't solve the case on your own." Recognizing Tipton's apprehension, Hensel steps closer to Tipton. "We'll help you figure out who the kidnapper is. You make the arrest. It's your investigation."

Tipton clenches his teeth and lifts the radio off his belt.

"Filmore, I want the men manning the roadblocks to look for a woman resembling Nina Steyer...yeah, I said Nina Steyer. And tell the other deputies we're bringing in the FBI." Tipton stares at Hensel and Darcy. "Let's bring Sandy Young home."

9

The farmhouse door closes, blocking out the howling wind and the unusual cold. Hensel and Darcy spent two hours inside the sheriff's department while Tipton coordinated with the FBI before she drove back to Laurie's, leaving Hensel with Tipton.

"So the FBI is coming to Scarlet River?" Laurie asks, falling into the kitchen chair.

Darcy sips from a mug of hot chocolate, the porcelain warm in her hands.

"The team flies into Atlanta in an hour."

"Amazing. I never understood how you did it, Darcy, dropping everything at a moment's notice and flying to the scene of a horrible crime. Wait, how is Agent Hensel getting around if you have your car?"

"It's an official investigation now, and Eric is on the clock. He'll get a rental. A perk of the job."

"I guess that means he won't be hanging around the house anymore."

"No. They'll get hotel rooms, probably in Millport."

Laurie's eyes can't hold still. They move from the windows to the door and back to the table.

"I should have taken the stalker more seriously."

"Hey," Darcy says, setting the mug on the table. "You acted natural, same as I would react in your position. Nobody wants to accept the worst-case scenario."

"And now it's part of a federal investigation. How did this happen to us?"

Darcy lowers her eyes to the table. She brought this on Laurie, just as she invited the horror of Michael Rivers into the lives of her children, Amy Yang, and the murdered girls of Darkwater Cove. If she'd finished the job and killed Michael Rivers in that dark house three years ago, none of this would be happening.

Footsteps crossing through the upstairs cause Darcy to lift her head.

"How long did it take before my kids rolled out of bed?"

Laurie smirks.

"Noon."

"Rise and shine."

"Ha. I was the same way. I never got out of bed before lunchtime on the weekends when I was a teenager. My parents would cut up sandwiches while I pulled a box of Wheaties down from the cupboard." When Darcy doesn't laugh, Laurie leans her elbows on the table. "Don't blame yourself, Darcy. You're a victim."

Darcy sips the hot chocolate. The sweet liquid cannot wash away the lump in her throat.

"Every night I fall asleep worrying what my kids' lives will be like when this is over. They've both been attacked and abducted, and the psychopaths following the Full Moon Killer want both of them murdered. How do you live with something like that?"

Darcy sets the mug down and leans her head on her palm, elbow resting on the table. "And now another girl is missing."

Laurie opens her mouth to argue and closes it. Her silence weighs heavily on the room as the fire crackles inside the wood stove. Darcy jumps when her phone rings. She checks the caller ID and breathes a sigh of relief upon seeing Hensel's name.

"I better take this," Darcy says, stepping onto the porch.

The cold grew teeth while Darcy was inside. Is this Georgia or Northern Maine? She curses herself for not grabbing a jacket on the way outside.

"How long before the team arrives in Millport?"

"Two or three hours, depending on traffic," Hensel says. "The roadblocks have been up since yesterday afternoon, but I'm concerned the kidnapper took Sandy Young out of the county before Tipton realized she was missing."

"No chance. He's here, Eric. He evaded the FBI and sheriff's department for a decade. This is where he feels safe, this is where he buried the girls. He would never leave his trophies."

Hensel pauses.

"You should give the profile."

"That will go over well with the FBI—a civilian delivering the profile. No thanks. I've probably gotten you into enough trouble by dragging you into this mess."

"Don't worry about me." Hensel moves the phone away from his ear and answers a question. Darcy recognizes Tipton's voice in the background. "Still, it feels weird without you working the case. You have a better sense for murderers than anyone I've worked with." There's a pregnant pause before Hensel speaks again. "I wish you'd get it together so you could come back to the FBI."

"I didn't realize I was so broken."

"Look, maybe I'm reading too much into things, but you

haven't been yourself since I came to see you in Genoa Cove. I asked you then about the medication."

"You think I'm a junkie, Eric?"

"I never said that."

"You didn't have to."

Why is Hensel bringing this up over the phone when he could have spoken to Darcy at Laurie's?

"Forget I brought it up. You should come back to the BAU. If you're not ready for full-time work, start as a consultant. The new profiler would learn a ton working under you."

Darcy blows the hair out of her face.

"So that's it. You just want me to coach up your new prospect."

"That's not why I want you back. You have a sixth sense for tracking down serial killers that nobody can teach in a classroom."

"I retired, Eric. There's no turning that ship around."

"But you didn't retire. You left to heal, and from where I stand I'd say you've made amazing progress. You can come back when you're ready. The ball has always been in your court. Listen, the crew we're bringing in is top notch. I'd like you to come by tomorrow morning for the briefing and meet everyone."

"Me?"

"The agent in charge of the briefing is smart as a whip but green. She could use a more experienced profiler looking over her shoulder."

"Eric, I couldn't."

"Why the heck not?"

"I haven't profiled in three years. My mind isn't wired that way anymore. It's not a switch I can turn on and off on a whim."

"Could have fooled me. You knew things about Amy Yang's murderer long before the police figured it out."

She sits on the steps and drops her head between her knees. The day she walked away from the FBI, she never envisioned returning. Her children already lost one parent. She can't risk leaving them alone in the world, two forgotten souls for child services to control. But she lost a part of herself when she retired, as though the cardboard box of her work belongings she packed and carried out to her car contained her soul.

"I get what you're trying to do, Eric. Invite me into the fold and give me a taste of the action so I miss the job. Well, you're too late. I already miss profiling, but I need to protect Hunter and Jennifer. That's not something I can do when I'm at work."

"I know," Hensel says. "And that's something else I need to discuss with you. I spoke with headquarters. They can get you, Laurie, and the kids out of the country under assumed names, including passports."

Darcy lifts her head.

"Eric, what are you suggesting?"

"Get out of Georgia after the briefing. Take Laurie and the kids someplace warm and tropical, a beach where you're surrounded by vacationers. Keep everyone off the Internet, even if you have to confiscate their phones. We can send an agent with you until the danger is over. I know it sounds crazy, but it's better than waiting until Rivers sends a murderer after your family. The moon is almost full, Darcy."

Darcy looks up at the bedroom window. Jennifer stands behind the glass, her body blurred by the dirt-smudged pane.

"No, I can't."

"Why the hell not?"

"This is my mess to clean up. Sandy Young won't be the last girl the killer takes. The horror is just beginning."

Hensel grunts, flustered.

"The offer stands. When you change your mind, call me."

Darcy stares at the phone. She forgets the cold, the wind.

In less than five minutes, Hensel offered an escape from Georgia and opened a door to the FBI Darcy thought had permanently closed. Knowing the BAU team is en route to the sheriff's office while she waits for word at Laurie's makes her feel out of the loop, a non-participant in a deadly game that affects her life. She wants to drive back to the office, meet the team and review their profile, making suggestions where needed.

Instead, she's an unmoving target. She should take Hensel up on his offer. To hell with Georgia. The kids are scared, nobody is happy. Summer temperatures and blue waters in December would improve morale.

Except the plan is fool's gold. Hensel can fly Darcy and her family to an uncharted island near the equator, and Michael Rivers will find her.

No. The horror won't end until she puts a bullet between the Full Moon Killer's eyes.

∼

When the front door closes and her mother steps outside, Jennifer's nerves twitch. Hunter sits on the bed, back resting against the headboard, knees drawn toward his chest as he pages through news stories. She knows he's reading about the North Carolina murders, about the two rapists who terrorized Smith Town and left Hunter beaten and bloodied. Soon, he'll discover the truth about Bethany. None of the media sites will include the victims' names, but Hunter will venture down the rabbit hole of comment sections and message boards until he stumbles upon a poster who craves attention and places their desires over the rights of the victims.

Or Hunter will break Mom's rules and text a former teammate. Most of the players acted hostile toward Hunter, but he got along with a few. Kaitlyn knows about the rape, so the entire school must have heard by now.

Jennifer needs to be the one who tells him. The results will be tragic if it comes from someone else. She doesn't doubt Hunter will get to North Carolina. And he won't visit Genoa Cove with the sole purpose of consoling Bethany. He'll do something unpredictable, something crazy. Maybe sneak a gun into the jail and get himself arrested. Or worse.

Her throat goes dry when she opens her mouth. Hunter catches her staring and lifts his palms and shoulders.

"What did I do?"

"Nothing," Jennifer says, frazzled and searching for the right words.

Who is she kidding? The right words don't exist.

Jennifer eases down on the edge of the bed. All 110 pounds of her, she's the only person between Hunter and the door.

"I sneaked out again last night."

Hunter sits forward and shifts his body to look at her.

"Dumb. Mom will drive Laurie's truck over your phone if she finds out. I hope it was worth it."

Hunter's hypocrisy bristles her. He's contacted Bethany twice since they came to Georgia. She swallows the anger burning in her chest. As if the ban on contacting her friends isn't bad enough, she harbors Bethany's dark secret.

"I talked to Kaitlyn, Hunter." Before he rolls his eyes and loses interest, and before she loses her nerve, Jennifer hurries on. "She told me something about Aaron and Bethany."

Footsteps clonk up the stairs. Jennifer holds her breath until the bathroom door closes. Hunter's glare causes Jennifer to misplace her words. He doesn't know what she's about to tell him, but he senses the impending doom, reads it on her face. Unable to hold the words inside any longer, she tells Hunter.

Jennifer can't tell if she disclosed the truth in a manner

gentle enough to prevent Hunter from exploding. His eyes go glassy, and he stares at the wall as if an alternate reality only he can see exists in the hallway.

A long time passes with neither speaking. When her worry grows, she touches his arm. Hunter flinches as if Jennifer prodded him with a live wire.

"I'm sorry."

Hunter opens his mouth. Pauses. His fingers curl and uncurl.

"How long have you known?"

"Since last night."

"You should have woken me up as soon as you knew."

"How would that have worked with Mom in the room with us?"

Hunter wears a tight-lipped grimace.

"I'm going back to North Carolina."

Here it comes. This is the response Jennifer expected. The bloom of his cheeks tells her his blood pressure is high, that he's a heartbeat away from stealing the car keys and driving to Genoa Cove.

"You can't take Mom's car."

"Why not? We're stuck here until God knows when. It's not like she needs the car, and Mom won't press charges if I'm the one who took it."

"Hunter."

He leaps off the bed, and she blocks him before he reaches the door.

"Get out of my way, Jennifer."

"You're acting crazy. Call Bethany, yes. Talk to her. Help her. But I know you're going after Aaron and Sam, and that's a terrible mistake. What do you think will happen if you walk into jail with a concealed weapon? They'll arrest you, Hunter."

Hunter's eye twitches. Shit, that's his plan. He wants the

police to arrest him so he can get at Aaron and Sam. Jennifer grabs the doorknob.

"You can't go back to North Carolina," Jennifer says, raising her voice so Mom or Laurie will hear.

He glares at her from the corner of his eye.

"That was stupid."

Jennifer's eyes turn glassy.

"Not if it means keeping you from getting hurt. I love you. You're my brother."

Her words disarm him, and a small amount of tension rolls off his chest. For now. It won't take long for Hunter's mind to return to Bethany. Panic and anger will set in, and Jennifer won't be able to keep him from driving away in the dead of night. She'll stay up all night and ensure he doesn't slip past her. But her plan isn't sustainable. Someone needs to talk sense into Hunter, set his mind at ease and keep him from falling off the deep end.

Bethany. Jennifer barely knows Hunter's girlfriend, but Bethany's number is in Jennifer's phone. Good plan, except Jennifer will need to admit she knows about the rape. A sick worm curls inside her stomach.

But she'll do it. As soon as she figures out how to sneak past her mother again.

∽

AFTER CLEANING THE DINNER DISHES, Darcy spreads her laptop on the kitchen table and waits for the aging machine to boot up. Hunter and Jennifer barely spoke during dinner, and now they're upstairs in the bedroom, criminally silent. They're hiding something. While she waits for the computer to load, Darcy moves to the bottom of the staircase and listens.

"Just like a government agent. Always assume guilt."

Laurie grins at Darcy from the couch, a Jack Ketchum book open on her lap. Laurie always loved dark horror, but Darcy wonders how she can read a horror novel when a real life menace hunts them.

"It's too quiet up there," Darcy says, tilting her head up the stairs. "When you have kids of your own, you'll see. Quiet means trouble."

Laurie unfolds the novel.

"Okay, Mom."

At the kitchen table, Darcy clicks the Internet browser and runs a search for Gil Waggoner. The search engine spits numerous identical names back at her, and Darcy narrows the search to Georgia and Scarlet River.

Bingo.

Waggoner ran into trouble with the law as a teenager when the sheriff's department caught him defacing the Baptist church. With spray paint. Could be a coincidence, but Darcy makes a note of the infraction and continues. Two drunk and disorderly convictions in Scarlet River, one ten years ago, another two years ago. Darcy locates the incident with the minor Tipton mentioned, the girl's name withheld.

It's clear Waggoner is trouble, but nothing screams that he's the kidnapper or affiliated with Michael Rivers.

Except his lecherous stare as he followed Jennifer through the supermarket. And the time line.

For eight years, Waggoner turned squeaky clean. Not likely for a man with his track record. Darcy runs a second search and determines Waggoner moved to Shatterstruck, Wyoming ten years ago. He returned to Scarlet River eight years later.

The Georgia child abductions and murders stopped around the time Waggoner moved to Wyoming. Darcy makes another note to have Hensel query the missing children's database for spikes in activity around Wyoming while Waggoner lived in the area. Waggoner might have abducted Nina Steyer and taken her to Wyoming. Google reveals Shatterstruck's population is a shade over 700, small enough for Waggoner to conceal a kidnapped girl for eight years.

And then what? He brought Nina back to Georgia and released her?

"What are you working on?"

Darcy jumps. She didn't hear Laurie come up behind her.

"Researching this Gil Waggoner guy that causes trouble in town."

"Oh, does the sheriff suspect Waggoner kidnapped Sandy Young?"

"Perhaps. They consider him a person of interest at the moment. Regardless, this guy is bad news, Laurie. Steer clear of Waggoner."

10

Darcy's stomach flutters with butterflies. She feels under-dressed and overwhelmed amid the throng of deputies and FBI agents. Hensel, who drove into Millport to purchase a gray suit fitting of an agent heading a kidnapping case, holds court in the corner with Tipton, Filmore, and a younger deputy Darcy doesn't recognize.

The BAU agents are recent hires, the profiler a pretty young woman with blonde curls, and the field agent an African-American man. Darcy hasn't met either, doesn't know their names. Time moved on without her at the BAU.

She checks her phone for messages from Laurie and the kids and finds none. No news is good news. Still, she feels uncomfortable with Jennifer and Hunter out of her sight. The probability that one kid sneaked out of the house the night before last continues to weigh on her. The mud on the bedroom floor was a dead giveaway. She's leaning toward Jennifer. Over the last day, her daughter vacillated between quiet and a little too bubbly with her friendliness. She's up to something. That either child slipped past Hensel disturbs her.

A long table along the side wall of the makeshift briefing

room holds three dozen assorted donuts. Plain, cinnamon, glazed, and jelly. The two agents assisting Hensel ignore the donuts. Better to let the deputies get their fill and not step on any toes. Hensel purchased the treats at the local Dunkin, an effective trick he's long used to get the locals on his side. You could spend thousands of dollars on outreach and conferences, or drop twenty-five bucks on three boxes of donuts. The latter won every time.

Darcy lowers her eyes when the female agent looks in her direction. Too late. She's coming over, black heels clicking the floor, the black power dress showing off the legs of a woman who must have been a track star in school. The woman offers her hand.

"Agent Gellar?"

Darcy glances up and pushes herself off the edge of the table.

"Darcy," she says, shaking the woman's hand. The agent's grip is strong. "I retired three years ago."

"Still Agent Gellar to me," the agent says, her smile showing off pearly whites. "I read your profile of Michael Rivers at the academy. Spot on. You were a huge influence on me. I'm Victoria Reinhold, but everyone calls me Reinhold like they forgot my first name."

"How long have you been with the BAU?"

"Three years with the FBI, a year-and-a-half profiling with the BAU."

"You moved up fast."

"Like you. I'm giving the profile on the kidnapper today, but I'd like your opinion after I finish."

Darcy nods, though her inferiority complex grows the longer she stands in the career-driven agent's presence. This is a woman who won't stop at the BAU. She'll hold a high position in CIRG, the FBI's Critical Incident Response Group. Spotting an opening in the conversation, the second FBI agent lends his hand. He's as tall as Tipton, black hair cut short and graying at the edges. His bifocals make him look like a college professor, but his body appears muscular beneath the silver-gray suit.

"Agent KC Fisher," the male agent says, clasping Darcy's hand in his. "I understand you helped convince the sheriff to invite us here. For that I thank you."

"I'm unsure I did much to—"

Tipton's voice quiets the clamor. The sheriff holds up a hand until he silences the last murmurs floating around the room.

"Okay, people. We're about to get started. For those of you who didn't notice yet, Agent Hensel laid out an impressive spread of snacks on the table. I'm not responsible for calories consumed."

"Especially for you, Grasser," Filmore says, smiling at the overweight deputy who accompanied Tipton to Laurie's house.

The sheriff waits for the laughter to die down.

"Grab a donut or two and take your seats so we can get the show on the road."

The deputies fill the half-dozen folding chairs. The room doesn't have a podium or a digital screen. Tipton wheels a laptop computer attached to a 60-inch high-definition television into the room and sets the cart beside a wooden table. Hensel, Fisher, and Reinhold take seats behind the table while Darcy meanders toward the back of the room, wondering why Hensel invited her. When the room quiets, Tipton points the remote at the television. A picture of Sandy Young, wearing a blue-and-white soccer uniform appears on the screen.

"Sandy Young went missing in Scarlet River forty-two hours ago. Witnesses report last seeing Young at Cass Park." Tipton's eyes move toward Darcy at the back of the room as though he still holds her in suspicion. "As you're all aware, we're manning checkpoints on all roads leading out of Scarlet River with the help of our friends at the state police. That the kidnapper hasn't attempted to pass the checkpoints with Young makes us think he's keeping her inside Scarlet River, or he took her out of the county before we erected the roadblocks. Let's hope that isn't the case." Tipton pauses. "To help us figure out who this man is and bring Sandy Young home alive, I brought in the FBI to help with this case."

Grumbling rolls through the room. Wounds from the decade-old failed investigation run deep, and it's easier to place blame on an outside entity than stare at the face in the mirror.

Tipton introduces Hensel and shoots the troops a stern glare. The grumbles stop, allowing Hensel to give a short introduction before he calls Agent Reinhold to the table.

Hensel slides into his chair as Reinhold strides to the computer. She clicks the mouse, and four pictures appear on the television, the four girls abducted ten years ago. Nina Steyer's full-color photograph draws Darcy, the quality much higher than the posters. Darcy can see every freckle and blemish, the glint of the camera flash bouncing off the girl's teeth, the subtle waves in her long hair.

"We're working off the assumption these abductions are related to the Sandy Young case. Which means the unknown subject is responsible for five kidnappings and at least three murders spanning ten years. But who are we searching for?" Reinhold advances the slide refuting common misconceptions about child abductions. "Most child kidnappers are family members, someone the child knows and trusts. The incidence of strangers abducting children is a fraction of a percent. But as children increase in age, the line blurs, and it becomes more common for kidnappers to seek sexual gratification in older girls. In all four of the cold cases, the girls were unrelated, ruling out a common family member kidnapping these teenagers."

Reinhold moves the presentation to the next screen, a summary of kidnapping statistics.

"Among stranger kidnappers, the offenders are overwhelmingly men. Over 95 percent. Less than half of stranger abductions result in murder, but those that do include the most violent and disturbed of offenders."

As Darcy edges closer to the deputies, Reinhold steps forward to grab their attention.

"Our unknown subject is a single male who seeks sexual gratification from his victims. He may have been in a relationship prior to the kidnappings, but he requires a solitary lifestyle to hide his activities from others. This man is an outcast, shy and uncomfortable in social settings. He has difficulty holding a job because he doesn't mix with coworkers, and if he has a job, he's the guy who hides in his cubicle all day and eats lunch at his desk rather than going out with others. And he was a victim of sexual abuse during his childhood."

Grasser raises his hand.

"We have a list of known pedophiles in the county to cross-reference."

"Our target won't be on any pedophile list." A murmur of doubt and disagreement interrupts the agent. Tipton looks over his shoulder and catches Darcy nodding in agreement. "The science is conflicted here. While pedophiles seek young teenagers for sexual gratification, kidnappers are too socially awkward to forge a relationship with a woman, and take to abducting girls so they maintain control."

"So they prefer older women but resort to kidnapping young girls?"

"Exactly."

"Sickos."

The other deputies nod at Grasser as Reinhold moves to the

next slide. Darcy's breath hitches when a photograph of Michael Rivers appears on the screen.

"As all of you are aware, the FBI remains concerned Michael Rivers, better known as the Full Moon Killer, plays a role in the recent kidnapping."

"How?" Deputy Filmore lifts his palms. "He's been in jail for...what, three years?"

"Indeed, Michael Rivers is serving a life sentence outside Buffalo, New York. Darcy Gellar, formerly of the FBI's Behavioral Analysis Unit, shot and captured Michael Rivers three years ago." The deputies turn in unison to stare at Darcy. She discerns respect in their eyes, but she's a zoo animal on display. "Last month, serial killer Richard Chaney murdered multiple young girls in coastal North Carolina, operating out of Ms. Gellar's village. Chaney abducted Ms. Gellar's daughter, but she shot and killed Chaney with the aid of Special Agent Hensel."

"Should have killed that Rivers bastard as well," Grasser says, winking at Darcy.

He means to compliment her, but the old frustrations over failing to kill Rivers resurface.

"The FBI uncovered evidence suggesting Michael Rivers hired Chaney to murder Ms. Gellar, and we have confirmation Rivers phoned her in North Carolina, threatening to kill her friends and family." The next slide shows the evil smiley face. "Then this painting, the mark of the Full Moon Killer, appeared on a house outside Scarlet River belonging to Ms. Gellar's cousin, Laurie Seagers. It's clear Michael Rivers has enlisted another killer, likely Sandy Young's kidnapper. In a recent development, Rivers called Ms. Gellar again and mentioned the Sandy Young kidnapping. He also promised more abductions and murders."

Even Tipton, who has remained skeptical of Rivers' involvement, leans forward with his elbows on his knees, eyes glued to the mark of the Full Moon Killer.

"Since Rivers is hiring murderers to kill for him, why not cut off his money supply? Freeze his accounts," Tipton says.

"The government froze Rivers' accounts at the time of the trial," Hensel says from behind the table. "Problem is Rivers amassed a huge sum of money as a free man and hid it well, much of it overseas. We've followed the money trail for three years to no avail. He's spreading money around by illegal means."

"Okay, but how does he get at his funds? He's a prisoner."

"Just as he buys off murderers, Rivers pays someone, possibly multiple people on the inside to get him phone and Internet access. Part of this investigation is discovering who helps Rivers at the prison."

Tipton sniffs.

"Prison guards don't make much, not enough to compensate them for the risks. Look for a guard who owns a car or house out of his league. Or someone planning an early retirement."

"And get me in on that deal," Grasser says, but only a few deputies chuckle.

"The profile will lead us to Sandy Young's kidnapper," Reinhold says, taking control of the briefing. "If we cross-reference suspects with people who've had contact with anyone at the Buffalo prison, we'll catch him faster."

The female profiler doesn't mention Nina Steyer. Darcy worries the FBI isn't taking the sightings seriously. Hensel turns the briefing over to Tipton, who gives closing remarks and assigns duties to his deputies. Spotting Darcy at the back of the room, Agent Fisher weaves through the crowd with a cup of coffee in each hand.

"You look like you could use a pick-me-up," Fisher says, handing her the Styrofoam cup.

"Thank you."

The first sip scalds her tongue. Then the liquid gold pushes Darcy out of her stupor.

"She's good, isn't she?"

Fisher raises his cup toward Reinhold, who holds court with Hensel and Tipton in the hallway.

"Sharp for a young agent."

Fisher sips his coffee and nods.

"We'll need your help, Darcy. You know Michael Rivers better than anyone in this room, so if you have any ideas that could help us figure out who took Sandy Young..."

"Do you have a daughter, Agent Fisher?"

"I do. Married with a newborn in Memphis."

Darcy nods and sets the coffee on the table, observing the deputies and agents as they mass around the snacks.

"My girl falls into the kidnapper's target age range. A young teenager. When Richard Chaney took my daughter, I couldn't bear the thought of life without her. So I know what Sandy Young's parents are going through. I don't know what I can offer to aid your investigation, but I'm available to you every minute of the day until the FBI locates Sandy Young."

Fisher touches Darcy's shoulder and moves on when Hensel approaches. Holding a glazed donut inside a napkin, Hensel is breaking his own rule about eating the locals' snacks. His drooping eyes suggest he skipped breakfast and didn't sleep well.

"What do you think of Agent Reinhold?"

"A solid profiler," Darcy says, though she can't decide why everyone wants her opinion of Reinhold.

"Fisher is helping the deputies scan the database for suspects who fit the profile. We'll catch him, Darcy."

"I looked up Gil Waggoner," Darcy says, pulling the notepad out of her bag. "Did you know the Georgia child murders and abductions stopped when he moved to Wyoming?"

She rips off a copy of her findings and hands it to Hensel. He scrunches his brow.

"Returned to Scarlet River two years ago," Hensel says, muttering as he reads. He raises his eyebrow. "Impressive track record. This guy's a piece of work."

"But you're not convinced he's a suspect."

"I look at Gil Waggoner and I see a bully, a lowlife, a scumbag with a kink for underage girls. But a kidnapper and murderer?" Hensel itches his forehead. "I'll talk to Tipton. It wouldn't be a bad idea to bring Waggoner in for questioning."

"He knows something about the kidnappings, Eric. If he's not our guy, he knows who is."

Hensel folds the paper and slips it into his jacket pocket. He glances off toward the door as the last remaining deputies file out of the room.

"There's something I need to tell you."

"This doesn't sound good."

"The FBI booked my hotel in Millport. I lobbied for commuting in from Scarlet River, but they want me leading the team."

Darcy braces against the shiver running down her spine. It was a matter of time before the FBI called Hensel back to Quantico or sent him to another case, but she'd hoped he'd convince the FBI to allow him to move back in with Laurie and Darcy. She should feel fortunate he's staying nearby, but the thought of the downstairs unguarded tightens her chest.

"I understand. Agents Reinhold and Fisher are staying in the same hotel, I presume."

"One block from the sheriff's department." Hensel touches her arm and prods her away from the door. "The hotel has vacancies, Darcy. You turned down a dream vacation, but there's no reason you can't move Laurie and the kids into the hotel. I'll check with the FBI, but I'm certain they'll pay for the rooms. Everyone recognizes you're the target."

Darcy searches for an argument but can't find one. Even if the FBI doesn't front the cost, she's happy to pay. She can't put a price tag on safety.

"Okay."

Hensel's eyes widen.

"Okay? That's it? I thought I'd need to drag you kicking and screaming to the hotel. Thank God, that's a load off my mind."

"Free Wi-Fi, breakfast, and the occasional car driving past. I won't need to twist my kids' arms to convince them. The hotel might be a tougher sell for Laurie."

Reaching into his pocket, Hensel removes his phone and locates the hotel's phone number.

"It's the Hampton Inn on Northland Avenue. How soon can you take the room?"

"Give me time to drive back and get everyone packed. We'll be at the hotel by eight."

Hensel's smile is infectious. The corners of Darcy's mouth curl up, the weight hanging off her heart not so heavy anymore. He holds up a finger.

"It's ringing. I'll set you up with the front desk. Grab Laurie and the kids and get there as soon as possible."

11

Jennifer doesn't require convincing when her mother suggests they move into the hotel. She spent the afternoon following Hunter around the house, clenching her teeth every time she lost sight of her brother. A bonus, Agent Hensel scored a second room for Laurie. Two queen beds and a sofa which pulls out to a cot. Humble compared to their home on Genoa Cove, but a huge leap in quality from the dusty, drafty farmhouse.

Her mother works in the kitchen with Laurie while Jennifer sits on the bed, watching Hunter pace the room like a caged rat. She calls his name twice. He doesn't so much as glance at Jennifer until her thumbs fly over the phone, composing a message for Bethany.

Need to talk to you about Hunter. Important.

Hunter stops and glares at Jennifer as if he senses what she's about to do. She narrows her eyes.

"What?"

He shakes his head and stuffs his hands into his pockets, resuming the infernal pacing. Jennifer has never seen Hunter this distraught. When he turns his back, Jennifer sends the message to Bethany. And waits for the carrier to deliver the text. She keeps waiting.

Jennifer curses under her breath when the signal strength drops to zero. Moving to the window, she grabs the pane and throws it open. A chilling gust lurches into the room and hurls the dust into a cyclone.

"Are you crazy? Close the freaking window."

Hunter never explodes at Jennifer. At least he hadn't before they moved into this godforsaken house in the middle of nowhere. But opening the window works, and for a brief second, two bars appear on the phone screen. Then the signal vanishes, the message undelivered and waiting for a higher power to whisk it away and push the text through the network. Slamming the window shut, Jennifer marches to the door.

"Don't go anywhere," she says over her shoulder.

The death stare he shoots her tells Jennifer he won't wait much longer. He'll leave tonight. Steal Mom's keys off the nightstand and slip out of the hotel room, the white noise from the fan masking his escape.

Jennifer stands in the hallway with her hand on the bedroom door as if a wishful part of her attempts to send her brother serenity and strength. As she treads down the stairs with Laurie's voice ringing out from the kitchen, she glances behind her. The doorway stands closed. Quickening her pace, careful to avoid the creaky steps, Jennifer creeps down the stairs. In the hallway, she hunches over and stays below the wall dividing the kitchen from the living room.

She pauses at the front door, certain she'll alert her mother when the night air pours inside. Gritting her teeth, she edges the door open and slides through the narrow opening, holding the knob so the mechanism doesn't click when she pushes the door shut.

Jennifer stands with her back to the door. Breathing and

waiting, breathing and waiting. When she's confident she slipped past her mother without drawing attention, she leaps off the top step and into the grass and hits the lawn running. She doesn't stop until she reaches the corner of the garage where she'd messaged Kaitlyn. Her phone hums when the message to Bethany sends. Two bars. That's enough.

A full moon beams eerie light into the dark yard, turning the meadow and surrounding hills ethereal. Crouching beside the wall, the splintered wood rough against her shoulder, Jennifer watches for Bethany's response. The wait is short.

Is something wrong with Hunter? You're scaring me.

Jennifer exhales. This isn't the response she desired.

Easier if you call me. Please. Won't take long to explain.

No sooner does the text send than the signal crashes again.

"You've got to be kidding me."

Jennifer holds the phone at arm's length and turns in a circle, and when that method fails, she stands on tiptoe and holds the phone toward the moon as though offering sacrifice to a pagan god.

The grass crunches behind her a moment before the hand reaches out of the dark and clutches her mouth. Instinctively, she bites down on the soft flesh and kicks back as a second arm snakes around her throat and drags her toward the brush. Toward the meadow and forest.

The powerful grip stifles her scream. Her arms flail and grasp blindly at the unseen attacker.

Jennifer's phone rings as it tumbles out of her hand. Lost to the night and the screaming moon.

∽

THE LUNAR LIGHT tainting the meadow looks wrong to Darcy. She dries the wine glass and places it on the kitchen shelf as she eyes the night outside the window. Laurie returns from her bedroom with an overnight bag thrown over her shoulder. She tosses the bag on the kitchen chair and places her hands on her hips.

"Your kids are awfully quiet tonight. You'd think they'd be bouncing off the walls waiting to get out of my house."

Darcy pulls herself away from the window, the growing trepidation that something is wrong threatening to cripple her. It's not like Hunter or Jennifer to nap during the evening. The kids are on their phones, she decides. Even if they're messaging friends, Darcy will allow the transgression. Soon they'll be inside a well-lit hotel with three FBI agents down the hall. For the first time since October, Darcy feels safe.

"Hunter? Jennifer? You up? We're leaving in five minutes."

After calling up the stairs, Darcy waits several heartbeats. She's about to yell again when Hunter sticks his head into the hallway. Then his eyes light with anxiousness, and he ducks inside the room.

"Hold on a second," Hunter says, and Darcy knows he's stalling for time.

Darcy shares a look with Laurie. The two women climb the stairs, Darcy taking the steps two at a time and racing ahead of her cousin.

"Where's Jennifer?"

Darcy carefully steps into the room as though land mines lay beneath the floor. She takes in the bedroom, Jennifer's bag packed beside Hunter's at the foot of the bed. But she's not here.

"Hunter, answer me. Where did your sister go?"

Hunter glances between Darcy and Laurie with frantic eyes.

"I'm not sure. Outside, I think."

"You weren't watching her?"

"I'm not in charge of—"

Darcy doesn't wait for Hunter's excuse. She throws the bathroom door open, knowing Jennifer won't be inside. Then Laurie's room. Empty.

Whirling around, Darcy bounds down the stairs with Laurie begging her to slow down before she breaks her neck. But Darcy doesn't care what happens to her.

The truth of what's happened dawns on her as she steps into the cold blues of the December night. Running through the yard, she spins and calls her daughter's name. Her voice echoes off the hills like a wraith screaming. She wishes she can turn the clock back, claw through time to reach her daughter before the night takes her.

Jennifer is nowhere. Gone.

Laurie hurls the garage door open and shouts inside. Hunter descends the steps like the dead walking, then he breaks into a sprint and screams his sister's name when the gravity of the situation hits him.

Darcy reaches her phone to call Hensel when Jennifer's ring tone plays somewhere in the yard.

"Jennifer! Where are you?"

Darcy finds her daughter's phone behind the garage, the screen glowing with the words *Bethany Calling* mocking her.

"I'm calling 9-1-1," Laurie says somewhere behind her.

Darcy falls to her knees and screams.

12

Darcy doesn't wait for the FBI and sheriff's deputies to arrive.

Sweeping her flashlight over the driveway and bordering meadow, she searches for fresh tire tracks, anything she doesn't recognize. Between the Prius and Laurie's truck, multiple tracks draw a confusing pattern as they come together and diverge. She shouldn't be able to make sense of the tracks, yet she does, her mind processing information at inhuman speeds as she recognizes the shallow grooves of her tires, treads incapable of cutting through mud or handling off-road driving. The uneven wear of Laurie's truck tires become clear, the tracks leading toward the front of the garage where Laurie parked. Besides the sheriff cruisers from the last two nights, no unidentifiable tracks exist. She can't locate evidence of another vehicle turning down Laurie's driveway.

"This is why I told you to stay inside."

Hunter, pushing aside grass and weeds as he examines the earth inside the meadow, flinches. Darcy immediately regrets her words. This isn't Hunter's fault. He is upset as Darcy.

Headlights flash across the meadow and blind Darcy. She

shields her eyes as Laurie runs toward the black SUV bouncing down the dirt and stone path. The driver kills the lights. Agent Fisher climbs down from the driver's seat and starts toward Darcy with Hensel and Reinhold behind him. Whirling lights through the trees announce the sheriff's cruiser before it pulls behind the FBI's rental. Another vehicle races down the lonely country road, and Darcy recognizes the Georgia State Police logo.

"She was just here," Darcy says, running to meet Hensel as Fisher's inquisitive eyes move from the house to the meadow and hills.

"We'll find her," Hensel says, wrapping Darcy in his arms.

A damn break of emotion bursts forth. She sobs against his shoulder, wanting her friend and old partner to bring Jennifer home. But she's been in his place too many times and understands the usual platitudes are meant to soothe and should never be taken as a guarantee. *We'll find her.* How? Jennifer vanished without a trace.

At the sound of dogs barking, Darcy turns her head. Search and rescue dogs. A bearded trooper holds one dog by the leash as Tipton walks over to meet him.

"Laurie, run upstairs and get me something that belongs to Jennifer," Darcy says, anticipating the trooper's request. "Any piece of clothing will do, but if she left dirty laundry in the bedroom, grab that first."

Laurie nods and runs back to the house as Tipton and the bearded trooper round on her. They'll have questions. How did Jennifer sneak out of the house, and what time did she disappear? Her mind races faster than her speeding heart. She takes a calming breath, but there can be no peace of mind until she finds her daughter.

"Ms. Gellar, this is Georgia State Trooper Max Quigley," Tipton says, introducing the trooper. Holding the leash, Quigley stands back with the sniffing bloodhound, keeping the dog away from Darcy and Hunter. "Trooper Quigley and I go back two decades, and there's no one better when it comes to search and rescue. We'll find your daughter. Do you have an item of clothing?

"Getting it for you now."

"Good. You're one step ahead of us."

Sucking air into her lungs, Laurie hands Tipton one of Jennifer's t-shirts. Darcy remembered seeing the shirt tossed into the corner of the bedroom, and for once she's thankful her daughter rarely picks up after herself. Tipton hands the shirt to Quigley, who places the clothing before the dog's snout. A series of loud sniffs, and the dog whirls on its leash and tugs Quigley into the meadow.

"Ask me anything you want, Sheriff, but I'm on the move. I'm going after my daughter."

Tipton nods. Then the sheriff turns and directs the deputies and FBI, fanning out the members into teams of two's and three's to cover the most ground in the shortest amount of time.

"How long since Jennifer disappeared?"

"Forty-five minutes at most," Darcy tells Tipton, handing him her daughter's phone. "We found her phone behind the garage."

"Show me where."

Darcy leads Tipton to the corner of the garage, a good place to hide from the prying eyes of anyone inside the house. Tipton kneels down and sweeps his hand through the grass as Deputy Filmore aims a flashlight over his shoulder. Tipton removes his own flashlight and walks in expanding circles, the beam stroking the grass. He stares at a spot in the yard between the garage and meadow. At first, Darcy sees nothing. Then she spies the matted grass, the spot large enough to be a footprint. Now Filmore joins Tipton, pointing the flashlights at the meadow, looking for evidence the kidnapper dragged Jennifer into the tall grass. The sheriff glances at Darcy.

"Ms. Gellar, do you know the passcode to your daughter's phone?"

"Sure."

Darcy takes the phone back from Tipton and punches in the six-digit code. The screen unlocks, and Tipton grabs the phone and scrolls through the message logs.

"Didn't you say Jennifer vanished forty-five minutes ago?"

"Yes."

"I see a message sent from Jennifer's phone to a Bethany Torres forty-seven minutes ago, and a callback from the same number a minute later. Is it possible this Bethany Torres has something to do with Jennifer's disappearance?"

"She lives in North Carolina," Hunter says. They all turn to look at him. "So no, she has nothing to do with whoever kidnapped Jennifer."

Tipton nods, unconvinced.

"Read Jennifer's message," Tipton says, tilting the phone toward Darcy. "It's clear she was desperate to reach Bethany Torres. I want to know why Torres called her back. Take nothing for granted."

Tipton's wasting precious time and following the wrong scent. Though Jennifer's need to speak with Bethany piques Darcy's interest, the North Carolina teenager didn't mastermind an abduction by providing a distraction.

"How was Jennifer's demeanor earlier?" Tipton asks. "Did you have an argument?"

"My daughter didn't run away," Darcy says. Heat builds through her cheeks. "And if she did, she wouldn't toss her phone on the lawn. She'd take it with her and text all her friends about what a terrible mother I am."

"I have to ask these questions, Ms. Gellar. Okay, so it's

unlikely she ran off. Are you certain you didn't hear another vehicle outside the house?"

Darcy turns toward the driveway.

"No, and I couldn't identify tracks besides ours and yours. Whoever did this, they came on foot."

Tipton raises his brow.

"I keep forgetting you worked for the FBI," Tipton says, removing his hat and wiping a cool sweat off his forehead. "Hard to abduct someone while on foot, but I suppose it's possible he parked along the road."

The bloodhounds disagree. The two dogs lead the troopers toward the end of the meadow, where moonlight reveals a break in the tree line—the trail. Are the dogs following the path Darcy and Jennifer took hiking?

Though Laurie insists Tipton allows her to help with the search, the sheriff orders her to stay in the house in case Jennifer returns. Darcy doesn't like the idea. Laurie will be alone if the killer comes back. Tipton waves Filmore forward, and they rush to close the distance on the bloodhound-led troopers with Darcy and Hunter close behind.

Darcy's concerns over the bloodhounds following an old scent fade when they begin the climb up the narrow incline. The dogs sniff and lunge up the hill, their barks echoing through the woods. The scent they pursue isn't old and weak. It's fresh, and the hounds drag the troopers as Tipton pushes through branches blocking their path. One branch snaps backward and cracks Darcy in the eye. Hot pain courses through her body as the trail turns blurry, but she pushes on.

Boughs snake together and form a thick canopy the moon can't penetrate. The forest turns an inky black, the flashlights pulling out the trail and the overgrowth reclaiming the path. A black void exists at the periphery of Darcy's vision. The path feels like a tunnel through the center of the earth.

She doesn't recognize her surroundings until the dogs veer right and pull the stumbling troopers onto the state park trail. The falls are ahead. Darcy hears the distant roar growing as they climb toward the ridge.

Please not the cliff, she begs. An unbidden image flashes in her mind—Jennifer's ruined body at the bottom of the chasm, the rocks sprayed black with blood.

As soon as the mist wets her face, the dogs twirl back and jab their snouts into the plants. She runs into Tipton, who steps back to give the dogs room. Relief pours through Darcy when the bloodhounds don't yelp at the edge of the cliff.

"Impossible," Quigley says. "They lost the scent."

The second trooper leads his hound to the bushes on the edge of the trail. The dog sniffs once and turns back to the path.

Tipton leans close to Quigley and whispers, "You think they went over the edge?"

But Darcy hears. She rushes to the lookout point and stands at the rail. Far below, shallow water gurgles over the rocks. The full moon pulls the details into sharp focus. No bodies in the river.

"Over there," the second trooper says, beaming his light off the side of the cliff.

Darcy's pulse quickens again before she follows the trooper's gaze. A steep, rocky grade leads down to the water. Traversing the grade would be treacherous in the daylight, impossible at night. But it's the only path the kidnapper could have taken.

"No way," Quigley says. "We can't take the dogs down the hill."

"Circle around," Tipton says, pointing back where the two trails converged. "Sure as hell beats falling a few hundred feet."

"How long will that take to go back?"

"Another half-hour to work our way to the stream, longer if we lose the moon."

Tipton glances at the full moon, its face a hanging man over the treetops. Quigley rubs his lips in consideration, then he kneels to pet his bloodhound.

"All right, Sheriff. You know these parts better than the rest of us. Lead the way."

As Darcy falls in line behind the troopers and deputies, the trees part. Tipton raises his gun. After a tense moment, he holsters the weapon, recognizing Hensel, Fisher, and Reinhold as they struggle up the hill.

"Anything?" Tipton asks.

"The dogs led you to the end of the trail, and that's it?" Hensel asks, shaking his head as he averts his eyes from Darcy.

"We think they descended the hill toward the stream bed. The water is shallow enough that we'd know if someone fell. There'd be a body at the bottom." Tipton's lips press together as he gives Darcy a sidelong look. "Sorry."

"No time for apologies, Sheriff," Darcy says.

With the dogs and troopers in front, the search party descends the hill. They take a shortcut through the woods, a trip that ends up taking longer when they're forced to struggle through the trees and scrub. But when they reach the stream, the dogs are silent. The scent disappears.

Like Jennifer, the scent vanished into the night.

13

Darcy slumps over the old wooden table, hand clutching one bandaged arm where a thorn bush took a bite out of her, one foot tapping out a nonsense beat on the freshly polished floor. Hensel offers her coffee. Darcy waves it away.

It's three in the morning. Nothing good ever happens at three in the morning. That's what her mother always told her. But now she tracks time by the number of hours since her daughter left their lives. Nine hours since they last spoke, and that was a trivial order to tidy up the bedroom before they left the house. Seven-and-a-half hours since Jennifer disappeared. She shouldn't be here. They should be safe in the hotel room, sleeping soundly and dreaming of a continental breakfast awaiting them downstairs.

Darcy let her family down. She had one task—protect her children and keep the monsters from breaking down the door. Instead, Jennifer sneaked past Darcy to bypass her idiotic rules and walked into the monster's clutches.

"Let me get you something to eat," Hensel says, sliding into the chair beside hers.

Darcy shakes her head.

"I don't need food or sleep. I need my daughter back, just like Sandy Young's mother and father need their daughter."

"Apparently, your son is on the same hunger strike. The deputies are having a helluva time keeping him in the building. He wants to search for his sister."

He sets a toasted bagel on the table. Slides it in front of her. She pushes it away and stares up at the florescent strip lighting.

"Okay," Hensel says with a sigh. "I'll leave the bagel in case you change your mind. Hang tight while I speak with Tipton. I'll be back in a few minutes."

He pauses and waits for a reply. After none comes, he marches out the door and leaves her alone. Just the harsh, buzzing lights and a window overlooking the dingy hallway.

Praying a message awaits from Jennifer, Darcy lifts her phone. She scrolls through messages from her daughter, the thread dating back to Genoa Cove after the police convicted Aaron and Sam for assault and battery. Her phone log displays no missed calls, but as she digs through the archives, she eyes the call from Rivers.

Before she talks herself out of it, Darcy presses the number and dials the phone. As expected Rivers doesn't answer. His helper inside the prison tossed the phone away after Rivers called Darcy, and now he has another disposable phone. Darcy jumps when she spots Hensel standing behind her, his reflection caught in the window. He's glaring at the phone.

"Who did you call?"

Darcy releases a held breath and tosses the phone to Hensel. "You already know."

He cocks an eyebrow and squints at the screen.

"I could have told you he wouldn't answer. Don't you think he got rid of the phone after the FBI attempted to trace the call back to the prison? Shit, Darcy. He won't tell you where Jennifer is."

"But he knows."

Hensel taps the phone against his palm, considering. He hands it back to Darcy.

"It's time we turn up the heat. I called the prison and left a message for Warden Ellsworth to contact me the minute he arrives this morning. Ellsworth might act like he has a rod shoved up his ass, but he runs a tight ship, and he won't take kindly to one of his guards aiding a murderer who's serving a lifetime sentence."

"We tried this already," Darcy says, burying her face in her hands as she remembers their visit with the Full Moon Killer. Rivers had refused to speak to the FBI after his incarceration, but he sang like a bird when Darcy entered the room, even if his intent was to cut her to pieces psychologically. By the end of the interview, Rivers almost had Darcy convinced Hunter was a budding serial killer. The combined efforts of Hensel and two prison guards stopped Darcy from leaping across the table to attack Rivers.

But she'd gotten to him. Psychologically turned the tables and broke down the invisible walls he'd built around him. She could do it again.

"Don't even think about it," Hensel said, reading her mind.

"No need to convince me. I'm not leaving Georgia without both of my children."

Perhaps Darcy need not travel to Buffalo. Other options exist to force Rivers' hand. She recalls a quip Hensel made at the prison. Something about Darcy bribing an inmate to jam a shank into Rivers' belly. During her first year with the FBI, Darcy and Hensel solved a series of mob murders in Western New York between Rochester and Buffalo. Who was the man the FBI aided?

Leo Vescio.

Vescio, a small-time operator out of Rochester, had been the next target in the turf war before Hensel's team crashed the party. The FBI took down Vescio's enemies, and the small-time operator grew in power after the dust cleared. Vescio had contacts inside the prison. And he owed Darcy.

Hensel checks his watch.

"Four hours until Ellsworth comes in. We'll catch the scumbag who's giving Rivers phone access, and then we'll put the pressure on Rivers. If he knows where the girls are, we'll find out."

The plan will fail. Darcy doesn't care. She's already searching for a way to contact Vescio without Hensel finding out.

~

JENNIFER'S EYES refuse to open. Too heavy.

Her head hurts. Stomach roils as though something crawled inside her belly and died. The memory of the callused hand curling over her mouth sends an icy lance through her body. She springs awake to a dark room. It's so cold she can see her breath.

She struggles to her knees, and chains yank her down. The links bite and pinch her skin. Jennifer trembles as she remembers floating through the forest as though weightless, the tree limbs and bramble scraping her flesh, dead leaves crackling against her face. Then the sound of water and a distant roar.

The falls.

Which means she wasn't far from cousin Laurie's house while the man carried her toward the water's edge. Jennifer isn't sure what happened after. She lost consciousness, though the floating sensation returns to her.

Her back scrapes against crumbling plaster. Grains pour off

the wall and cascade to the floor as if someone opened a salt shaker. Listening, she can't hear the falls anymore. Just a gentle susurrus that could be a river or the wind. She could be anywhere, but the pitch dark means it's not morning yet, and she doesn't remember being inside a car. They couldn't have gone far.

As her eyes adjust to the dark, she picks out details in the room. A cot in the corner with a blanket bunched at the foot of the makeshift bed. A second cot, disturbingly coffin-like, rests against the opposite wall. Her gaze travels to the half-open doorway, through which gray light spills as though a light shines in a hidden corner of the house.

Jennifer almost misses the bulk curled beside the second cot. She locks her eyes on the form. Unlaundered blankets or a pile of clothes? A yelp escapes her lips when the bulk moves. A subtle shifting.

It's a girl, Jennifer realizes. And she's alive.

The unknown girl moans. Her arms reach toward the dark ceiling, searching for a parent or someone to save her from this house of horrors. The pitiful croak which emanates from the girl's chest tells Jennifer she's sick and in a great deal of pain. Perhaps dying. Instinctively, Jennifer struggles toward the girl. Then the chains dig into her arms and ankles and tear soft flesh.

When Jennifer cries out and falls against the wall, the girl squeaks and draws her knees toward her chest. The clink of chains echo back to Jennifer, proof the kidnapper bound both girls. Even in the gloom she sees the girl tremble like a frightened mouse. The girl is too groggy to know Jennifer is here, only realizes someone is in the dark with her.

Jennifer's attempt to speak to the girl ends when a black shadow fills the doorway. Hinges creak as the door drifts open. The man steps into the room, his face concealed by darkness. He sniffs the air, animal-like. Then he strides forward, walking straight at Jennifer. She rolls away until the wall traps her.

"Leave me alone," she says as the man hauls her into a sitting position.

"You fight too much," the man says, bending closer so she smells the rank of his breath.

The feminine pitch of his voice surprises her. It belies his tall, strong body. With his face close to hers, she makes out his features now. He's a walking dichotomy, ugly yet handsome. High cheekbones for a male, face smooth except for a long scar over his left eye. The face of the devil, a voice whispers inside Jennifer's head.

Bringing up a knee, she kicks him in the chest and knocks him back on his heels. The backhand slap twists Jennifer's head. Stars burst in her eyes as pain spreads through her cheeks. She promises herself she won't cry. A part of her realizes that's what he wants...to watch her grovel and plead as tears flow down her cheeks. A shock moves through her when his callused hands grope beneath her shirt and slither toward her chest. She kicks him again, and this time his face twists in anger. Grabbing her hair, he shoves her head against the wall. Agony forces Jennifer to sob, shaming her.

When she's certain he means to rape her, he turns toward the door, stopping only to study the other girl on the floor. The unknown girl makes a duck-like cough and rolls onto her belly, too weak to defend herself. Jennifer looks away. She won't watch him rape the sick girl.

"You're so beautiful," the man says, looking back at Jennifer. "He wants you for his own, but there's no reason for you to die. Stay with me. I can make you so happy. He doesn't need to know."

The man kneels to brush the hair off the other girl's face.

"So beautiful."

Jennifer clamps her eyes shut. Refuses to watch. But the room is quiet now. The only sound is her own breathing.

He's gone.

A scream pops her eyes open. The man's shadow passes the open doorway with another girl slung over his shoulder. A third kidnapped girl. Then a door slams, and the screams become muffled, fading in volume until Jennifer can't hear the girl anymore.

She shifts her body around and faces the wall where the chains hook against an antique radiator. Wincing, she kicks the radiator and drives the heel of her foot against the brass padlock.

Then she hears him coming back.

14

When did she fall asleep?

Darcy bolts up in the chair and grabs her aching neck. She's still inside the sheriff's department briefing room, the quality of the light stronger as gray daylight seeps down the hall and slides across the window. Voices travel from the hallway. When she tries to stand, the cramp worsens. As if someone pinches the back of her neck with pliers. That Jennifer is missing keeps jolting her nerves with electrical shocks. She can't put two thoughts together.

Rubbing the knot out of her neck, Darcy shuffles to the door and opens it a crack. Hensel, the jacket gone and his dress shirt wrinkled, runs a hand through a rat's nest of hair. Black shadows circle his bloodshot eyes, and as he speaks to Agent Fisher, Hensel totters like a tree close to toppling. Grogginess can't dampen his anger. He spins on his heel and stomps toward the briefing room. When Hensel sees Darcy in the doorway, he pulls up, surprised she's awake. He starts forward again and itches the top of his head.

"How long did you sleep?"

"Longer than you," Darcy says, leaning against the frame. "Fisher looks rested. Let him run the show for a while."

He waves away her concern.

"I can go another twelve hours. Hey, I just got off the phone with Warden Ellsworth."

Darcy stands a little straighter.

"What did Rivers say?"

"They can't break him, Darcy. He refuses to speak, and short of the guards clubbing the hell out of him behind a locked door, Rivers will outlast them."

"What about his phone access?"

Tipton calls Hensel's name from the end of the hall. Hensel holds up a finger so he'll wait.

"Ellsworth takes offense to the notion one of his workers betrayed him to aid a serial killer. He promised to look into it, but—"

"Forget it, Eric. It's not Ellsworth's daughter. Why should he give a shit?"

Flustered, Hensel tries to reply as Darcy slams the door in his face. She hears him breathing in the hallway. Several seconds pass, and he knocks softly. She doesn't acknowledge him. Darcy didn't lock the door, so if he wants to barge in, there's no stopping him. A pang of guilt hits her when his footsteps trail down the hallway.

Craning her neck at the window, she verifies the hallway is empty. For added security, she draws the blinds.

Before she fell asleep, she called a contact at the Buffalo Police Department, a balding detective named Brady who aided the FBI in cracking the mob ring. The detective remembered Darcy. If he knew she'd left the FBI, he didn't say. And she didn't offer. A little smooth talking won her Leo Vescio's phone number. The mob boss was the new kingpin of Western New York, a title which put the target squarely on his forehead if the authorities decided Vescio had grown too powerful. That meant he was likely to cooperate and stay on the government's good side. Vescio needed a friend in the FBI. And like Brady, Vescio didn't need to know Darcy's employment status.

An uncertain *hello* greets Darcy when Vescio answers the phone. Rechecking the hallway, Darcy fights her shaking voice until she gains control.

"Sure, I remember you, Agent Gellar," Vescio says. "To what do I owe this pleasure."

"You've come a long way, Leo."

"Top of the world," he says with a snicker, quoting Jimmy Cagney. "I hope you haven't forgotten how instrumental I was in helping the FBI."

She senses a threat beneath the words.

"Nobody here has forgotten you, Leo. Which is why I'm offering you an opportunity to maintain your good neighbor status."

"Forgive me, Agent Gellar, but you speak as if it's already in question."

"Perhaps with some of my colleagues, Leo. But I worked closely with you and understand your intentions are good, if a little misguided from time to time."

"We all make mistakes."

This feels like a dance to Darcy. One misstep will blow everything. While he's still on board, she tells him about the trouble Michael Rivers is causing the FBI.

"He's a pedophile, Leo. It doesn't get any lower than that."

"But you locked the Full Moon Killer away, Darcy. For life, I believe I read."

"He wields a great deal of power from his jail cell," Darcy says, recalling the picture Vescio once shared of his teenage daughter. He was attempting to convince the FBI he was a good man. As though only a good man could raise a beautiful daughter. "Unfortunately, we can't track the money flow, but Rivers pays child abductors to kidnap teenage girls and send him... videos."

"I see."

The disgust in his voice is clear. Darcy hit her target.

"If something were to happen to Michael Rivers..."

"Are you recording our conversation, Agent Gellar? You're straying toward entrapment."

"I'm not a fool, Leo. If my superiors caught wind of our conversation, I'd be in a lot more trouble than you."

Vescio goes silent. She can hear the wheels turn in his head and senses he's a hair away from ending the call. Darcy clamps her eyes shut and bites her lip.

"So this isn't an official call, I presume," he says.

"Let's just say there are those who need to know inside my agency, and those who don't. Regardless, this offer stays between the two of us."

Vescio smiles through the phone.

"What do you have in mind, Agent Gellar?"

When Darcy ends the call, she bites her hand and cries. The door opens, and she shoves the phone into her pocket and turns her head away. A moment later, the door drifts shut. Swiveling her head around, Darcy spies Reinhold through the crack in the blinds as the profiler seeks Tipton, giving Darcy space. A minute earlier, Reinhold would have walked in on Darcy's conversation with a mob boss.

Reminding herself of the phone call stiffens Darcy's spine. She made a deal with the devil and will pay dearly. Her bank account, most of it funded by Tyler's life insurance payout, is dangerously low, and she hasn't worked as a freelance graphic designer since the madness began at Darkwater Cove. Whatever price Vescio demands, it will cripple Darcy financially. Any price to get her daughter back.

After opening the blinds, Darcy ventures into the hallway. Voices come from all directions inside the building, so she follows Hensel's voice toward the break room. She pulls up when Hunter rounds the corner with Laurie. Laurie whispers in Hunter's ear and stands back, leaning against the wall as Hunter advances. Laurie gives a half-hearted wave and lowers her head.

"What are you doing to find Jennifer?"

The aggression in Hunter's eyes knocks Darcy back a step.

"Search parties are working around the clock, and the sheriff and state police are stopping vehicles—"

"No, what are *you* doing to find her?"

Darcy folds her arms and looks over Hunter's shoulder. His raised voice draws Hensel and Tipton out of the break room.

"Everything I can."

"She's gone because of you," he says, curling his hands into fists. "Do you know that? Because of your stupid rules. What good did banning us from talking to our friends do? Did it keep us safe, Mom? Did it keep Jennifer safe?"

Laurie hurries forward and grabs Hunter's arm, imploring him to walk away. He shrugs Laurie off.

"That's not fair," Darcy says in a soft voice. "You're upset, Hunter."

"I'm *upset*? Tell me you didn't know about Bethany."

"What about Bethany? Hunter, we've been away from home for almost a week."

"But you must have heard. You know everything that goes on in our lives and never let us breathe."

"Come inside the briefing room so we can talk about this in private."

He spins in a circle, taking in the stares of the deputies and FBI agents. Raising his hands, eyes wide, he sends out a silent challenge to anyone who wants to silence him.

"They raped Bethany. Aaron and Sam. Her own fucking brother!"

Darcy's knees buckle. She didn't know. She reaches for Hunter, but he backs away with a wild grin on his face.

"I couldn't even talk to her," Hunter says, laughing as tears roll off his face. "Because it was so important to keep us away from our friends. That's why Jennifer sneaked outside—to talk to Bethany. She was safe in the house. You did this to us."

Darcy pulls Hunter into her arms. He spins away and slams his fist against the wall. Fissures crawl through the plaster.

"I'll kill them. Aaron and Sam are dead when I get back to Genoa Cove."

Before Darcy can grab him, Hunter wheels around and rushes for the exit. Tipton steps down the hallway with his fingertips brushing the holstered gun.

"Let him go," Darcy says to Tipton. "Hunter won't hurt anybody. You heard what he said about his girlfriend, so surely you understand why he's reacting like this."

Tipton nods to Filmore.

"Bring that boy inside. I want eyes on him until I'm certain he isn't a danger to himself or anybody around him." Recognizing the protest forming on Darcy's lips, Tipton raises his hand. "He's not under arrest. But I'll be damned if I'll let him storm through downtown after he threatened to kill two people."

Deputy Filmore hurries down the hallway. Darcy's pulse thrums with the possibility Hunter will resist.

"Go with the deputy," Darcy tells Laurie, who nods and runs to make up ground on Filmore.

Tipton and Hensel follow behind. When Darcy joins the chase, Hensel shakes his head, a warning not to get involved. After the fight, Darcy's presence will only make things worse.

She feels thankful Hensel is with Tipton, because the sheriff's hand remains uncomfortably close to his gun. Almost as if he's looking for an excuse to shoot her son. Holding her breath, Darcy watches Filmore and Laurie round on Hunter in the parking lot. Laurie's calming effect on Hunter is immediate, and the tension drains out of Filmore after Hunter calms down. Though she can't read their lips, Darcy can tell they're getting through to Hunter. Laurie leans forward and levels her eyes with Hunter, then she looks toward Darcy. Hunter's eyes follow Laurie's, and guilt sags the boy's face before he lowers his head.

Another minute passes, then Hunter follows Laurie and the deputy into the building. Tipton's hands relax, and Hensel gives Hunter a gentle slap on the shoulder as he passes.

Laurie offers Darcy a tight-lipped smile. The instant her cousin breaks into tears, Darcy pulls Laurie into a hug and rubs her back.

"Whatever you said to Hunter, thank you."

"I can't believe this is happening. I keep thinking I'll wake up, that this is just a crazy nightmare."

Over Laurie's shoulder, Hensel hangs back and gives Darcy and her cousin space. Darcy waits until Laurie stops crying. When she's finished, Darcy grips her by the shoulders.

"This isn't your fault or mine. We both need to stop blaming ourselves, okay?" Laurie nods. "Right now, I need you to be Hunter's favorite cousin again and keep him company while I speak to Agent Hensel. Can you do that?"

"I've got this."

After the door clicks shut behind Laurie, Hensel sighs and drapes his arm over Darcy's shoulder.

"Let's get you a bite to eat before you drop."

Darcy leans on Hensel as he walks her to the break room. Tipton waits inside, arms crossed. Deputy Grasser microwaves a sandwich and does a hot foot dance when he burns his fingers on his lunch. Grasser's face turns weary as Tipton impatiently waits for the deputy to clear the room.

Darcy collapses onto a plastic chair and rests her head against the wall. When Hensel hands her a bagel, she breaks into a thin, forced smile that inspires little confidence that she'll finish the food. She takes a bite and chews. It slides down her throat like wet cardboard as if her taste buds withered and flaked off.

Tipton pulls out a chair and flips it around. He sits backwards on the chair, arms resting on the seat back.

"You want to tell me about Aaron and Sam?"

Darcy swallows and sets the bagel down.

"I'm sure you read the Genoa Cove PD files. Aaron Torres and Sam Tatum are two of the boys who attacked Hunter."

"The night you and Agent Hensel shot Richard Chaney." Darcy gives him a blank nod. "Bethany was the girl who last called Jennifer's phone. What's this about a rape?"

Darcy, reeling from Hunter's revelation, pieces the story together for Tipton.

"Christ," Tipton says. He sets his hat on the table and rubs the exhaustion off his face. "If I was in your son's shoes, I'd react the same way. But I'm uncomfortable letting him out of our sight, at least for the rest of the day."

"I'll worry about keeping my son in line. Find my daughter."

Tipton convenes with the FBI inside his office, shutting Darcy out. Through the window, she spies a topographic map on the wall of Scarlet River, Millport, and the surrounding county. Two little flags mark where the girls disappeared. Agent Reinhold takes over the meeting. She's passing out sheets of paper containing the latest profile updates. Darcy would love to be inside the room, partly because she isn't confident the young profiler has the requisite skills to find Jennifer and Sandy.

When Darcy's phone rings, she sees Margaret's name on the

screen. Walking toward a quiet spot in the hallway, she answers the call.

"Agent Gellar? Nina was here again. Not over two minutes ago."

Darcy glances into Tipton's office. They're debating the profile now.

"Are you sure it was her?"

"It was the same girl as the other times. She tried to break into a truck. The owner chased her off."

Eyeing her car in the parking lot, Darcy pulls the keys from her pocket and angles toward the door, the others too preoccupied to notice.

"Tell me you still see her, Margaret. I can be there in twenty minutes."

"No, she got scared and ran off. But I took another picture."

"She couldn't have gone far on foot. Keep your eyes peeled. I'm on the way."

The dashboard GPS displays a network of roads converging on Maury's Diner on the border of Scarlet River. Most of the roads are rural and farm-to-market, a good choice to walk along if you don't wish anyone to see. Darcy crisscrosses the roads, improving the odds she'll pass Nina. But she finds nothing but open countryside and farmers' fields gone to winter.

Darcy slaps her hand against the dash as she pulls into Maury's parking lot. Standing out front with her arms clasped against the chill, Margaret notices the Prius and takes an uncertain step toward the car.

"I'm sure it was her this time," Margaret says, holding the phone screen aloft while Darcy climbs out of the car. "I did my best, but we had so many customers, and I had three tables."

"Don't apologize. Your job is with the diner, not tracking Nina Steyer."

"I zoomed in close." Margaret hands Darcy the phone and

pulls out a copy of the poster. "Now look at the eyes. They're the same, right? I mean the hair is different, and her complexion is so pale compared to the girl in the poster, but that has to be her."

Darcy studies the two pictures. Though Nina is in the act of turning, Margaret's photograph captures the girl in full profile. Neither Tipton nor Hensel can deny this girl is Nina Steyer.

Margaret touches her mouth.

"That new kidnapped girl. Her name is Gellar. Is that—"

Darcy glances up.

"Margaret?"

"Agent Gellar, is that your daughter? I'm so sorry. I should have put two and two together. With two girls kidnapped in less than a week, everyone is too scared to think straight."

"I'll find my daughter, Margaret, and I'll find Nina."

"Nina has something to do with the kidnappings. That's why you want to find her, and I lost her again."

Margaret's assessment is correct. Nina's appearances are related to the abductions. When Darcy figures out the connection, she'll find Jennifer and Sandy Young.

Darcy's eyes glaze over. She scans the parking lot and spots where Nina stood in the picture.

"You last saw Nina a half-hour ago?"

Margaret sniffs and checks her watch.

"Yes."

Impossible. Nina Steyer couldn't disappear that quickly, even running at a full sprint. Darcy examines the roads leading away from the diner with the GPS map overlaid in her mind. The county route runs straight into the horizon toward Millport. A handful of dead end roads branch off the route, but the closest is two miles away. Across from Maury's, the bisecting road leads to the center of town. Darcy's eyes stop on a residential road a half-mile away. Paint-chipped houses and trailers dot each side of the street, and beyond the road, the terrain climbs into forestland.

"Margaret, where does that road lead?"

"Harrison Street? Nowhere, really. It's a dead end."

"But if I were to park at the end of Harrison and walk up that incline, where would I end up?"

Margaret rubs her chin.

"I guess you'd hit the state park trail after two or three miles. You wouldn't go that way, though, not with access points to the trail at the far end of town."

"That's the trail that ends at the falls?"

"Yes, ma'am."

The falls...where the dogs lost Jennifer's scent. Sickness bubbles through her stomach. There's a voice inside Darcy's head, an insidious voice that says she'll never see Jennifer again. Darcy battles to suppress the voice, but it grows louder by the minute.

"You did well," Darcy says. "Should Nina come again—"

"I promise I'll call you."

"Anytime, day or night."

Darcy thanks Margaret and climbs into her car. Margaret's head hangs over the car door, the wind throwing the waitress's hair across her face.

"I'll pray for your daughter, Agent Gellar."

Tipton confers with Deputy Grasser outside the sheriff's office when Darcy returns. With Nina's picture loaded, Darcy holds her phone in front of the sheriff.

"We had another Nina sighting at the diner, and this time the waitress took a clear photograph. That's Nina. There's no denying it anymore."

Tipton squints at the picture and presses his lips together.

"I suppose it could be her. People change a lot over ten years. Hard to say."

Darcy unfolds the poster of a younger Nina and covers the hair in both pictures.

"Focus on the eyes, the face. If this doesn't convince you, nothing will."

Tipton's tongue presses against his cheek.

"What would you have me do, Ms. Gellar? I've got two missing girls, one of them your own daughter. There's no time to chase ghosts."

"The waitress told me Nina tried to break inside a vehicle. Could be she wanted to get out of the cold, but I don't think so. Twice she tried to hitch rides at the diner. I think she meant to steal the vehicle."

"For what purpose?"

"Wherever Nina has been the last ten years, she's ready to leave."

"So why not go back to Millport? To her mother?"

"I can't place myself in her shoes or get inside her head. What if she escaped from the man who took Sandy and Jennifer? She can tell us where to find the girls."

"Deputy, can you give us a minute?"

Grasser glances between Tipton and Darcy and gives a quick nod. Tipton waits until the hallway empties.

"Look, Ms. Gellar. I barely have the manpower to search for two abducted girls. As much as I'd like to help, I can't let a cold case get in our way. This theory you have that Nina knows where Sandy and Jennifer are is just that. A theory. You know the old saying. *If you chase two rabbits, you will lose them both*. Help me in any way you can to find Jennifer and Sandy, but I don't have time to chase a woman who resembles a girl who died a decade ago."

Darcy's mouth hangs open as Tipton strides into his office and slams the door. This is the second time Tipton acted emotionally over the Nina Steyer case. No sooner does the sheriff enter his office than his phone rings. As she scans the hallway for the FBI team, Tipton's door flies open.

"Grasser!" Tipton shouts down the hall as his deputy emerges around the corner. "Get me those FBI agents."

"What's happening sheriff?"

Tipton's eyes hold alarm and pity as he brushes past her without comment. She starts after him and freezes. Only two possibilities explain the sheriff's reaction. Either the kidnapper took another girl.

Or someone found a body.

15

"Keep breathing, Darcy. We don't know it's her."

Hensel sits ramrod straight beside Darcy in the rental's backseat. He's trying to calm her down, but his body language is wrong. He fears what they'll find in the farmer's field outside of Scarlet River.

The farmer found the body in his field, a stone's throw from the road. He estimated the dead girl's age at fourteen or fifteen. They're less than a minute from the body now. Darcy bites her lip and closes her eyes.

Pressing the accelerator to keep up with Tipton's cruiser, Agent Fisher checks his mirror for Filmore's cruiser. Reinhold rides shotgun beside Filmore. The crime scene investigators are en route.

The silo rises above the earth like an unmoving tornado, boards missing from the barn's roof and walls. A man in dusty blue jeans and a Carhartt jacket waves the caravan down as they pull into the dirt driveway fronting the barn. Tipton and Grasser climb out first. Fisher shuts off the engine, and the silence inside the car rings in Darcy's ears. Her heart pounds, body rigid as Hensel makes a show of checking his pockets. He's giving her time, allowing her to breathe and melt the ice off her bones. When Fisher glances over his shoulder, he avoids looking at Darcy.

"Okay, I think I'm ready," says Darcy.

As she walks between Hensel and Fisher, the field seems to drift toward Darcy. It's as if she stands on a conveyor belt. Walking beside Tipton, the farmer points into the field. Darcy can't recognize the body yet. From here, it's a pale bulk glowing under the hazy light. Faceless, nameless, unclaimed by the benevolent god who allowed this sin.

"Farmer saw a hand sticking out from under the dirt and dug her out," Hensel says while he walks, focusing on the facts to disassociate himself from the potential the dead girl is Jennifer. "The flesh wasn't rotted, so he thought the girl might be alive."

Tipton holds up his hand to stop the farmer from advancing. The sun-parched man watches Darcy and the others pass as if viewing a funeral procession. Footsteps hurry behind. Darcy looks over her shoulder at Reinhold and Deputy Filmore, the profiler carrying a camera. Reinhold appears as if she wants to talk to Darcy, then she pulls her eyes toward the young girl's torso.

Tipton kneels beside the girl. She's naked and staring up at the sky. Purple bruises the size of silver dollars cover her body, and ligature marks circle her neck. Someone beat and strangled the girl.

Darcy's breath catches at the spill of dark hair fanned against the brown earth. Hensel reaches for Darcy, but she's already on her knees beside the girl's head.

It's not Jennifer. She's sick with guilt for feeling relieved, but that doesn't stop her from muttering a prayer of thanks. Tipton meets Hensel's eyes, and the agent shakes his head to indicate this isn't Darcy's daughter. The sheriff removes his hat and looks up at the sky, then down at the girl. His haunted eyes are unmistakable. He sees the bodies of girls ten years dead and wonders why this nightmare came back to claim him again.

"He beat her first," Reinhold says, clicking a photograph. "The killer was angry. Why?"

Hensel points at the bruising around the girls neck.

"Notice the ridging around the ligature marks. As if the killer strangled her with a thin piece of rope."

"Maybe twine," Tipton says, his face green.

Pulled into the examination, Darcy lends an observation. Her voice cracks, causing everyone to look at her.

"Sorry." Darcy swallows the lump in her throat. "She wasn't his type. That's why he beat the girl and tossed her away."

"We only have two girls to construct the profile from," Fisher says, brushing a fly off his face. "This girl's hair is dark like your daughter's, while Sandy Young's is lighter."

"No need to refer to this girl as if she's a Jane Doe. Her name is Emily Vogt."

"What?"

"The girl. She's Emily Vogt." Darcy fires a glare at Tipton. "She went missing outside Atlanta. I believe that's what you said. I told you the cases are related."

Fisher clears his throat.

"You said this girl isn't his type. How do we determine what his type is when we only have three kidnappings to go on?"

Darcy waits for Reinhold to answer. When the profiler doesn't, Darcy clears her throat.

"We have seven girls, not three. Four from ten years ago, three this week. They're all between the ages of twelve and sixteen, thin and pretty. Emily was too heavy for him."

Darcy cringes at the callousness of her words, but the heavy thighs on the dead girl set her apart from the others. Including Nina Steyer.

"Isn't that the age range the Full Moon Killer targeted?" Filmore asks.

Hensel nods and sneaks a look at Darcy, who clamps a hand over her stomach.

"You okay?"

"I feel sick, Eric."

"No reason for you to be out here. Head back to the vehicle. I'll meet you in a few."

The clumped earth tries to trip her up as Darcy staggers toward the barn. When she passes the farmer, the man's gaze locked on the dead girl in his field, a van clambers into the driveway. The CSI team piles out to collect evidence. Soon the poor girl will lie upon the medical examiner's table, and her parents will face the horror Darcy dodged.

She closes the door and slides down in the backseat, the shuffling feet and measured voices of the crime scene techs outside the windows as they make their way toward the field. A cold Darcy can't shake follows her into the rental while she rests her head against the seat back. The phone hums inside her jacket. She'd silenced the phone before examining the body. Recognizing Leo Vescio's number, Darcy raises the phone to her ear.

"Leo?"

"Agent Gellar, we have a deal."

16

The light through the hallway seems wrong. Tainted and soiled.

Jennifer's eyes blink open to the shadowed bedroom. Twisting onto her side, she forgets the chains and yells when the links tangle around her midsection and dig into her ribs. When she rises onto her knees and lifts her head, she notices boards cover the bedroom's windows. The harsh light bathing the hallway tells her it's daytime. Her eyes stop on the girl across the room, bound and unmoving. Dirt and dust mar her light-colored hair, the strands slick with sweat and matted to her face. The girl's chest rises and falls too quickly, breath unsteady and garbled as if dragged over broken glass.

This must be Sandy Young. Jennifer overheard her mother and Laurie talking about the kidnapped girl. She knew the FBI was in town, helping Sheriff Tipton search for Sandy. That gives Jennifer a sliver of hope the authorities will find them.

Without a window view, she can't recognize the landscape. But they couldn't have gone far last night. Her captor is strong, but carrying a hundred pounds of dead weight for several miles is unrealistic. She thinks hard, tries to recall sounds and smells while she eased in and out of consciousness. The strange floating sensation returns to her. Weightlessness. Drifting on the wind.

And colliding against rocks.

The scents of rubber and fresh water come back to her. Yes, she was inside an inflatable raft. Which means the kidnapper could have taken her a long distance. How far does the stream extend past the falls? Without a map as a guide, she can't know if she's a few miles or ten miles from Laurie's house.

Sandy groans. Pitching glances into the hallway, Jennifer crawls toward the girl. Her chains rattle and grate. If the kidnapper is inside the house, he'll hear.

"Sandy," Jennifer whispers. "Sandy Young."

If the girl hears, she doesn't acknowledge. She lies on her side in a fetal position, hands tucked between her knees as she faces the opposite wall. Jennifer struggles forward. Sandy's sweat-beaded body curls beyond Jennifer's fingertips. She strains against her bindings, reaches for the girl's shoulder. If only the girl awoke and rolled a foot to her left. But like Jennifer, she's at the edge of her boundary, the chains stretched taut.

"Wake up. We need to find a way out of here."

A door creaks open down the hall. Footsteps.

Jennifer scurries back to the wall as the shadow grows across the hallway floor. The footsteps stop outside the door. He breathes and listens, patient. The floorboards squeal when his weight shifts. As Jennifer falls back against the wall, the chains clink together. She senses his smile a moment before he steps into the bedroom.

His face hides in darkness with the light at his back. But as he strides into the room, the gray dimness of the room pulls his face together. He's the same unmemorable man from last night. His face is plain, no discernible features which make him stand out beside the scar. If he entered a room with a dozen people, he'd be invisible, the man no one recalled talking to. Yet he's familiar. Jennifer ponders where she's seen him, then she recalls the man in the mall watching her and Hunter. Yes, it's the same man. She's certain of it.

"You're awake. I hope you had a good night's sleep."

Jennifer pulls her hands to her chest and neck. His grin displays too many teeth. The kidnapper slides down the wall and sits beside her. His gaze moves over Sandy's prone form, and sadness touches his eyes.

"She's sick," Jennifer says. "You should let her go so she gets help."

"No help out here." His stare is blank. "Nobody but us. There's nothing to do now but wait."

"Wait for what? Sandy is dying."

His head swings toward Jennifer.

"You know her name. How is that possible? You're not from Scarlet River."

Without another word, he pushes himself to his feet and kneels beside Sandy. Placing a hand on her hip, he brushes the hair from her face. The girl shivers and mutters in her sleep, asking for her mother. The man looks back at Jennifer.

"Time grows short for Sandy, but we don't need her. It could be just the two of us. He doesn't need to know. Nobody does."

Who is *he*? She remembers the kidnapper referencing another man last night. A father figure, she senses. Someone who holds sway over him. Then his hands slither over Sandy's chest.

"Get away from her, you piece of shit!"

Jennifer's vitriol spins his attention back to her. There's a new aggression to his step when he approaches. She screams when he digs his hand into his pocket. Instead of removing a knife, he produces a key. He jiggles the key into the padlock, and the lock springs open. Jennifer sighs, the pressure and weight of the links finally off her body. Before she works the feeling back into her hands, he slaps a handcuff over her wrist and uses the other cuff to rip her to her feet. She bites her lip when the force almost yanks her shoulder out of socket.

"There's no shame in crying, little one. Scream, if you must. Nobody will pass judgment on you here."

While he pulls her toward the hallway, she half-crawls, half stumbles across the dusty floor. The light in the hallway is stronger than a million suns. Her watering eyes adjust. Before she makes out her surroundings, he hauls her into a kitchen. The floor lacks several tiles, and two long rust smears mark where a refrigerator once stood in the corner. There's a small refrigerator in its place, the size a student takes to college. A roach lies belly-up on the counter, and a black spider the size of Jennifer's palm hangs in the corner, presiding over a graveyard of flies and mosquitoes. But it's the spray painted face on the wall that makes Jennifer's heart race—the same leering smile painted on their house in Genoa Cove. The mark of the Full Moon Killer.

Using the handcuffs, the kidnapper locks Jennifer to the leg of a wooden table. She curls on the floor while he runs water in the sink. The liquid comes out brownish-gray before it clears, then he fills a glass and sips.

When the hair tingles on the back of her neck, she senses they aren't alone in the kitchen. Someone else is here.

A strange girl stands in the entryway. Her arms hang at her sides as if clipped to her body by thumbtacks. The girl's eyes appear lost and vacant. At that moment, Jennifer thinks this is the girl the kidnapper carried down the hallway last night. No, that girl appeared heavier and younger, no older than Jennifer and Sandy. This new girl looks older. At least twenty. And there isn't an ounce of fat on her body.

"What are you staring at?"

The new girl jumps when the kidnapper speaks. She opens her mouth to respond and closes it, defeated. Her eyes drop to the floor, and she flinches when the man closes on her. Is this his wife? Daughter?

"You're too dull to answer," he says, gritting his teeth. Consumed by fury, he makes a concerted effort not to strike the girl. "I don't want to look at you today. Go to your room, or get lost in the forest for all I care. It's no skin off my back."

The girl's eyes move to Jennifer on the floor. When she sees the handcuffed prisoner, her lips tremble and her eyes glass over.

"Don't look at her!" Spittle flies from his mouth when he screams at the older girl. "You'll never capture her beauty."

The older girl spins and vanishes from the kitchen. Footsteps trail from room to room as if the girl can't find the exit. Then the front door opens and closes, and the house becomes quiet again.

Until the older girl fled, Jennifer held onto a fleeting hope the girl might fight on their behalf. Even now the possibility exists the girl will bring help, but the girl's submissive demeanor convinces Jennifer she won't turn on the kidnapper. Jennifer is abandoned, left for this madman to rape and murder her.

Something breaks inside Jennifer. She cries, gulping sobs that burn her chest and scar her lungs. This isn't a nightmare she'll wake up from. She will die in this rundown house, and no amount of fantasizing over heroes breaking down the door will change her fate. Nobody knows where she is. If anyone did, they would have found Sandy already.

The rim of the water glass presses against her chapped lip and splits the surface. She tastes blood as he nudges the glass forward, squeezing her lip against her teeth.

"Drink." She shakes her head. "Drink or you'll die."

He shoves the rim into her mouth, drawing more blood

when he gouges her gums. With her free hand, she swats the glass away. Water splashes against the walls as the glass shatters on the floor. Silent tension follows like the moment before a bomb drops. Enraged, he snags her by the ponytail and wrenches her head back. A hard slap knocks her neck sideways.

When her eyes clear, she spies a piece of broken glass beside her knee. She snatches the shard between her fingers and slices it at his face. Quicker than Jennifer, he clutches her wrist. Squeezes until she feels the brittle bones crackle under the pressure. He pulls back on her hand, bending until her knuckles are inches from her forearm. The pain is exquisite, maddening. But it's proof she's alive and fighting, not teetering on death's edge like Sandy in the dark bedroom. Finally, the pain is too much to bear. Her fingers release the shard.

"You will learn to obey," he growls, snaking his arms under her chin and around her neck.

She squirms and flails. With the muscles of his forearm and bicep acting like a vise against her carotid artery, she blacks out and goes limp in his arms.

The dreamlike levitation invades Jennifer's thoughts as it had the night he captured her. She imagines herself riding atop a black and purple storm cloud, the skies bruised, a tube tornado shattering a small town as she floats weightless above the storm. When she awakens, she's handcuffed to Sandy, wrist attached to wrist. The dying girl's eyes open and stare, and there's fear, intimidation in Sandy's eyes. It isn't until they lock that Jennifer realizes Sandy's nose bleeds, her top lip split.

Jennifer twists her head around and finds the kidnapper leaning against the door frame. He studies the two girls the way a hurtful boy watches a bee inside a jar after introducing a hornet.

"You beat her? Why?"

The kidnapper folds his arms and smiles.

"I did nothing of the sort. You did this."

"I heard screaming and came inside to find you hurting Sandy."

"That's bullshit. You put me to sleep. How could I hurt anyone?"

"You're a violent girl, Jennifer." Her spine turns to ice. He knows her name. "You had your hands around Sandy's throat, and you kept striking her face. I pulled you off before you went too far. So angry, so much hatred. But I don't blame you for wanting to hurt Sandy. She'll only get in the way. It proves you're the only one for me."

Jennifer rubs her eyes. The room shifts out of focus for a second. Cuts from her forearm to her wrist mark where the handcuffs tore at her flesh while she slept. Her knuckles are red with blood, but not all the blood is hers.

"No, you grabbed my arm while I was asleep and made me hit her. You just want to turn us against each other." Jennifer touches Sandy's arm. The girl flinches as though electrocuted and slinks away, dragging Jennifer's hand with her. "Please, Sandy. You can't believe I did this."

But no words can convince Sandy that Jennifer doesn't mean her harm. The kidnapper strolls to Jennifer and tugs her into a sitting position by her shirt collar.

"Now, watch and learn. The next time she goes to sleep, you put your hand like this and cover her mouth and nose."

His hand engulfs Jennifer's face and suffocates her. With her free hand, she digs her nails into his arms and scrapes. Two nails break off as she carves thin rivulets of red down his arm. He doesn't seem to notice. As she bats at his hand, he squeezes harder, crushing her nose. Her struggles slow as her brain grows foggy.

Everything goes dark.

17

Emily Vogt. The girl who could have been Jennifer.
As Darcy expected, Tipton matched Vogt's picture to the girl in the field. The girl's parents are en route to the coroner's office to ID their child.

Inside the warm break room of the county sheriff's office, Darcy sits alone at the table with a cup of tea bleeding condensation circles. The department ordered out for dinner, and the roast beef sandwich Deputy Grasser handed her sits untouched on a cheap porcelain plate with floral markings. Lettuce and mustard spill onto the plate, and the onion scent tempts Darcy to wrap the sandwich in a plastic bag and stuff it into the garbage can. But she knows she has to eat, needs to sustain herself if she wishes to pull night-long vigils until she finds Jennifer. She takes a bite. Chews. Swallows. It's a mechanical process geared toward survival rather than pleasure. The pieces sit like lead on the bottom of her stomach. After two bites, she pushes the plate aside, unable to look at the sandwich anymore.

She taps her thumb over the contact list on her phone, deciding whether the time is right to call Hunter. Laurie took him back to the hotel before Darcy returned from the farmer's field. She wants to tell him the incredible news, that there's a strong chance Jennifer is still alive. But that's only because the FBI discovered another family's daughter murdered.

Instead, she lifts the dinner plate, intent on hurling it against the wall. She stops herself at the last second and sets the plate aside.

Emily Vogt. She repeats the girl's name as a mantra. She hates herself for being relieved the dead girl was anyone but her daughter. When Vescio's contacts inside the prison beat Rivers within an inch of his life, she hopes he suffers worse than Emily did.

After taking a deep breath, she dials Hunter. He answers with a groggy voice.

"You doing okay now, Hunter?"

He sniffs and tells Laurie that Darcy is on the phone.

"Better than before."

"I didn't know about Bethany. It was wrong of me to keep you from talking to her."

She pictures Hunter rubbing the sleep from his eye.

"I talked to Bethany a few times, so it's not like I lost contact, but that was before I learned about Aaron and Sam."

The admission doesn't surprise her. Darcy had only wanted to prevent their enemies from tracking Hunter and Jennifer, but she'd pushed too hard.

"God, I can't imagine what she's going through. I knew Aaron Torres was a sociopath, but I never believed he was capable of this. How is she doing?"

"She's seeing someone," Hunter says with a yawn.

"A counselor?"

"Yeah, I guess that's supposed to help. Her parents won't accept Aaron did this, but that's expected. They're no better than Aaron."

"You don't mean that."

"No?"

Darcy digs her nails into her palm.

"Hunter, leave Aaron and Sam to the courts. They're going to jail for a long time. You can't be there for Bethany if the police arrest you."

Hunter pauses.

"Jennifer told you."

"No, she didn't need to. Besides, you shouted your intent in front of the FBI and County Sheriff today."

"I wouldn't have gone through with it."

"You're upset. So am I. But you need to be careful what you say around people." He mumbles an apology Darcy barely comprehends. "I'll make this right, Hunter. I'll find Jennifer, and Michael Rivers will pay for what he put us through. Sorry I woke you up. Go back to sleep. It will be all right."

Daylight wanes when Darcy leaves the sheriff's department. She doesn't tell Hensel and Tipton she's leaving. They'll only try to stop her. She tucks a dogeared Georgia road atlas under her arm and tosses it on the passenger seat with the pages open to the Millport-Scarlet River area. She studies her scribbled notes about the killer and copies key locations to the car's GPS. Laurie's house, Cass Park where Sandy Young disappeared and a stalker followed Laurie, the last scent the dogs caught of Jennifer near the falls, Maury's Diner. One point sticks out from all the others: the discovery of Emily Vogt's body. The farmer's field lies five miles outside the clustered points. As if the killer dumped Vogt outside the town limits to throw them off. Or maybe she disgusted him, and he wanted her as far away from his comfort zone as he could deposit her without abandoning Sandy and Jennifer.

Checking her mirrors, Darcy confirms nobody saw her leave. She turns out of the parking lot and allows the GPS to direct her to Cass Park. It isn't until she's outside the bustle of Millport that Darcy notices how dark the road has become. She flips on the high beams, the headlights like flaming swords cutting into an endless abyss of dark. Farms pass to either side of the car, but she can't see them, only the flare of a faraway light through a window. Silo shadows tower over the flat countryside. Nightfall over the great unknown reanimates her fear of the dark, and she reaches inside her bag and searches for the bottle of anti-anxiety medication, fingers prodding and searching. Before she leans on the crutch, she yanks her hand back and forces her fingers to curl over the steering wheel.

Darcy takes a deep breath, checks the mirrors again, and keeps inhaling and exhaling until the tremors subside. Lights at the outskirts of Scarlet River cannot settle her nerves. The town appears alien to her, secretive and dangerous. Even with the GPS as a guide, she turns herself around and gets herself lost after she passes the supermarket. Two blocks later, she finds Cass Park and pulls the Prius into the empty lot. A sign hanging off the fence warns visitors the park closes after dark, the new rule in effect since Sandy Young's abduction. One point of contention eats at Darcy. The kidnapper abducted Sandy Young in broad daylight inside a busy park. Yet nobody heard a scream or noticed a man dragging a struggling girl into the parking lot. Somebody would have noticed a stranger stuffing a teenage girl into a vehicle. What if he didn't drive to the park?

Before she shuts the car off, she zooms in on the GPS until the map pulls the trail into detail. The path meanders through a copse for a mile and loops around a pond, circling back to the playground equipment on the opposite side of the woods. But it's the creek at the end of the copse that catches her attention, for the stream originates at a larger body of water. Dragging the map to the left, she follows the twisting creek for a few miles until it wraps around a ridge and merges with a river. The falls. A short walk from Laurie's house.

She glances out at the night-shrouded park and back at the map, getting her bearings. Killing the engine, Darcy steps outside and edges the door shut.

Inside the park, Darcy passes the swings and jungle gym as the cool night bites at her ears. She shrugs her head into the hood of her sweatshirt and zips her coat, one hand buried in her pocket while the other holds the doused flashlight. The Glock rests on her hip. When she's beyond view of the parking lot, Darcy switches the light on and sweeps the beam over the grass until she locates the trail.

As she walks, she pictures her surroundings from the killer's perspective, a trick from her nascent days as a profiler. The trail seems too close to the park, too populated during daylight hours. A kidnapper wouldn't feel comfortable here. A half-mile down the path, Darcy works the chill out of her bones. The medication calls her, promises to take away her fear, but she left the temptation inside the car. The trail narrows. Moonlight reflects off the pond's surface.

When she hears the gurgling creek, she stops, concerned she walked too far. Shining the light through the trees, she searches until she spots water glinting fifty yards off the trail.

But there's no safe path to reach the creek. Covered with deadly bramble and deep pockets of mud, the land drops off like a miniature cliff. Darcy stops at the edge of the trail and focuses the light on the thorns, which snake together undisturbed. The killer didn't come this way.

An owl hoots. Darcy jumps and looks back the way she came. Night conceals the path, cuts her off from civilization. Paralleling the stream, Darcy follows the trail until the border thins and the land beside the path levels. Parting a wild shrub, she locates a grass and weed clearing that slopes down to the creek. Using her imagination, she almost convinces herself a thin line of grass lies matted down as if someone passed through the field recently.

Heart beating in her ears, she descends the terrain until she reaches the rocky creek. The flashlight confirms an unauthorized pathway along the water. It runs as far as her eyes can travel, ultimately toward Laurie's house and the falls.

Curiosity makes her want to see how far she can get. Too dangerous. She isn't sure how rough the climb is, and the tiny swamps girding the creek make her worry about alligators. Darcy backtracks to the parking lot with a frozen image of the creek in her head. She'll mark the position on the map and check for roads close to the track the killer took.

Or might have taken. She's grasping at thin strands of hope, her mind honing in on any piece of evidence that might lead her to Jennifer.

Darcy spies the shadowed park equipment on the horizon when her phone rings. She bristles for forgetting to silence the ringer as her finger hovers over the answer icon. *Hensel* looks more like a shout than the caller's name when it flashes on the screen.

"Where the hell are you? And don't tell me you're out for a walk or grabbing a late dinner. I called Laurie, and she hasn't heard from you since this afternoon."

Darcy clutches the phone to her ear and hurries past the playground as though the ghosts of dead girls watch her in the dark.

"It's not your business where I spend my time, Eric. I'm not under house arrest."

"Warden Ellsworth called ten minutes ago. There was a near riot at the prison this evening, but I don't suppose you'd know anything about that."

Darcy stops beside the car and holds her breath.

"What does that have to do with me?"

Hensel grinds his teeth.

"You damn well know. Dammit, Darcy. Five men cornered Michael Rivers and threw him into a utility room. Six people walked into that room. Only one walked out."

Fumbling the keys, Darcy steadies her voice.

"What are you saying?"

"The five attackers sustained stab wounds to the chest and stomach. The guards found one with his throat slit, and another gutted like a—"

"Stop! Just stop. I don't want to hear anymore."

"Rivers got his hands on a weapon, though the guards can't seem to find it. For Christ's sake, Darcy. He murdered five inmates."

The door unlocks. Darcy slumps over the seat and swallows the sick rushing up her throat. Her head spins, pulse slams until she's sure she'll faint.

"I figured it out, Darcy. Lou Vescio. I mulled over the people who could help you get to Rivers, and then I thought of Vescio. He trusted you. I wonder what Vescio thinks about Agent Gellar tonight."

Darcy straightens in the seat before leaning over to spit the wretch out the door. Her hand shakes as she wipes it across her lips, craving something to take the edge off. Just two pills to help her process five dead inmates and a serial killer bent on revenge. Two pills to block the images of Emily Vogt left for dead in the farmer's field. Two pills to keep the black night from crashing through the window. Then she'll quit.

"Darcy, answer me."

She fumbles the bag and spills its contents over the seat.

"I'm here, Eric."

"Tell me where you are."

Before she can answer, a text pops up on the screen. It's from an anonymous sender, but Darcy knows who the messenger is.

Nice try. I'll gut you and watch you bleed, you pathetic bitch. Right after my friend rapes your daughter.

Darcy deletes the message and blocks the sender, though Rivers will contact her from a different phone next time.

"I'm coming to pick you up," Hensel says.

"That's not a good idea."

"Why the hell not? Whatever you've gotten yourself into, tell me where you are and I'll take you back to the hotel. Look, I don't know where you got the money to hire Vescio, but it's over. Ellsworth and Tipton don't need to know what you did, but you have to promise me you'll never pull a stunt like this again."

Darcy can't hold the pill bottle. It slips and tumbles into her lap, where she wrestles the cap off and flings it across the car. She pops two pills. Swallows. Then two more.

"Don't lock me out, Darcy. Give me your location. If you don't want to see me, I'll send Fisher or Reinhold to pick you up."

"I was wrong, Eric. I failed everybody."

"Wait, don't—"

She ends the call and sits back in the driver seat. Already she senses the medication trickling through her body. Soothing. Numbing. Hensel calls back, and she presses ignore and stuffs the phone in the bag.

Darcy pulls the Prius out of the parking lot. She shouldn't feel calm yet, not this fast, but the brain's power of persuasion is a powerful force. It won't be long before the pills kick in, robbing her ability to drive. No chance she can drive back to Millport.

But Laurie's house is a ten-minute drive. The key to Laurie's front door dangles off the chain. She throws the car into drive. Maintaining speed is a game of chicken. Too fast and she'll lose control of the car. Too slow and she might black out before she arrives.

Laurie's house blends with the night before the headlights pull it from the shadows. Dark windows look back at her with soulless eyes. She half-walks, half-stumbles up the steps with the keyring hanging off her fingers. Fitting the key into the lock proves difficult, then the mechanism clicks, and Darcy lurches into the frozen house and flicks the wall switch. She doesn't understand why the interior feels as cold as the outside until she remembers the wood stove. Sighing, she tosses her bag and keys on the table beside the holstered Glock and rubs her eyes on her way to the living room. The coals have burned down to ash, no residual heat left inside the chamber as she strikes a match and lights the kindling. The flame catches her thumb, and she tosses the match into the stove with a shout. It only takes a minute for the dry kindling to catch, and after she loads two split logs into the stove, she rubs her hands together as the fire grows higher.

Heat rolls off the stove when Darcy closes the door and drags herself into the recliner. Though she regrets leaving the kitchen light on, she doesn't have the strength or motivation to turn it off. Instead, she closes her eyes against the harsh glare, the light pink and orange against her eyelids as the fire drives back the cold and thaws her bones. A forgotten portion of her brain accosts her for abusing the anti-anxiety medication, screams for her to shake the cobwebs off and find her daughter. The numbing comfort of the pills quiets the internal arguments, and soon she drifts into sleep.

Darcy doesn't know how long she's been asleep when her eyes shoot open. The kitchen light seems darker than before as if the night saps its power. Inside the wood stove, a log snaps. Then she remembers what woke her. A sound. Something in the night.

Her eyelids bat under the weight of too many pills. Fingers tingle with pins-and-needles, body struggling out of a murky bog. She lifts her head off the recliner a moment before a shoe swishes through the grass below the window.

The glass implodes. A dark shape plunges through the

opening and leaps toward her with a raised knife. Instinctively, she reaches behind her for the bookcase and closes her hand over the hilt.

Darcy jabs the hidden knife into the attacker's arm. He howls and strikes her face with his fist. Her head snaps back, and she tumbles over the armchair with the man atop her.

Legs kick out as her feet find purchase on the hardwood. His fingers curl around her neck. She bridges hard and bucks him off her hips. When he reaches for his knife, she finds the steak knife on the floor and jams it into his shoulder. The man screams and falls back, the knife stuck in his shoulder as he backs away. Seeing she's weaponless, he regains his confidence and thunders across the living room. Unable to reach the other hidden weapons, Darcy reaches for the fireplace tools and swings the poker. The iron rod clips him above his eye and draws a bloody gash.

Now she climbs to her feet, the weapon held in front of her, adrenaline driving the haze away. He climbs through the broken window and rushes into the night. Darcy grabs the gun off the kitchen table and turns toward the entryway. She hurls the front door open, expecting headlights to blind her. But hers is the only vehicle in the driveway. The killer is on foot, too far away for her to catch him.

It doesn't matter.

She saw his face.

18

Jennifer awakens to the chains around her body. He bound her again, but something is different. Her skin crawls from recent contact, and when she pulls her shirt up to her chin, she sees the hand marks across her belly and chest. Automatically, her body performs an inventory, each nerve at high attention.

Did he touch her in other places? No, she doesn't think he did. Still, she feels the ghosts of his fingers pinching and prodding.

It's dark outside, the light in the hallway seeping through the floorboards. She knows she slept a long time before the front door opened and edged shut. Someone is in the house.

Across the room, Sandy is an immobile bulge. For a panicked second, Jennifer doesn't hear the girl breathing. Then the girl coughs and chokes, rolling onto her stomach in a tangle of chains to clear her windpipe.

"Sandy, I didn't hurt you. He did it. That creep put my hands around your throat while I was asleep."

The girl doesn't answer. Her eyes flutter for a second and shut again.

"That other girl who was here last night. I saw him carry her down the hallway. Do you know her name? Is she still here?"

What she wants to ask is, *is the girl alive?* But in the dark corner of her mind, she already knows. The kidnapper killed the girl, and he'll murder Sandy and Jennifer too. It occurs to Jennifer the silence inside the little house is deeper than before. Absolute.

He's not here. Whoever is inside the house, it's not the kidnapper. This is her last chance to escape before the killer finishes the job. She pulls on the chains, searching for a weak point. Five minutes later, she's no closer to freeing herself than she was when she started.

"Wake up and help me!"

Screaming doesn't rouse the prone girl. Falling to her back, Jennifer pushes against the radiator with her feet. The struggle causes a headache-inducing racket, but the heater holds firm. She curses and slaps her hand against the floor. Immediately, she pays for losing control. Jennifer clutches her hand and rocks back and forth, flesh stinging, bones and tendons bruised.

The shadow in the doorway touches her face. She retreats toward the wall, but it isn't the kidnapper watching her from the darkness. The older girl has returned, and as Jennifer expected, the girl hasn't brought the sheriff and FBI with her.

For an uncomfortable minute, Jennifer and the older girl glare at each other from across the room, neither speaking.

"What are you staring at?"

Jennifer's anger backs the girl into the hallway where she stands like a statue. Moonlight touches the girl, and a flood of emotions twist her face. Terror, desperation, disgust. When the girl edges into the doorway again, Jennifer lowers her voice.

"Why do you help him? He treats you like an animal."

No response. On the floor, Sandy's body shifts, legs twitching. Jennifer wants to believe the girl is waking up. More likely a nightmare haunts the girl...images of Jennifer's hands wrapped around her throat and squeezing the life out of her.

"If you won't help me, please help Sandy. She's sick and needs a doctor." Jennifer lifts her hands and displays the chains. "Help me break these chains, and I'll make sure Sandy gets to the hospital."

When the girl's eyes lock on the chains, a shudder rolls through her body. But she doesn't move.

"I can't break them by myself," Jennifer says. "Maybe he left a key for the locks. Or he keeps tools, something you could smash the chains with."

The girl clutches the door frame as if the world is a spinning ride she'll fly off of if she doesn't hang on. It seems insane to Jennifer the girl won't help, and that rekindles the suspicion the girl must be the man's wife or daughter, always in his service. The girl's unwillingness to help breaks Jennifer's spirit. She collapses against the wall where she huddles in a ball and sobs. Nobody will help her escape, and Sandy won't open her eyes. She cries in the thickening darkness until a sound pulls her head up. The floor squeals with each careful step into the room.

Now the girl stands above Jennifer. She's bigger, older. Jennifer is at the girl's mercy should she turn violent and attack. But the girl doesn't hurt her. Instead, she looks down upon Jennifer, lips quivering. Jennifer believes the girl wants to free her but can't smash through the mental barrier holding her in place.

Her hand reaches out. Touches the chain and darts back as though the links burn. After a long period of indecision, she kneels before Jennifer and pulls the chains through her hands until the padlocks prevent further stretching. Then she shifts to the radiator and examines the locks as one might a bizarre new flower growing amid weeds and bedrock.

"Does he leave the key?"

Each time Jennifer speaks, the girl jumps back. Jennifer walks a tightrope, balancing discretion with her need to prompt the girl into action.

"If not a key, then a hammer. Or an ax. We can split the chains and escape before he returns."

The older girl shakes her head as if at war with herself.

"We'll run until we find help. Just you, me, and Sandy. The sheriff will come and arrest him. He'll never hurt us again."

The girl chews on the corner of her mouth. Her eyes swing between the two chained girls as Jennifer nods in encouragement. But the girl turns and runs from the room, terrified.

"You bitch! Don't leave us here!"

The front door slams. She's gone.

19

Moonlight beams down on Laurie's farmhouse, the rising sun hours away. Darcy lifts her head off the floor at the sound of two vehicles rolling down the driveway. She checks the clock, realizing with a start she fell asleep again. Asleep with the killer outside.

Hensel's voice calls to her as he pounds up the steps. The front door opens, and he blinks at the mess covering the downstairs. As he rushes into the living room, Fisher and Reinhold appear in the doorway. Both agents have their weapons drawn. Kneeling beside Darcy, Hensel raises a hand toward his partners.

"Give us a second." When Reinhold gives him a questioning stare, Hensel points at the staircase. "Clear the upstairs while I check on Darcy."

A second glare from Fisher tells Darcy the agent knows nobody else is inside the house. Still, the agents clamber up the stairs and move from one room to the next as Hensel turns Darcy's head to face his.

"There's bruising on your neck. He strangled you?"

Darcy touches her neck, the attack more dream than reality

until she remembers the killer's hands squeezing the life out of her.

"Eric, I saw his face."

His eyes light with hope. They extinguish a moment later.

"Look at you. You're abusing the meds again. How many this time? Three? Five? More?"

"It's not important."

"Yes, it's damn important," he says, moving two fingers in front of her eyes. "A good lawyer will blow holes in the testimony of an intoxicated witness. What time did the attack occur?"

Darcy closes her eyes and concentrates.

"An hour ago. Maybe longer."

"Shit. You don't know."

"Stop harassing me, Eric! I'm not the one on trial."

Hensel puffs air through his lips and rubs the back of his neck.

"I can't defend the decisions you made tonight, but I get it. Jennifer is your daughter, and if I had a kid of my own, I wouldn't think rationally if something happened. But put your FBI shoes on again and see things from the law's perspective. You're our only hope for identifying this guy, and I doubt we can use your testimony in court."

"I don't care about a trial. I want this bastard dead and my daughter back."

Hensel places a finger over his lips when Fisher and Reinhold start down the stairway.

"Not a word of Lou Vescio or how many pills you took," Hensel says, whispering next to her ear. "Fisher and Reinhold don't know."

"Upstairs is clear," Fisher says, cocking an eyebrow at the glass shards sparkling on the floor.

The open window invites the gelid night inside, a cold the

wood stove can't overcome. Darcy recounts the attack for Fisher and Reinhold. She's firm with her estimation that the killer broke inside an hour ago. Hensel shifts his jaw, unconvinced.

"And he left on foot?" Fisher asks, brushing a piece of glass aside so he can lean his head through the window.

Darcy nods.

"But you didn't see which way he ran," Reinhold says, studying Darcy.

"No."

"If he's on foot, that significantly narrows the area we need to search," says Hensel, rising to his feet. He touches the fireplace poker with the toe of his shoe. "Did he swing this at you?"

"No, I used it in defense."

"That's all you needed to fight him off?"

Darcy glances around for the steak knife before she remembers it was still buried in the killer's shoulder when he fled.

"No. The hidden knives, remember?"

"You hid one in the bookcase."

"Good memory."

Fisher kneels down and shines his flashlight on the floor.

"Blood," Fisher says, looking over his shoulder at Hensel. "And Darcy isn't bleeding."

"Get me a CSI team. This prick left DNA." Another pair of headlights flare against the kitchen window. "That will be the sheriff."

Darcy grabs Hensel's arm as he rises.

"I don't want Laurie and Hunter to find out about this. They're under enough stress."

"It's your cousin's house. She needs to know." Seeing Darcy's protest forming, he clears his throat. "But we can't allow Laurie inside until the techs finish collecting evidence. So I'll forget to contact her for another hour and let her sleep."

Hensel's gaze slides from Fisher to Reinhold. They nod in agreement.

When Tipton enters the house, he looks like he fell asleep an hour before the call came in. His long face droops and sags, the lines under his eyes heavy with sleep deprivation. He takes one look at the shattered window and overturned furniture and mutters a curse.

"Anybody get a look at this guy?"

Hensel fills Tipton in. The sheriff glances in Darcy's direction when Hensel tells him she saw his face.

"Okay, here's what I want," Tipton says, scanning the downstairs. "Before the CSI team arrives, I want every deputy yanked out of bed to search the grounds. If this scumbag pulled that knife out of his shoulder, I want it found. That will give us a first guess at the direction he headed, and we'll have more DNA to nail him on. You two," Tipton says, glaring at Hensel and Fisher. "Pull up a map and figure out where this guy could have run off to. He's on foot, so there's a good chance he lives around here."

"Or has a place he takes the girls," Reinhold suggests. "An abandoned cabin."

"Fewer theories, more results. I want Sandy Young and Jennifer Gellar found. After the paramedics check Ms. Gellar, get me a police sketch artist. Bring him to the hospital if you need to."

"I don't need a doctor," Darcy says.

"You'll do what the paramedics tell you. This isn't up for debate."

The ambulance arrives fifteen minutes later. A skinny boy in glasses who doesn't appear old enough to drive checks Darcy over. Except for the bruises on her neck and a scrape down her arm, she's uninjured and doesn't require a hospital stay. The paramedic gives her the usual catch-all advice—follow up with her own doctor in the next few days and get extra rest.

"I'm running low on a prescription," Darcy says, scratching her arm.

"Sorry, Ms. Gellar. I'm not authorized to write prescriptions. But if you take my advice and visit the hospital..."

"No hospitals."

Three CSI team members wearing baggies over their shoes pour over the evidence. The fireplace poker departs the scene in a plastic bag, and a young woman with sharp, green eyes dusts the living room for prints. She pulls a partial print off the windowsill and what appears to be a thumbprint from the hardwood where Darcy and the killer fought.

The police sketch artist arrives an hour later. She's a middle-aged woman with strawberry blonde curls. The artist wears designer reading glasses on the end of her nose, and when she glances at Darcy, it's always over the tops of the glasses as though she's peeking over a wall at a strange animal she doesn't recognize. Remembering the attack makes Darcy's skin crawl, but sitting steps from where the intruder broke inside sharpens her memory, clears away the medication's cobwebs. During her run with the FBI, Darcy worked with police sketch artists. She understands the process, knows the prompts before the artist gives them. But Darcy allows the woman to sketch the attacker at her own pace.

She's surprised the work is already complete when the woman puts the pencil down and rotates the pad so it faces Darcy.

"Is this the man who attacked you?"

The sketch depicts a white male in his late-thirties to early forties, as average as apple pie at Thanksgiving. An upturned celestial nose appears accurate, as is the short, round chin and the unshaved stubble on his face. The spacing of the light brown eyes looks perfect, as is the thin scar on his forehead, but what strikes Darcy is the vacant stare in the picture. The sketch artist captured the killer perfectly. This is their guy. Now it's a matter of spreading the picture around until someone recognizes him.

While Darcy huddles in the kitchen under a blanket, Hensel, Fisher, and Tipton spread a map across the table. When she tells them about the trail she found leading out of Cass Park, Hensel narrows his eyes.

"You investigated the park without backup after dark," Hensel says, shaking his head. "Any more surprises I should know about?" He turns to Tipton. "Take her back to the hotel."

"No, you can't lock me out of the investigation."

"I can and I did. You're not law enforcement, Darcy, and the way you conducted yourself tonight, I can't trust you to contribute."

"A maniac kidnaps my daughter, and you blame me for generating leads. That's just great, Eric."

"Our sole focus is finding Sandy and Jennifer. Go back to the hotel, Darcy. We'll discuss this after you've slept."

"Fine. You don't need to take me. I have my car."

"You're in no condition to drive. Take her keys."

Wearing the grimace of a disappointed father, Tipton sweeps Darcy's keys into his hands and tosses them to Agent Reinhold. To Darcy, the move feels childish as if the agent and sheriff play an immature game of keep-away.

Anger and hurt stab into her chest. Hensel never turned on her before. Slapping her palm on the table, she pushes past the agents. Awaiting Darcy at the door, Reinhold pockets the keys and leads her into the predawn dark. Darcy doesn't realize she still has the blanket draped over her shoulders until she climbs into the SUV and yanks the door shut. Reinhold hasn't looked at her, and Darcy is thankful the roar of the engine replaces the uncomfortable silence. They're on a desolate strip of farm-to-market road between Scarlet River and Millport when Reinhold finally speaks.

"I'll have a deputy drop the car and keys at the hotel this morning."

Darcy glances over and mulls over the petulant responses popping into her head.

"I could have driven myself and saved you the trouble."

"Doubtful." Reinhold glances at Darcy as she navigates the dark roadway, and her eyes hold the cold, interrogatory stare Darcy witnessed during the briefing. "You're not fooling anybody, you know?"

"Excuse me?"

"Come on, Darcy. The constant drowsiness—"

"Try to sleep when your daughter is missing."

"—memory loss, questionable decision making, hostility."

"Oh, for Christ's sake. Don't fucking profile me."

Reinhold bites her tongue, considering.

"You clutch that bag against your hip like you're afraid it might vanish, and every few minutes, you touch the zipper. If I weren't here, you'd go the next step and plunge your hand inside the bag. What's in the bag that you can't live without? You're on a sedative."

Darcy nudges the bag away and folds her arms, keeping her searching fingers pinned beneath her elbows.

"I'm not a junkie, Agent Reinhold. It's a prescription. I'll be happy to show you the bottle, if you'll get off my back."

"Regardless of what the bottle says, you're taking several times the prescribed dosage. You hold prescriptions from multiple physicians and keep a bottle everywhere you go, no different from an alcoholic concealing bottles in a desk drawer at work. Now you're running low, and you've constructed a list of area doctors so you can get another script filled."

"It must feel like a game to you to tear into my character flaws."

"I'm not judging you, Darcy. Just the opposite. I came here

hoping I could pick your brain, snag pointers from the woman Agent Hensel calls the best profiler to come through the BAU in the last decade. You're angry with him for not letting you contribute, but you're compromising the investigation. Stop blaming Eric. With the state you're in, he had no choice."

Darcy gives Reinhold the cold treatment until they pull into the drop-off lane at the Hampton Inn. As Darcy gathers her bag, Reinhold rests her hands on the wheel.

"Don't hate me, Darcy. I'm only trying to help. If you want to talk to someone about—"

"Goodnight, Agent Reinhold."

Darcy slams the door and marches past the front desk. The woman manning the desk cranks her head up as if she'd dozed off and gives Darcy a weary smile. Darcy produces her room key to allay the woman's suspicions. Inside the hotel room, Darcy swipes her phone on so she can see in the pitch black. Hunter's head pokes out from under the covers. Letting him rest, she curls onto the cot and falls asleep before her head hits the pillow.

The sun singes Darcy's eyelids. She awakens to Hunter sitting on the edge of the cot with a tray of breakfast in his lap. Laurie is on the chair, one leg crossed and a Grisham novel open on her lap. Her eyes slide between the pages and Darcy, lips parted as though she has something to say.

"You slept past breakfast," Hunter says, handing her the tray. "I grabbed you eggs and waffles. Hope that's all right."

Though she can't bear the thought of food, Darcy smiles and cuts into the waffle with the plastic fork and knife.

"This is perfect. Thank you for thinking of me."

Even with the waffles soaked in syrup, she can't taste the sweet comfort food.

"Anything new with the search?"

It hurts Darcy that Hunter doesn't say Jennifer's name. He's compartmentalizing, opening doors a sliver so the terrors don't escape. From the glare Laurie gives her from the tops of her eyes, Darcy knows Hunter hasn't heard about the attack.

"The FBI has a few leads. We should hear something in the next two days." Darcy swallows the rest of the waffle and sets the tray aside. "Can you watch my food for me? I need to speak to Laurie next door."

Hunter carries the plate to the refrigerator and places it inside. Darcy, who fell asleep in her clothes, follows her cousin on unsteady legs into the hallway, the bag glued to her shoulder. Laurie's room is brightly lit, the shades open to the noon sun. Whereas unlaundered clothes and pillows littered the floor in Darcy's room, Laurie's is neat and clean, the bed recently made. Laurie closes the door and throws the bolt. Turning on Darcy, she folds her arms.

"You want to tell me about the stunt you pulled last night?"

Darcy brushes the hair from her eyes and sinks into the chair.

"I'm sorry about the window. Let me pay for the replacement."

"I don't care about the window, I care about you. What were you thinking going to the park alone at night?"

"I used to be an FBI agent, Laurie. I can take care of myself, and I carried a weapon."

"Don't agents take partners for backup? And I know why you ended up at my house. Hensel says you're abusing the meds again and couldn't drive back to the hotel. He wants you in rehab, and I agree."

A hundred curse words poise behind Darcy's lips. But Laurie is right. Darcy is spinning out of control, a train that clattered off the tracks three years ago.

"I can't go into rehab. Not with Jennifer missing. But there's a reason I risked investigating Cass Park last night. If I hadn't, I wouldn't have figured out how the kidnapper took Sandy Young with no one noticing. And when I find out where he took her, I'll know where he's keeping my daughter."

"What does nearly overdosing on anti-anxiety pills have to do with catching a child predator?" Darcy bends over and rests her face in her hands. Laurie grabs the trash basket and sets it at Darcy's feet. "If you're going to throw up, aim for the trash. I'm not cleaning up your mess."

Darcy waves the trash can away.

"You can't imagine what it's like to fall asleep seeing the face of a serial killer every night. Or what it's like to be terrified of the dark, though the only man I need to be afraid of is locked away for life. You think I want to take pills so I can function?"

Pushing the container away, Laurie kneels in front of Darcy and takes her hands.

"I want you to promise me you'll get help when this is over." Laurie holds her eyes until Darcy nods. "Until then."

Laurie opens her hand.

"What?"

"Give me the bottle."

"Seriously?"

"Do it."

Darcy groans and digs the pills out of the bag.

"Happy?"

Keeping her eyes locked on Darcy's face, Laurie turns the bag over and spills the belongings on the carpet.

"Swear to me you aren't hiding another bottle."

"Not anymore." When Laurie glares at Darcy from the corner of her eye, Darcy raises a hand as if taking an oath. "I finished the other bottle. I'm out."

"Shit." Laurie twist the cap off and spills a dozen pills onto her palm. "I'm no doctor, but this is a legitimate prescription, and stopping cold turkey might do more harm than good."

She counts out three pills and drops them into the bottle. The rest she folds into a tissue, which she stuffs into her pocket.

"The prescription says one per day." Laurie hands Darcy the medication. "In two days, you will produce the bottle, and there'd better be one pill left, or so help me I'll drag you to rehab myself."

Darcy lowers her head. Tangles of hair conceal the red around her eyes.

"I've failed everyone," Darcy says, hitching.

Laurie lifts her chin.

"Like hell you have. You're the strongest woman in my life. Nobody could hold it together as well as you have. But from now on you lean on your family and friends when you need help, not a bottle of pills."

Darcy releases an injured sob. She's hidden her demons for too long. Dragging them into the open humiliates her. Yet it frees her. Nothing to hide, nothing left to lose.

Laurie places a call, still holding Darcy's gaze. After a moment, Darcy hears a man's voice through the receiver.

"She's ready," Laurie says, ending the call.

"Who was that?"

A knock on the door follows before Laurie can answer. Rising to her feet, Laurie checks the peephole and opens the door. It's Hensel, and he has Fisher and Reinhold with him. A fresh wave of embarrassment crashes into Darcy. She rakes the snags out of her hair as her former partner, dressed in a suit that looks like a million bucks compared to her wrinkled outfit, edges into the room.

"She'll be fine now," Laurie says, giving her a stare that warns Darcy not to let her down.

20

"Waggoner is in the interrogation room awaiting Tipton and Reinhold," Fisher says as a way of hello when Darcy accompanies Hensel into the briefing room at the sheriff's office in Millport. The agent doesn't pull his eyes from the map laid out on the table. He's circled Cass Park and the falls, and Darcy is happy to see Fisher is on the same wavelength.

"There's no official trail from Cass Park to the falls area," Darcy says, leaning over Fisher's shoulder. "But you can walk along the banks."

Fisher gives an unconvinced groan.

"Problem is Sandy Young weighs 110 pounds. That no one heard her scream tells me he knocked her out, possibly drugged her. Let's say our kidnapper is strong enough to carry her a half-mile, longer if a deputy is on his trail and his adrenaline is spiking. But all the way to the falls? Not a chance."

"He could have taken rests," Hensel says, tracing an invisible line with his finger toward the falls.

"I talked to a hydrologist out of the local weather office. He says that creek runs around a foot deep during the fall, but the region experienced a stormy summer and a tropical depression last month. The stage sat at three to four feet over the last two weeks, and that's plenty deep enough to support a small craft."

"Like a canoe or kayak," says Darcy, picturing the creek under the moonlight.

"The wife and I take inflatable kayaks on the river back home. We get weird looks, but the inflatables hold up well, bouncing off rocks instead of smashing against them. A small creek with this many turns, I'd use an inflatable. But this creates another issue. The stream runs twenty miles, so the theory that this guy lives close to the falls has holes in it."

Tipton and the FBI profiler emerge from the sheriff's office. He holds a folder which he taps against an open hand as he blows the hair off his forehead.

"You want in on the interview?" Tipton asks Hensel.

"We'll watch through the glass," says Hensel. "Agent Reinhold will take my place. She'll switch up the line of questioning, if she thinks he knows the kidnapper."

Tipton nods and leads Reinhold across the hall. Darcy follows Hensel into a neighboring room barely large enough to hold the two chairs facing the glass. A reciprocal mirror divides the interview room from the tiny viewing room. While the interrogation room is bright, the lights are off in the viewing room to create the illusion of one-way transmission.

Darcy didn't smell Hensel's cologne earlier, but it's overwhelming in the observation room. He twists the chair backward and sits down, arms resting on the chair back as he drums his fingers. To Darcy, the room feels ten degrees warmer than the rest of the building. Sweat beads over her brow. It's the huge bearded man seated across from Tipton and Reinhold who spikes Darcy's blood pressure. This isn't the man who attacked her at Laurie's house. The two men couldn't look more different. Yet the possibility exists Waggoner is the kidnapper which means a child abductor and a serial killer could be stalking Scarlet River.

Tipton adjusts his hat while Reinhold flips open her notebook and clicks a pen. Waggoner sits with his arms folded, a confident, bemused grin on his face. His eyes wander to the glass. Though Waggoner can't see past the mirror, Darcy's skin crawls. He seems to be looking right at her, a mirage made more convincing when his tongue slithers out to lick his lips. It's the same hungry leer he gave Jennifer.

"Something funny, Mr. Waggoner?"

Waggoner wipes the smirk off his face, but the challenging stare he gives Tipton says they can't intimidate him.

"I understand you were at the Fresh Mart on the fourth of December," Tipton says, clasping his hands together.

"So what if I was? That's not a concern for the sheriff's department."

"Getting an early start on the week's groceries?"

"Something like that."

Tipton sneaks a peek at Reinhold, who jots a note on the pad.

"What did you buy?"

"Excuse me?"

"You shopped for groceries. So what did you buy?"

Waggoner shrugs and tips back in his chair. The chair back clicks against the wall.

"Food and stuff. That's why people go to grocery stores."

"Funny, the video footage from the store security cam shows you abandoned an empty cart in the produce aisle and bought nothing."

"Now that I think about it, I bought groceries over at the

Wal-Mart in Millport. Damn Fresh Mart is too expensive, so I took my business elsewhere."

"So you just left?"

"Yeah, I left without buying anything. Are you gonna charge me with illegal browsing, or should I leave?"

Waggoner stands up from his seat, and Tipton glares at him.

"Sit down, Mr. Waggoner. I have an eyewitness who says you followed an underage girl and her mother through the store."

"Well, now. I don't have any recollection of that."

"Says you confronted the mother in the parking lot and threatened her."

Darcy's back stiffens. If Waggoner tells Tipton she pulled a gun, she'll lose whatever goodwill she gained today. The sheriff will be hard pressed to arrest her—she can claim self-defense—but the gun incident will complicate matters.

"Oh, that." Waggoner waves the accusation away. "I was in the beer aisle minding my business. Never said a word to that woman. She confronted me in the parking lot and claimed I was checking out her daughter, which was bullshit. We shared a few choice words, but nothing came of it. Haven't seen her since. Did that bitch claim I started the fight? Because it's a lie."

"Bitch," Reinhold says, setting down the pen. "Do you frequently refer to women as bitches?"

Waggoner clicks his tongue.

"If the shoe fits."

Reinhold removes a paper from the folder set between her and Tipton. She scans the page and sets it down so Waggoner can see.

"Two years ago, Sheriff Tipton arrested you for trying to coax a fifteen-year-old girl into your truck."

"A gross exaggeration. I'll bet your report also says the sheriff released me the same day because I didn't do nothing wrong.

Girl said she needed a ride across town. No harm in helping a local girl."

"Picking up a hitchhiker is illegal."

"That's if you pick up a stranger. But everyone knows everyone in Scarlet River. I didn't know the girl's name, but I'd seen her around, so I guess you could say I knew her."

"Just a Good Samaritan helping out a girl in need."

"I mean, yeah."

"Did she have a long walk?"

"Huh?"

"A long walk home."

"Long enough."

"Can you be more specific?"

"About two miles."

"So you knew where she lived. You make a habit out of learning the addresses of underage girls?"

Waggoner scowls.

"Now you're the one being the bitch, trying to put words in my mouth. I told you it's a small town. We speak to our neighbors. This ain't D.C."

"Mr. Waggoner," Tipton says, regaining control of the interview. "Where were you between the hours of three and five P.M. on December the sixth?"

The bearded man leans back again and itches his beard.

"I'm a busy man, Sheriff. Can't say I recall."

"Try, Mr. Waggoner. It was only four days ago. Did you visit Cass Park?"

"Now why would I go there?" asks Waggoner, but his eyes shift from Tipton to the door.

Tipton removes a photograph of Sandy Young from the folder and slides it in front of Waggoner.

"Recognize her?"

Waggoner picks the photograph off the table, his thumb

poised over the girl's breast as if he wants to caress it. He studies the picture, eyes moving up and down the top half of the girl's body, before he hands it back to Tipton.

"Might have seen her around."

"Girl's name is Sandy Young. She disappeared from Cass Park four days ago during the late afternoon, and you can't seem to verify your whereabouts."

For the first time since the interrogation began, Waggoner's face shows alarm. He raises his hands.

"Hold up. I heard about a kidnapping on the news, but I didn't put two and two together until now. Sandy Young, sure. Her name is all over the papers, but I never kidnapped no one. And now that I think about it, I was at Patsy's Bar and Grill on Chestnut Street between three and five."

"So if I ask around at Patsy's, they'll remember seeing you."

"Damn right."

Undeterred, Tipton slides Jennifer's picture across the table. Darcy tries to avert her eyes, but she can't.

"Recognize this girl?"

"I think I need a lawyer."

"Now, now, Mr. Waggoner. You're not under arrest. We're clarifying important details." Tipton taps his finger on Jennifer's photograph. "This is Jennifer Gellar, age fourteen, the same girl my eyewitness says you followed at the Fresh Mart. She was kidnapped two nights ago, just five days after you trailed her through the store."

"No way did I hurt her, and I don't know nothing about kidnapped girls. I think I want that lawyer now."

Hensel leans over and whispers to Darcy.

"They've got Waggoner off balance. Time for Tipton to find out what the scumbag knows."

Darcy's heart thumps. Did this man kidnap her daughter?

"Another interesting coincidence," Reinhold says. "Ten years ago, you moved to Shatterstruck, Wyoming. Is that correct?"

"Yeah. I suppose there's a law against moving from Georgia."

"Four teenage girls went missing ten years ago, three murdered and one girl we never found."

"I remember. That was a bad time for all of us."

"Funny thing. The abductions and murders stopped after you moved to Wyoming. Now you're back in Georgia, and we've got three new kidnappings and another murdered teenage girl on our hands."

"Add in the fact that you harassed one of the missing girls five days ago," Tipton says, leaning across the table toward Waggoner. "And this doesn't look very good for you."

Inside the observation room, Darcy glances at Hensel and says, "It's all circumstantial."

Hensel grins and tilts his head at Waggoner.

"But Waggoner doesn't know that. Check him out. The S.O.B. is sweating bullets."

The mood changes in the interrogation room. Gone is Gil Waggoner's sarcasm and swagger. His eyes dart between Reinhold and Tipton like moths caught amid streetlights.

"Hey," Waggoner says, waving his hands. "I might have a thing for pretty girls."

"Pretty underage girls," Reinhold interjects.

"But I never hurt anybody. All I did was look. If these girls don't want guys staring at them, they should put on clothes. Stop walking around in crop tops and shorts cut up to their pussies. I mean, maybe someone ought to arrest these girls for indecent exposure and stop blaming every guy who notices."

"Mr. Waggoner, I'd like you to review this transcript from an Internet chat room."

As Reinhold hands Waggoner the transcript, Darcy gives Hensel a questioning look.

Hensel winks and says, "We followed his IP address and caught him soliciting teenage girls in a private Internet forum. According to his profile, he's seventeen."

The papers tremble in Waggoner's hands as he flips from one page to the next.

"This isn't me," says Waggoner, jabbing his pointer finger at the paper. "I don't go in chat rooms. Hell, the Internet is nothing but whiny liberals bitching about people who work for a living."

"We can prove it's you," Tipton says. "An IP address is a lot like a phone number, Mr. Waggoner. We traced your screen name, so let's cut the bullshit. Ever meet any of the girls you chat with?"

Waggoner appears ready to protest and stops himself. He stuffs his hands into the pockets of his jeans, his shoulders curling inward.

"No."

"Never?"

"It ain't illegal to talk to girls."

"Mr. Waggoner, please turn to page three," Reinhold says, flipping through her copy of the transcript. Waggoner wastes time, turning the sheets over as though page three is difficult to locate. "Go back one page, Mr. Waggoner."

"Okay, I think I found it."

"Direct your attention halfway down the page. You solicited nude pictures from a teenage girl with the screen name *S-Cato4*."

"I was joking around. And she never sent a photo, which tells me she ain't who she claims she is, anyhow."

"No, she didn't send you a nude photo." Waggoner grins at Reinhold's admission, his arrogance returning. "But you had quite the conversation. It goes on for almost an hour, and three times you offer to meet her."

"Again, it's nothing but fooling around. Flirting. These girls realize people hanging out in chat rooms aren't who they claim to be, and that's part of the turn on. It's all fantasy. I wasn't serious about meeting her."

"So you never got together with anyone you met during a chat session."

"Course not. That's sicko stuff."

Again, Waggoner drops his eyes, a tipoff he's lying. Reinhold removes her reading glasses and sets them on the table.

"Except you met this girl, didn't you, Mr. Waggoner? *S-Cat04* is Sandy Young."

The blood drains from Waggoner's face. He opens his mouth to protest and nothing comes out.

"Admit it," Tipton says, knocking his knuckles on the table. "You met Sandy Young at Cass Park and abducted her, just like you kidnapped Jennifer Gellar after you stalked her from the store to the parking lot."

Waggoner's eyes widen to white saucers. He fidgets in his seat as if he needs to use the restroom, the bright lights making his eyes squint.

"No...no. I didn't kidnap no girls."

"But you know who did. Is there something you want to tell us?"

The big man slumps over and slides his hands over the table, cleaning up an invisible spill.

"I ain't never hurt these girls, and I sure as hell never met no Sandy Young. But maybe someone else did."

Tipton slaps the folder shut and tilts his head at the notepad. Reinhold slides him the paper and pen.

"Start talking."

"There's this guy. He comes into the chat room now and then, but he don't say much. And before you ask, no, I don't know his name. He might have asked me to talk him up, make the girls think he was the real deal."

"Meaning?"

"A lot of them girls thought we were putting them on about being teenagers, but I vouched for this guy. Said he was a college student, but he was shy, not comfortable meeting girls."

Tipton grips what little hair he still has in his fist and lets it go.

"So you lied to teenage girls and convinced them your friend was their age. You're a real upstanding citizen, Mr. Waggoner. What happened next?"

Waggoner rubs his temples.

"I may have set up *S-Cat04* to meet this guy."

The table shifts and screeches over the floor when Tipton leans forward.

"So you're saying you told Sandy Young to meet an adult posing as a teenager at Cass Park," Tipton says, scribbling the pseudo-confession on the notepad.

"No way. I only suggested Sandy give the guy a chance. Nobody told me where they met. Their conversation went dark."

"Dark?"

"Private."

"They messaged in private?"

"Yeah. I mean, I guess so."

Tipton's temple pulses. Realizing the sheriff borders on an explosion, Reinhold tries to wrestle control of the interview away from Tipton.

"But you didn't suggest Sandy Young give an adult male a chance," she says. "You tricked her into believing he was a teenager."

Tipton tilts his hat down his forehead.

"Gil Waggoner, you're under arrest for conspiracy to kidnap Sandy Young."

The interview erupts with Waggoner's protests. On the other

side of the glass, Darcy falls back in her chair, fingers tingling with anxious energy.

"Find out who the second man in the chat room is," Darcy says, turning to Hensel. "That's how we'll find Jennifer and Sandy."

"The BAU is tracing his activity. Whoever this guy is, he covers himself better than Waggoner, using multiple servers. But we'll nail him. Hopefully, in the next twenty-four hours."

"The girls don't have twenty-four hours, Eric."

21

A groan in the floor pulls Jennifer's head up from slumber. Her lips stick together, dried and caked with a white paste. Parting her lips tears the flesh and spills blood as she battles up to her knees. Two days after the abduction, she can't recall the last time she ate a full meal. Besides the madman forcing water and food scraps past her lips, she hasn't eaten. The ache in her bones and congestion tell her she's sick, no surprise given the lack of sleep and the constant chill bleeding through the uninsulated wall. She shivers, pulls her knees to her chest, and eases her back against a radiator which hasn't pumped heat during her captivity.

Sandy's lungs gurgle when she breathes, the girl's deterioration accelerating. Jennifer wonders if the teen contracted pneumonia. Worry creases Jennifer's face. She might have the same sickness Sandy caught. In fact, the chances are high considering their abductor locked them together for almost forty-eight hours.

Multiple attempts over the last two days taught Jennifer she can't reach Sandy unless the girl rolls toward the center of the room. Jennifer lifts her arms to try, but the weight of the chains and the lingering illness drag them down. Jennifer blinks and studies the door. Something about the ribbon of black beneath the door unsettles her. It's almost indecent, like a tongue protruding from an open mouth. She knows he's there. Listening. Footsteps quietly pad away and confirm her suspicion, and she releases a held breath.

When she's certain he's too deep into the house to hear, she clears the phlegm from her throat and swipes her nose with her shirtsleeve.

"I'm worried about Hunter," Jennifer says, though she knows Sandy is too sick to comprehend and hasn't met her family. "He'll go to North Carolina and do something stupid, and Mom won't be able to stop him because she's too busy trying to find us."

Sandy shifts onto her side and trembles, a sound close to a death rattle.

"I used to say Hunter was the responsible one between us, but I don't know anymore. I mean, I can't blame him for being angry. What those boys did to Bethany...I shouldn't tell you this stuff, but we're kinda like sisters now, and I know you'll keep it a secret. I try to put myself in Hunter's shoes, but I don't know what I would do if two people hurt someone close to me. How far would I go? It's easy to say I'd let the police handle it, but I'm not sure. I mean...if someone gave me a gun, would I..."

Jennifer wills Sandy to awaken. In her fantasy, Sandy's eyes pop open, and the girls form a silent bond to protect each other until they escape. Then Sandy will spot the obvious escape route Jennifer keeps missing, and the girls will be free. The sick girl mumbles, and Jennifer bolts to her feet, the chains stretched taut. But it's only ramblings inside a dream. Jennifer hopes it's a happy dream, even if the thoughts result from pneumonia-induced delirium.

She sits down and knocks her head against the radiator,

searching for a way out of this room. Then she remembers the older girl, the one who could have released Jennifer. By now, Sandy should be under a doctor's care while the kidnapper sits in a jail cell. Jennifer's fingers close over the links and squeeze. The strange girl is just as guilty as the man who abducted them. If she gets the chance, she'll hurt the girl. Make her pay for serving a psychopath.

When Sandy mutters again, Jennifer loses herself in the fantasy conversation.

"There's no reason to act like we're alone when we have each other, Sandy. So if you feel scared, I want you to tell me. I have your back. That's what a good sister does." But Jennifer remains furious over the older girl's unwillingness to help and bites down on her tongue, drawing blood. "And Mom *will* find us, Sandy. She profiled killers for the FBI. A few years ago, she shot the creep this guy works for. I guess that's why he wants to hurt me, but I suppose psychos don't need a reason. Anyhow, I know you're scared. I'm scared too. But we don't need to be. The FBI is in Georgia, and they'll find us if we hold out a little longer."

Jennifer gasps when the door slides open. How long had the man listened from the hallway?

Like a shadowed wraith, he glides across the floor of the darkened room and stands over Sandy. Jennifer's spine stiffens.

"Get away from her, creep."

"Looking out for your *sister*?" Jennifer can't see the grin spread across the man's face, but she hears the amusement in his voice. "I'd very much like your mother to find us, little one. That would save me the trouble of going after her again. And how I'd love for you to watch when I slit her throat."

Jennifer tugs at the chains. The kidnapper chuckles, a dry, ugly sound like rats crawling over old newspaper.

"I hope you've given a thought to my proposal," he says, pacing toward the corner where he stands with his hands clasped at his waist. She notes one of his arms hangs gingerly as if he nurses a shoulder injury. "There's no need for this ugliness between us. We're perfect partners. I can give you a good life."

"If you want to give me a good life, start by letting me go."

"Of course, we can't stay here," he says as though she hadn't spoken. "He'll find us if we stay here. But nobody finds me unless I want them to. Yes, we must leave and not tell a soul. Find another quiet place where nobody will bother us. We can leave immediately, if it pleases you."

"Why would I run away with you?"

"Because you were made for me. You're young yet, but I trust your mother taught you about love."

"My parents fell in love and had children. It had nothing to do with a sicko who hides in the woods and kidnaps young girls."

His back straightens, and suddenly he seems very tall. When he closes the door, the darkness thickens and turns suffocating. He crosses the room to Jennifer. The open palm slap stings her cheek. Her eyes adjust to the deeper darkness, and she stares into his crazed eyes.

"You're undisciplined. It's time you learn about consequences and loss."

As she clutches the welt rising on her face, he swivels and marches toward Sandy's prone body. If the girl senses his presence, she doesn't react to him looming over her.

"What are you doing?"

"Your sister, as you call her, cannot come with us. She'll never survive the journey."

"Then let her go."

His head tilts back at Jennifer.

"Why would I do such a thing? Even if I unchain her, she'll curl into a ball and lie here until she rots. Don't you see, Jennifer? There's nothing left to do."

"She has a bad cold and needs a doctor."

The kidnapper shakes his head.

"No doctor can bring her back. Listen to her, little one. Do you hear that? That's the sound of death. Better I leave Sandy here and remember her as she was when we first met."

Jennifer's head drops between her knees.

"No, I'm not going with you, and I'll never leave Sandy alone."

"You act as though you have a choice. We leave tonight, just the two of us, but not before you learn what happens when you disobey me."

From his pocket, the kidnapper removes a key. While Jennifer watches in stunned silence, he unlocks the two padlocks and pulls the chains off Sandy's arms and legs.

Wake up, Jennifer wills the sick girl. The man is nonchalant as he drags the chains to the corner, leaving Sandy alone in the center of the room. Jennifer prays the girl plays possum. If Sandy springs to her feet and runs for the door, he won't catch her. The girl's legs twitch, and Jennifer's heart leaps with hope.

But Sandy doesn't move. Only trembles on the cold, wooden floor as the madman strolls back to the center of the room. His head turns toward Jennifer.

"One day you'll forgive yourself for what you did to Sandy."

Panic shoots through Jennifer when she realizes what he intends. The chains yank her back toward the radiator as the man kneels atop Sandy and grips her by the throat. The attack shocks Sandy awake. Her eyes go wide as the maniac's hands encircle her neck and squeeze.

"Oh, God, don't do this! Stop!"

Jennifer's pleas spur the madman to squeeze harder. Sandy coughs, her legs bridged against the floor as she tries to buck him off her hips. Pulling up on Sandy's neck, he grips her head before smashing it against the floor.

Sandy's legs scramble with frantic desperation as he grins down at the teenager. Turning her head, she clamps her teeth down on his wrist, eyes clenched shut. He forms a fist with his free hand and pummels the side of her face. She bites harder, drawing little rivers of blood that flow off his hand and slick his skin.

Jennifer rips at the links and throws herself toward the fight. The chains chew crevices into her flesh and trip her up. Her vision goes black when she slams against the floor. Sharp agony in her shoulder tells Jennifer she popped it out of socket, but she ignores the pain and drags herself toward the dying teenager.

She's down on the grimy floor, breathing in the dust as tears flow off her cheeks and puddle on the hardwood. To her horror, Jennifer realizes Sandy is still three steps away. Sandy's face turns toward hers. Desperation pours out of the girl's eyes. Desperation and acceptance.

Sandy's hand slaps the floor. Her sneakers beat uselessly against the wood, a last ditch signal for someone to intervene. No one hears or helps. Her legs flail ever slower. When Sandy's eyes lock on Jennifer's, her body goes limp.

"No, you can't die!"

Jennifer begs the girl to fight back.

Sandy stops breathing.

22

The anti-anxiety medication's siren song is loud in Darcy's ear.

Riding in the passenger seat of Hensel's rental, she hides her hands inside her coat pockets so he won't see them shake. The western horizon burns with the sun's remnants, and the darkness that pours off the sea and floods the Georgia countryside makes Darcy wish for the bottle of pills. But they're locked in the hotel room a dozen miles away as the black SUV barrels through the night. Scarlet River's lights glimmer in the distance while Darcy concentrates on the white dividing line, averting her eyes from the blackening sky.

"You're doing great," Hensel says, sparing Darcy a glance after navigating a winding curve.

I can't hide the panic attack, she says to herself. Removing her hands from her pockets, she sets them on her lap. Her fingers fidget with a loose thread hanging off her pants.

"Darcy, look at me." She does. The dashboard lights his face in strange greens and reds, but his dead certainty they'll find Jennifer steels Darcy and replaces the fear with determination. "Any minute now, we'll hear from the BAU on the chat room trace. Fisher and Reinhold are canvassing Scarlet River, and Tipton's team is ready to roll the second we get a name."

Darcy nods and turns her attention back to the dividing line, the white stripe grounding her by giving her mind something to focus on. When he sets his hand on her wrist, she realizes her fists are clenched, nails digging holes into her palms. She forces her fists to open and takes a deep breath.

"I'm all right. Just get us there."

Hensel gives her a cautious glance and sets both hands on the wheel a moment before he presses down on the gas. The SUV jumps forward at seventy mph, the *Welcome to Scarlet River* sign a mile ahead. Hensel intends to revisit Laurie's house in case they missed a piece of evidence during the investigation. Darcy wants to help. Anything to stay busy and put herself in a position to rescue Jennifer when the FBI locates the killer.

A half-mile outside the town border, Darcy catches a ghostly shape striding down the shoulder in the pitch black. The headlights catch her face. Nina?

"Stop and go back!"

"Why?" Hensel taps the brakes and slows the SUV before it scoots past the intersection. "What's the problem."

Darcy throws the seatbelt off and twists around in her seat. The thin girl walks with her head down, hands in her pockets.

"That looked like Nina Steyer."

"Are you sure?"

Could it really be Nina? They're down the road from Maury's, the location of recent sightings.

"Back up, back up. Come on, Eric. Before she disappears."

Already the girl is a shadow against a dark backdrop of sky and open meadow. Hensel looks over his shoulder and shifts the SUV into reverse. The brake lights cast the girl in red, and she gives an anxious glance back at them as the black SUV closes on her.

Then she does the unexpected. The girl darts across the road behind the vehicle as Hensel screeches to a halt. The SUV rocks and settles, but the girl is already leaping the opposite shoulder and hurrying toward the side street running perpendicular to the country route.

This is the road that leads toward the state park trail, Darcy recalls as she leaps from the SUV before Hensel can stop her. She hears him curse and fumble for the window controls as Darcy closes the gap on the fleeing girl. When the girl looks back, Darcy recognizes Nina Steyer from Margaret's picture. She's wearing the same faded, beaten blue jeans, her head hidden inside the hood of her gray sweatshirt. A windbreaker with a rip down one sleeve isn't staving off the chilly evening, but Nina doesn't miss a step as she pushes through a row of shrubberies and hurries past a rundown one-story house with a sagging porch.

"Nina, don't run. I just want to talk to you."

A dog barks in the night. Somewhere a car door slams. Nina vanishes into the shadows when she runs through a backyard. Darcy follows, listening for the girl's sneakers swishing through the long, frosty grass as she ducks beneath a clothes line. Hensel's headlights sweep across the homes as he swerves up the lane and speeds up. Darcy worries he'll spook Nina, but if he gets ahead of the girl, she might double back and run into Darcy.

Nina materializes two properties ahead of Darcy. She's running for the trees. Darcy sprints until her lungs burn, closing the distance. Sensing Darcy coming up behind her, Nina runs harder. Though Darcy stays in shape by running, she's no match for Nina when the girl kicks into high gear. The woods loom ahead. Once they lose the girl inside the trees, they'll never catch up. As Darcy struggles to keep pace, Hensel exits the SUV running and aims for the tree line, aiming to cut Nina off. When the girl sees Hensel, she spins around.

And crashes into Darcy's waiting arms.

Darcy and Nina struggle until the former FBI agent wraps her arms around the girl.

"Please don't fight me, Nina. I promise I won't hurt you."

Hearing her name gives the girl pause, and she relaxes for a heartbeat. Darcy keeps a tight hold on the girl. If she lets her guard down and Nina escapes, Darcy knows she won't catch her again.

"That's right. I know your name, Nina. Many people have been searching for you. Shh...you're safe now."

Nina's back stiffens when Hensel approaches. The agent stops several paces away and holds his hands up.

"It's all right," Darcy whispers into Nina's ear. "Agent Hensel works for the FBI. He'll keep you safe and make sure you get back to your mother."

The girl's eyes swing to Darcy's. Disbelief sharpens her glare, and her forehead furrows in confusion. Nina's body slackens a split-second before she twists around and almost wiggles out of Darcy's grip. Hensel shifts his body in front of the girl and extends his arms, a net cast to catch Nina if she breaks free.

Hensel returns Darcy's glare. Nina panicked when Darcy promised they'd return the girl to her mother. Was Cherise Steyer involved in her daughter's abduction? Darcy recalls crazier revelations during her brief FBI career, but Cherise couldn't be working with the kidnapper. Darcy looked into the mother's eyes and saw injury, loss, and a frantic need to find her daughter. So why did Nina run at the mention of her mother?

"A friend of mine saw you at the diner. She said you tried to hitch a ride on a tractor trailer. Are you running from somebody, Nina?"

The girl's lower lip quivers, and her gaze travels down the

hill to the busy parking lot beside Maury's. The outside world troubles and confuses Nina, but she understands travelers come through Scarlet River and stop at the diner. For a girl searching for a way out of town, the diner's parking lot is her ticket.

Hooking elbows with Nina, Darcy leads her down the grassy hillside as Hensel lifts the radio to his lips. Tipton and his deputies will be here soon. This worries Darcy. A cruiser or ambulance pulling curbside might send Nina into hysterics. She's already too petrified to stand near Hensel. So Darcy diverts Nina's attention, all the while keeping a grip on the girl. Someone locked Nina away ten years ago, and discovering his identity is key to rescuing Jennifer and Sandy Young. Did Nina escape? Though time ticks against the abducted teenagers, Darcy steers the conversation toward calming subjects, things Nina experiences daily and understands.

"You amaze me, Nina. It can't be over forty-five degrees tonight, and I can't stop my teeth from chattering. Yet you're outside in a light jacket and doing fine."

Nina's eyes dart from the houses to Hensel, then back to the diner's parking lot. She's focused on escaping Scarlet River, even if it means never seeing her mother.

Darcy glances at the warm SUV up the hill. It's too soon to coax Nina into the vehicle. Not until Darcy builds trust.

"Tell me why you want to leave Scarlet River, Nina." The girl's head swivels toward Maury's again. "If you're afraid of someone, I'll protect you. And so will Agent Hensel."

Hensel pockets the radio and edges closer. Darcy appreciates the care with which he approaches the terrified girl. When Nina's hands grasp Darcy's jacket, Darcy assumes the girl is cowering from the agent and wants protection. To Darcy's shock, Nina speaks.

"He told me he killed Mommy."

23

Darcy paces outside the van. Emergency lights from the two cruisers swirl hot and frozen colors across her face. An ambulance idles curbside while looky-loos mass in their yards for a better look at the commotion. Two paramedics lean with folded arms against the van and whisper back and forth. A second SUV, belonging to Reinhold and Fisher, stands behind Hensel's vehicle.

Reinhold, Hensel, and Tipton are inside the van with Nina, the door closed as the profiler interviews the girl. The sheriff, his face pale after seeing Nina up close, phoned Cherise Steyer and told her they found a girl they believe to be her lost daughter. Darcy expects Cherise Steyer's car to squeal to a halt outside the van any second now, though the sheriff implored the mother to allow the FBI to interview the girl first. Cherise Steyer must be in a state of shock, Darcy expects. Darcy imagines the reunion and pictures Jennifer.

Until the FBI convinces Nina to direct them to her abductor's home, there's nothing for Darcy to do but fret and wear a groove in the blacktop. When she can't wait another second for Reinhold to coax Nina into talking, Darcy marches to the van just as Agent Fisher climbs down and blocks the entrance.

"Hold your horses, Ms. Gellar. They're almost finished with Nina."

Sipping from his coffee, Fisher offers a second cup to Darcy. She accepts, knowing the hot drink will burn the chill off her bones.

"Please tell me she knows where Jennifer and Sandy are."

Fisher gulps the coffee and stares with squinted eyes beyond the emergency vehicles. Whatever the agent learned inside the van, it shook him.

"Getting to the truth with that girl is like prying a stuck lid off a jar. This guy abducted Nina and kept her for a decade. Imagine someone buries you inside a time capsule, shutting you off from news of the outside world, then unearths you ten years later. And somehow you didn't age during the process. That's Nina Steyer. She's an adult, but mentally, Nina's still a kid."

"The kidnapper told Nina he murdered her mother?"

"From what I overheard, he told Nina many things to break her."

"So he brainwashed her." Darcy paces to keep the cold from catching her. "The killer kept her alive after murdering the other girls, so he considered Nina special."

"Nina filled some need for him, so he chose not to kill her. That explains why the abductions and murders stopped. He found what he was looking for."

Darcy can't imagine someone stealing her from her parents and locking her away for ten years. No chance she'll allow him to do the same to Jennifer. Is Jennifer a replacement for Nina?

"He started hunting again when Nina became too old for him," Darcy says, the explanation ringing true in her head. "And he killed the girls who didn't fit his type. But how did Nina escape?"

Fisher squints thoughtfully and moves his gaze over the forested hill.

"I don't think she did."

"Are you suggesting he let her go? Why?"

The agent narrows his eyes and strokes his chin.

"It's like you said. Nina outgrew her usefulness."

"She could have run to the sheriff the moment he allowed her to walk."

"Yet she didn't. Put yourself in Nina's shoes. For ten years, she believed her mother was dead. This guy fills her head with all sorts of insanity and leaves her with nothing. Then he tells Nina he loves her, she's special, and he'll give Nina the life her mother couldn't give her. Allow water to ripple through a stream bed for long enough, and even the sharpest stone becomes smooth."

Darcy clasps her hands over her head and walks in a circle.

"She began to see him as her protector and ally. Stockholm syndrome."

Fisher snaps his fingers.

"Good theory."

"That explains the aimless wandering. He shunned her, and she doesn't have anyone to turn to. Now she's lost, but she retained enough logic and survival instinct to inspire her to hitch a ride."

"Remember she's from Millport, not Scarlet River. Nina Steyer might not realize she's been living this close to her hometown all these years. He could have told Nina they were in Oz, and she would have believed him."

Darcy rubs the tension out of her neck as she wills Hensel to exit the van with the kidnapper's location. The FBI is taking too long to trace his Internet activity. With every passing hour, she fears a farmer will discover another dead body in the field, and this time it will be her daughter they find staring into the sky.

"Nina can only walk so far," Darcy says, looking up the hill toward the forest. "The kidnapper must live close to the falls."

"We assumed that much. But there aren't any residences once you get past the state park."

"He's living off the grid. That makes him harder to find, but he can't hide in plain sight."

"You'd be surprised how simple it is to disappear with a little know-how."

Another van climbs the hill, this one with a satellite fixed to the roof.

"Looks like the media vultures found out about Nina," Darcy says.

Deputy Filmore moves into the street to prevent the vehicle from getting too close. Following on the van's heels, a blue, rusted sedan skids to a stop before it blasts into the van's bumper. Darcy recognizes Cherise Steyer when she whips open the door. She rushes up the hill as a cameraman leaps from the back of the van to capture the drama. A second deputy joins Filmore to keep Cherise and the media back. A red-haired woman in heels thrusts a microphone in Filmore's face.

"Is it true you found Nina Steyer?" the woman asks the distraught Filmore as Cherise shouts her daughter's name.

The reporter's questions cause murmurs among the growing onlookers. Several people raise their phones to record the scene. When Darcy fears the deputies will lose control of the situation, the van door opens, and Hensel and Tipton step out. Reinhold and Nina remain inside.

"We've got a rough location," Hensel says. "Nina's confused, didn't even realize she's still in Georgia. She estimates the walk to the diner takes her about three hours. Given the harsh terrain, I can't see her keeping a fast pace, so that tells me he's about six to eight miles from Scarlet River."

"Can she take us there?" Fisher asks, digging the keys out of his pocket.

Tipton shakes his head.

"Not unless you want to kayak down the river in the dark. Once you pass Laurie's house, there aren't any roads beyond the falls."

"Helicopter?"

"That's an option," Hensel says, checking the time. "But a copter makes too much noise. Remember, he's holding two girls. God only knows what he'll do if he hears us coming."

Darcy's hands move to her hip. Her gun rests beneath her jacket, but Hensel must know she's armed.

"Then drive as far as you can, and we'll go the rest of the way on foot," Darcy says, causing Hensel to narrow his eyes.

"You're a civilian, Darcy. I can't take you."

"That's my daughter. The night I lost Jennifer you allowed me to help."

"You were a member of the search party, not on a rescue mission." She argues, and Hensel holds up his hand. "The answer is no. Stay back and let us save Jennifer."

Hensel hands her a key.

"What's this?"

"The key to my rental. I may be a hard ass, but I'm not stranding my old partner by the side of the road. Keep your phone on. I'll keep you in the loop throughout."

Darcy clenches her jaw, then shoots Hensel a tight-lipped smile.

"I'll give you two hours, Eric. After that, I'm going after Jennifer, with or without your help."

Hensel groans and marches past the reporter, ignoring her questions. Fisher gives Darcy a sympathetic nod over his shoulder. Should she take the gesture as an apology or a promise to save Jennifer and Sandy? One of Tipton's deputies piles into his cruiser with the two FBI agents, while Tipton stays behind until Reinhold finishes with Nina. The emergency lights swirl before the deputy executes a three-point turn and wheels the vehicle down the hill. The brake lights flare, then the cruiser disappears around the corner.

Darcy twirls the keyring on her finger, deciding her next move. No matter what Hensel says, she won't sit by her phone and wait for news. This is her daughter, her flesh and blood. A hand on her shoulder spins Darcy around. She expects to find the reporter firing off another round of questions. Instead, Cherise Steyer wrings her hands in front of Darcy as her eyes dart toward the van.

"I know you," Cherise says, swiping a tear off her cheek. "You're that lady from the restaurant in Millport."

"I am."

"You saw the girl Sheriff Tipton says is Nina. Please tell me. Is my baby inside that van?"

Cherise's eyes won't sit still, and her hands flutter like trapped birds when she speaks.

"Yes, that's your Nina."

Cherise releases a breath. Her shoulders slump forward, and she places a hand over her heart.

"I knew it. All these years I prayed God would bring my Nina back to me. Everyone told me she was dead, but I'm her mother. I'd know if my baby left the earth. When will they let me see her?"

"An agent is finishing up with Nina now, and then you'll see your daughter. But I want you to understand the agents will have more questions for Nina."

"Because they want to find the man who took her."

"That's right."

Cherise nods and lifts her chin.

"Nina is a strong girl, she always was. But if it's true those people saw Nina at the diner, why didn't she come home after she got free?"

Darcy bites her lip, remembering the kidnapper convinced Nina he'd murdered her mother.

"We'll find out more soon. Take comfort in knowing your daughter is alive, and you have the rest of your lives to make up for lost time."

Cherise chews a nail and stares at the van door. It's all she can do to keep from rushing the van and pulling her daughter into her arms. Darcy wants nothing more than to do the same to Jennifer. How can two days feel like forever? She can't imagine how Cherise kept herself sane for ten years, but it's clear Nina inherited her mother's strength.

"Hey, how come you're not with those FBI agents? I heard you work with them."

"Not since three years ago."

"You found my daughter. I don't care whether you work for the sheriff or the FBI or anybody. I owe you my life."

A vehicle door slams. Cherise jumps, but it's a newspaper reporter climbing out of his car. Though Cherise wants to see Nina, she's petrified. There's so much she doesn't know about Nina's abduction and the last ten years of the girl's life. Cherise's imagination fills in the details, and it's devouring the poor woman.

"Cherise, I can't imagine what Nina went through, but she made it this far. When you see your daughter, be there for her, but give her room."

Darcy wonders if the speech was for herself or for Cherise. The woman cups her elbows and gives a quick nod, then her eyes return to the van. The door opens, and Agent Reinhold supports Nina by the elbow as they step down. Cameras flash, and the two reporters shout a litany of questions as Filmore prevents them from advancing.

"Who kidnapped you, Nina?"

"Did he rape you?"

"Where is he keeping the other girls?"

Darcy ignores the reporters. She's a statue frozen in place as Cherise takes a hesitant step toward her daughter. Agent Reinhold whispers into Nina's ear and points at Cherise. The girl gives the profiler a frightened look, and Reinhold pats Nina's shoulder and nods. Nina stumbles toward her mother as if walking on stilts. Cherise's mouth quivers, and she lets the tears roll down her cheeks as she forces herself to wait for her daughter to come to her. When Nina is two steps away, Cherise opens her arms. The chasm closes between them, and Darcy's heart splits as mother and daughter reunite.

As Darcy moves aside to lend Cherise and Nina privacy, Reinhold finishes a call and hustles to Darcy's side. Filmore fields a call at the same moment, and Darcy's heart pounds as news spreads among the law enforcement contingent.

"We know who the kidnapper is," Reinhold says, answering the question on Darcy's face. "Eric Stetson, twenty-six Spruce Street in Scarlet River. Turns out he's active in plenty of chat rooms geared toward teenage girls."

Tipton points at Reinhold, who nods. She grabs Darcy's arms and holds her eyes.

"Listen, you're a civilian, but this is your daughter, and you'll beat us to Stetson's address if we leave without you. You're welcome to ride with us or follow in Hensel's SUV, provided you leave the investigation to us. Your choice."

"I'll follow, but this makes little sense. Nina's directions point to a remote area downstream from the falls."

"Yes, Stetson has a secret location, somewhere private to take the girls, but he owns property in town. With any luck we'll catch him at his official address."

Darcy draws in a breath.

"Okay, lead the way."

"But promise me you won't interfere," Reinhold says as they walk toward their vehicles. "You need to stand back while we enter Stetson's house."

"Deal."

Keeping Hensel's rental on the road proves challenging as Darcy's nerves unravel. The discoveries of Stetson's locations came too late. If only they'd found Nina a day earlier or brought Gil Waggoner in for questioning when Darcy first told Tipton about the incident at the grocery store. Something terrible happened to the girls. Darcy feels the truth in her bones.

Stetson's house is a decrepit two-story that appears as if no one has inhabited the residence in years. The porch leans to one side, and the white paint on the front of the house peels away to old, weathered boards. Blue paint covers the side of the house, an unfinished renovation for a dwelling Stetson doesn't care for. A tall wooden fence protects the backyard from prying eyes, and Darcy wonders what Tipton might find if he digs into the earth.

Darcy grips the steering wheel to keep herself from flying off the spinning earth. The engine ticks with leftover heat as she parks beneath a line of old trees. From the curb, she watches Tipton scale the porch steps while Reinhold circles around the back of the house. The female agent struggles to find footing as she scales the fence. Then Reinhold's athleticism and agility surprise Darcy when she pulls herself up and over. Darcy cranes her neck, but the fence hides Reinhold from view.

Tipton slips inside. The silence doesn't last long. As Darcy steps out of the vehicle, a gun blast flashes across the window and booms through the night. Instinctively, Darcy hits the pavement. Then she crawls over the curb and places her back against the oak, pulse thrumming as she slides the Glock out of her holster. Inside the house, a deadly silence runs as deep as the darkness at the windows. Where is Reinhold?

She can barely hold the phone as she calls Hensel. The phone rings and rings. He might not have cell coverage beyond the falls.

"Dammit, Eric. Pick up."

As Darcy races to the porch steps, she kills the call and dials 9-1-1. The male dispatcher sounds overwhelmed when he answers.

"This is Darcy Gellar at Eric Stetson's address on Spruce Street in Scarlet River. Shots fired in the house. Tipton is inside."

"Do you have eyes on the sheriff?"

"Negative. It's been a minute since the shot. No sign of Tipton."

The dispatcher requests backup, but the sheriff's department is stretched thin. With the last remaining deputy taking Nina and Cherise back to the station, Darcy worries the department won't have another cruiser to send.

From inside the house, footsteps pound toward the front door. Darcy raises her gun as the door slams open, and a pale-faced Agent Reinhold stumbles onto the porch. Blood covers her hands.

"Tipton's been shot," she says.

"Help is on the way," says Darcy as Reinhold races back inside to aid Tipton.

Two sirens scream from the far side of Scarlet River—one sheriff cruiser and an ambulance.

24

It's after nine when the paramedics wheel the gurney out of Stetson's residence. With Reinhold, two deputies, and the paramedics surrounding the sheriff, Darcy can't get a good look at Tipton. What she sees tells her the sheriff's situation isn't good. There's too much blood. It covers Tipton's button-down shirt and stains his hands. The door slams, the siren fires, and the ambulance speeds away from the curb with the cruiser in close pursuit. Filmore stays behind to investigate the house, but the stricken look on his face tells Darcy his heart isn't in it.

Reinhold shuffles toward Darcy, the profiler's eyes blank and lost as she shakes her head.

"It was a trap," Reinhold says, leaning over with her hands on her knees. "The bastard rigged a shotgun with a tripwire. No way Tipton could have seen it until he turned the corner into the living room. The damn fence slowed me down. I didn't even make it to the back door before I heard the gunshot. If I'd gotten to him sooner..."

Darcy kneels beside Reinhold and brushes the hair from the profiler's eyes.

"Don't go there. You did everything you could."

"No...no, I should have hit the back door when Tipton entered the house. This is my fault."

Darcy grasps Reinhold's chin and turns the agent's face toward hers.

"I could tell you plenty about the dangers of digging holes you'll never climb out of. Don't blame yourself. I went through first aid training before I became an agent, same as you. You believe either of us could have saved Tipton? We're not paramedics or doctors."

Reinhold nods without conviction.

"I know."

"Do you? Twenty-four hours ago, you talked me off the ledge. Allow me to return the favor."

Reinhold shakes the cobwebs out of her head and climbs to her feet. Her color looks better, and she doesn't wobble.

"I need to go back inside and help Deputy Filmore. What are you going to do?"

"Find my daughter," Darcy says.

She climbs into Hensel's SUV and fires the engine. A quick check of her phone shows no calls or messages from the search team. Speeding toward the other end of town, Darcy reminds herself wireless coverage is nonexistent beyond the state park and she shouldn't expect Hensel to pick up. But that doesn't stop the doubt from creeping up on her.

Stetson hid in plain sight for ten years. He's resourceful. While the rigged shotgun suggests organizational skills, it screams paranoia. Stetson has an escape route ready should the authorities converge on him. But no roads exist in the wilderness. He'll use the river. Stepping on the accelerator, Darcy steers the SUV toward Cass Park.

The park is pitch black when Darcy turns into the lot. Rocks ping the undercarriage, loud amid so much quiet. She finds a parking space beneath a tree at the back of the lot, reducing the chance Stetson will see the vehicle. The trail winds into the great unknown. As she touches the door handle, her phone rings. But it's not Hensel calling with an update. It's Laurie.

"Hunter's gone. I can't find him anywhere."

At the sound of Laurie's voice, the air rushes from Darcy's lungs. No, this can't happen. Not now.

"What do you mean he's gone? Weren't you with him?"

"Yes, I stayed in your room with Hunter. I had to use the bathroom, and when I came out, I couldn't find Hunter, and my keys are missing."

Darcy grips her hair in her fists and pulls, teeth gritted as she fights to keep control. Yes, she left Laurie in charge of Hunter, but she can't blame her cousin. This isn't Laurie's fault anymore than it's Reinhold's fault Tipton walked into a trap. Hunter planned this. He's on his way to North Carolina now.

"Okay, slow down," Darcy says as Laurie goes breathless. "This is on me. I should have seen this coming."

"Darcy, he was so quiet. I knew he worried about Jennifer, but he seemed to have it together."

"All right. Think, Laurie. Did Hunter act differently before you left the room? Maybe he received a text and looked upset."

"No, nothing stands out. Should I call the sheriff?"

Darcy pictures Tipton on the operating table, the doctors fishing a slug out of the open wound in his belly.

"No, let me call Hunter and talk some sense into him."

"I let you down, Darcy."

"You didn't. This is Hunter's doing."

She ends the call and leans her head back, eyes clenched shut. After she vets the furious responses firing through her head, she takes a breath and calls Hunter's phone. But her son doesn't answer. She should call the Genoa Cove PD. Give them fair warning and an opportunity to diffuse the situation. How does she tell Detective Ames her son intends to murder Aaron Torres without guaranteeing the police open fire the first time Hunter slips a hand into his pocket? It will take Hunter eight hours to drive to Genoa Cove. That buys her time to free Jennifer and get through to Hunter.

Darcy hops down from the SUV and locks the door, cringing at the loud beeps. After she scans the park for movement, she steps across the lot, her sneakers making scuffing noises on the stones. Chin up, Darcy blocks out the darkness. The night seems to slither around her, spinning around the playground equipment and dropping off the trees like an unspeakable evil. She's halfway across the grass when her limbs lock and her spine turns to ice. Darcy realizes she can't venture forth into the dark. Not alone. Willing herself to outrun her fears, Darcy struggles past the swings and toward the trail. She can see the path now, a silvery ribbon cutting through the heart of the copse.

It isn't until she's beside the towering slide that Darcy realizes she's stopped moving. It's the worst thing she could have done. Like standing on quicksand. Her legs freeze in place as her heart races at a dangerous speed. Her head spins, but she refuses to turn back. She can't let Jennifer down. Cursing, Darcy tries to step forward, but an invisible wall stands between her and the trail. Her legs give out.

"Please, not now," she mutters with her elbows on her splayed knees, fingernails digging into her scalp.

When a pair of headlights sweep across the playground, Darcy ducks her head and slides the gun from its holster. Ducking behind a tree, she watches the lights grow brighter as the vehicle turns into the parking lot. The lights are too high to be from Reinhold's SUV, and the unknown vehicle isn't a sheriff's department cruiser. It's a pickup truck. The killer?

The truck idles in the lot with the high beams flaring into the park. Then the engine cuts off. Darcy rubs the red imprints off her eyes as the dark becomes absolute again. A door opens. Footsteps track toward Hensel's SUV and stop as the unknown person examines the rental. It's quiet, the figure lost in the shadows. The footsteps angle across the lot, and Darcy glimpses the man's silhouette as he stops at the gate and searches the park.

"Mom?"

Darcy sobs with relief. It's Hunter. He's not driving to Genoa Cove, thank God. He's halfway across the park when Darcy crawls out of hiding and runs to meet her son.

"What are you doing here?"

"I came to find you."

Darcy wraps Hunter in her arms, relief pouring out of her that at least one of her children is safe. Holding her son against her, Darcy realizes her paralysis vanished the moment her son's presence distracted her from her fears. She hates herself for being too weak to rescue her daughter.

"You shouldn't have run off like that. Do you realize how much you frightened Laurie?"

"Tell her not to worry. I'll bring the truck back in one piece."

"But you should have checked with her first."

"Really, Mom? It's not like she would have given me the keys if I asked."

"That doesn't justify stealing the truck." Darcy peers over Hunter's shoulder. The park is empty except for them. "How did you know I'd be here?"

Hunter shows Darcy his phone. The Nina Steyer story headlines the *Millport Times* website.

"There's an update at the end of the story that the sheriff's department learned the kidnapper's name, and I knew Agent Hensel wouldn't allow you to join the rescue team."

Darcy remembers telling Hunter the kidnapper abducted Sandy Young at Cass Park. He put the clues together on his own.

"Listen, Hunter. It's a long shot the kidnapper will flee through the park."

Hunter raises an eyebrow.

"Then why did you come here?"

He's too smart for his own good, she thinks. It's dangerous for Hunter to be in the park, and she worries how he'll react if her theory comes to fruition and the killer arrives with Jennifer. The risk is worth it. Better to keep her eyes on Hunter than let him run off to North Carolina. And perhaps Darcy will better cope with her phobia now that she isn't alone.

"Fine, but stay behind me if the kidnapper shows up."

Hunter drops his hands on Darcy's shoulders.

"Mom, he's not leaving the park with Jennifer. She'd risk everything for us, so we'll do the same for her. I won't let her down."

Darcy's eyes glaze with tears. Her children are inseparable, and they'll defend each other against any odds.

"Then don't let me or Jennifer down by doing something stupid. I'm taking both of my children back to the hotel tonight, and I'm never letting either of you out of my sight again."

"Seriously? I'm going to college after next year."

"If I have my way, you'll earn your degree online."

They enter the trail side by side, mother and son against the dangers of the night. As was the case last night when Darcy investigated the park alone, the trail becomes too difficult to see once the tree canopy blocks the moonlight. Branches brush against her arm as she strays to one side of the path.

"You said the kidnapper took Sandy Young through the back of the park. How far until we get there?"

"Another ten or fifteen minutes. We should keep our voices down until we're sure we're the only people in the park."

Slowly, Darcy's eyes readjust to the dark. The heights and shapes of the trees make her skin crawl. The trees look like giants glaring down at them as they follow the path of dirt and leaves. Darcy's phone buzzes. She sighs with relief when Hensel's name appears on the screen. But as she brings the phone to her ear, her heart thunders with the possibility of tragic news.

"Hensel? Where's Jennifer?"

Darcy hears Fisher's voice in the background.

"The kidnapper must have taken Jennifer and run off. We found the house. It looks like a long abandoned home he discovered and fixed up. But Darcy, we found Sandy Young's body inside a bedroom."

Darcy drops to one knee. A cold sweat breaks along her brow as her stomach roils.

"Mom? What happened to Jennifer?"

Darcy shakes her head at Hunter and holds up a finger.

"Jesus, Eric."

"Sandy Young's body was still warm when we found her. No rigor mortis, so that indicates he's only an hour or two ahead of us."

"But you don't know which way he fled."

"We think we do. Fisher discovered several oars and a punctured raft behind the house. Appears you were right about this guy using the creek. The state police set up additional road blocks around the county, but we think he's heading for Cass Park." Hensel sounds short of breath. He's walking as he talks. "Reinhold is on her way to the park with Filmore, and the state police are sending a helicopter."

Darcy clears her head and struggles to her feet with Hunter's aid.

"Where are you now?"

"The three of us are following the creek. Just passed the falls and found shoe prints in the mud where he cleared branches and dragged the debris ashore." Fisher says something in the background. "Okay, Darcy. I gotta go. I promise I'll keep you in the loop."

"Thanks, Eric. You'll see me soon, regardless."

"Come again?"

"We're inside Cass Park right now."

"Who's we?"

"I'm with Hunter."

"Darcy, you can't be there with your son. Stand down. Let Reinhold and Filmore handle the rescue."

"Then you better tell them to hurry. I'm not going anywhere until his escape route closes."

He's mid-argument when Darcy ends the call.

"I take it you pissed off Agent Hensel again?"

Darcy glances at Hunter, the confirmation her theory is correct quickening her pace.

"I don't give a damn how many bridges I burn tonight. Jennifer is coming home with us."

25

The wind touches Jennifer's face and drags her out of her haze. She blinks and stares up at the starry sky, where the moon shimmers and leers down from the heavens, its eyes always following. The sight of the nearly full moon causes Jennifer's body to turn cold and rigid.

The raft hits a bump and bucks, a reminder of where she is. She recalls the kidnapper binding her wrists and ankles with rope before he filled the inflatable raft with an electric pump behind the house. It was the first time she'd examined the terrain surrounding the property. Though she'd hoped for a revelation of her location, she felt more hopeless than ever. The expanse of forest extended to the horizon, no sign of civilization anywhere.

Her head aches. She recalls the man striking the back of her head and neck when she refused to sit still while he readied the raft. The ropes prevent her from rubbing away the pain. Jennifer attempts to lift her head, but it's too heavy, bogged down and clouded. She can't see her kidnapper, but the raft leans toward his weight. The swish of water redirects the raft to the left, and she imagines him paddling around the rocks with an oar.

She forces her drooping eyelids to stay open. Closing them conjures memories of Sandy flailing while the monster murdered her. The lump in her throat can't compare to the one pushing sick up from her belly. Focusing on the night sky, she breathes and inventories her ankles and wrists. That's when she realizes the ropes around her wrists aren't as tight as those on her ankles. Furthermore, the floor of the raft puddles with water, greasing her skin. Given enough time, she might work her wrists free, but she senses his gaze and knows he expects an escape attempt.

Though doing so will haunt her with images of Sandy dying, Jennifer allows her eyes to drift shut. She hopes he didn't see her awaken. Flat on her back, she wiggles her wrists and bites her tongue as the ropes dig and burn into her skin. When he doesn't react, she pauses for the blood to rush back into her hands and fights with the ropes again. A strange whirring in the distance tempts her to stop and look. The sound fades as quickly as it began, and Jennifer wonders if she imagined the noise.

The raft smashes to a stop, causing Jennifer to pop her eyes open. They're not moving. She glances around and sees him climbing out of the raft. Before she can feign sleep, he grasps her shoulders and hauls her from the boat.

"Don't play games. I know you're awake."

While she squirms on her side, he grabs her legs and saws through the ropes with a knife. The feeling hasn't returned to her ankles when he stands her up and demands she follow. She spits at the maniac, catching him below the eye. The callused hands close around Jennifer's forearms and shake her until she screams in his face.

"Get away from me!"

"Move it, or you'll be joining your sister."

The whirring sound comes again, and Jennifer sees the cause of his consternation. A helicopter flies low in the sky, aiming a spotlight across the ground as it follows the stream. Tossing her onto the rocky shore, he drags the raft out of the water and jams a knife into the side. Air hisses from the tear as he plunges the blade into the opposite end. When the watercraft deflates enough to fold, he conceals the remains beneath a stand of shrubs. Then he drags her off the shore and behind the tree line just as the helicopter rounds the bend.

Gripping his hand over her mouth, he pulls her down before the spotlight sweeps over the trees. The helicopter passes overhead, the landing skids almost clipping the trees. Jennifer's heart sinks as the clamor fades, but already she hears the helicopter turning around for a second pass.

"Don't make a goddamn sound, or I swear I'll snap your neck. I can find another girl. You're not irreplaceable."

She bites his hand. Crying out, he shoves her to the ground and stomps on her shoulder. She grits her teeth, refusing to cry. But when he plants the toe of his shoe in her stomach, she curls into a ball and sobs into her arm.

"Get the hell up."

Wrenching Jennifer's arm, he pulls her up and prods her forward. As he steps ahead and parts a tangle of branches, she spots the handgun sticking out of his back pocket. The lesson with Agent Hensel on how to fire a gun seems like it occurred years ago, and he taught her with a rifle, not a handgun. What more does she need to know other than to point and shoot? She isn't sure. But he's left the grip exposed, the weapon taunting her to reach out and steal it from his pocket.

As she wiggles her wrists, the ropes loosen.

26

Darcy rounds a bend in the trail, paranoid she missed the secret path down to the stream. It seems they've been walking for too long before Hunter spots a break in the flora where Darcy fought her way to the water last night. He moves toward the opening, and she grabs his arm as an unexpected noise comes from the far end of the valley.

"What's wrong?" Hunter asks.

Darcy listens. Something in the sky. She's about to write off the sound as her nerves playing tricks on her when the distinctive chop and whir of helicopter blades travel over the stream. Leading the way into the thicket, Darcy ducks when the spotlight slashes across her face. The light blinds her, and when her vision clears, the helicopter has already swooped over the park and circled back.

Searching for an opening in the canopy, Darcy waves her arms at the helicopter's second pass. Wind generated by the blades sets the trees in motion and whips dead leaves into a cyclone. As they shield their eyes, Darcy and Hunter grab hold of the trees and descend the steep drop-off, the moon shimmering off the waters below.

A snapping sound pulls Darcy's head up. As if someone stepped on a fallen twig. She places her hand over Hunter's mouth to keep him quiet while the helicopter shoots over the creek.

There's no time to react before the gunshot explodes through the copse. The bullet ricochets off a tree trunk. An explosion of bark clips Darcy's forehead above the eye. She drops to her back, stunned, her vision black as she claws at the sodden earth above the creek. Hunter's warning rings out a moment before the next shot gouges a hole in the earth. He yells and falls behind Darcy, clutching his knee.

Darcy's vision clears, but her ears ring, the sounds of the forest muffled as if smothered under a blanket.

"You've been shot," she says, throwing her body over her son's chest to cover him.

"No, the bullet missed. A rock got me in the knee."

"Don't move."

He protests and tries to roll her off before another explosion flattens them, Darcy's hands covering the back of her head. She scans the forest down to the stream. The kidnapper must be close. No way he could see them inside the copse from across the stream. She slips her own gun from the holster and swings it across her field of vision. The next shot burrows into the earth a foot from her head. A blast of pebbles peppers her face and draws blood as mud and sediment rain down on her hair.

Setting her elbows on the ground, she aims the gun between the trees, eyes fixed on a narrow clearing between a stand of elms that might give the killer a sight line. At the same time, she maneuvers herself over Hunter and gestures toward the thick trunk beside them.

"Get behind the tree."

He shakes his head.

"Hunter, you don't have a gun."

He tenses his jaw and crawls on his belly toward the tree. Darcy exhales in relief when her son gets to safety, but then he limps to the next tree, and Darcy realizes he means to circle around the shooter and cut him off. Another blast drops Hunter to the ground. Darcy holds her breath until she spies his shadow slinking into hiding. It occurs to her she hasn't heard the helicopter in the last minute. Either the pilot set the helicopter down, or the helicopter is too far downstream. Someone must have heard the gunfire.

Light flashes across the water, and Darcy shoots the Glock. She rolls behind the trunk, expecting return fire. A second after she vacates her position, the ground erupts with gunshots. The killer fooled her, attempted to draw her out. He could have reflected the moonlight with a knife.

Unable to see the killer, she's terrified to shoot. Jennifer might be in the line of fire, but Darcy's daughter solves the problem by crying out. There. A hundred feet off to the right.

Just past the shoreline, a shadow ducks behind a small cliff. Darcy edges down the hill to the next trunk, her heartbeat loud in her ears as she searches for her daughter. A slap follows a muffled scream, and Darcy knows the killer struck Jennifer when she tried to warn them. As Darcy slips closer to the cliff, the helicopter rounds the high terrain of the state park and angles down the stream. The spotlight no longer sweeps the ground. It focuses on the cliff. The state police must have eyes on the killer.

Anticipating he'll grab Jennifer and flee, Darcy studies the land for an escape route. Either he reverses course and runs along the stream in full view of the state police, or he drags Jennifer up the hill and attempts to reach Cass Park. As Darcy leaps from behind the tree and moves along the hill to intercept the killer, three shadows emerge ahead of the approaching helicopter. Hensel's team. Darcy's heart fills with hope before the bullet slices across her thigh with white fire and drops her to the forest floor.

Blood soaks her pants leg. Pulling herself forward, crawling on her elbows, she ducks when another shot whistles past her ear. Unable to see the killer, she fires the Glock to the left of the cliff and toward the stream, hoping she can pin him down until Hensel closes in.

More shadowed figures descend the hill off to her right. Though she can't make out their faces, she recognizes the shapes as Reinhold and Filmore. They've hemmed the killer in, but the killer might murder Jennifer in his last stand.

Darcy catches the glint of moonlight reflecting off his gun when he rounds the cliff. Darcy is ready. She pulls the trigger.

The bullet clips the killer's kneecap and spins him around. As he stumbles beside the stream, the gun tumbles from his hand and vanishes beneath Darcy's sight line. Reinhold and Filmore are coming fast now, but they're still a long way up the hill. The three members of Hensel's team struggle along the rocky shore, shutting off the killer's escape route, but they won't reach the killer in time if he attacks Jennifer. Hunter climbs down the other side of the ridge, hangs over the cliff face, and drops to his feet, doubling over when his knee buckles. Hunter struggles toward the madman, diverting his attention. They've cut off all escape routes, but Darcy knows nothing fights harder than a cornered animal.

Darcy screams for Jennifer to run when the killer climbs to his feet with a knife. She focuses the gun on the killer, prepared to strike him down if he turns on her daughter. But Jennifer wavers on her feet in the line of fire. Spotting the agents cutting across the stream, Hunter yells for Hensel to hurry. But the FBI has the same problem as Darcy—Jennifer stands between their guns and the killer.

Why won't Jennifer run? With blood pouring from the killer's knee, he's in no position to beat her in a footrace.

Jennifer's chin hangs against her chest as if overcome by exhaustion. Ropes bind the girl's wrists behind her back. Darcy's breath hitches when one of Jennifer's hands slips free from the bindings. She uses her other hand to clasp the ropes against her back so the killer doesn't see them fall away.

While Hunter steps over rocks to cross the stream, the killer brandishes his knife so everyone can see. He wants everyone to stay back, realizing nobody will shoot through the teenage girl to get to him.

But there's one problem. He's blind to Jennifer's hands and believes the girl is about to lose consciousness when she feigns dizziness.

"Freeze! FBI. Drop the weapon."

Fisher's voice.

Under the moonlight, the killer's smile gleams as he stalks toward Jennifer. The world moves in slow motion, Darcy begging the FBI to open fire as she spins past Reinhold and Filmore for a better angle...the helicopter blades driving mist off the stream, turning the killer's hands slick...Hunter wading through the water and into the heart of the impending firestorm.

When the killer is almost upon her, Jennifer drops to her knees and grabs the fallen gun off the rocks. The man freezes, eyes wide. Jennifer squeezes the trigger.

Nothing happens.

The safety. Jennifer doesn't know how to unlock the pistol's push-button safety.

But the pause is all the FBI needs with Jennifer on her knees. Fisher's shot thunders into the killer's shoulder and twists him around. Darcy and Reinhold open fire. One bullet slams into the man's chest while the other grazes his forehead.

Yet the man maintains enough strength to lunge at Jennifer with the knife. But Hunter knocks his sister out of the way and Hensel drives his shoulder into the small of the man's back.

The killer's body slams into the shallows with Hensel atop him. There's a crackling sound as the man's head bashes against the rocks. His legs flail out, spasm, then drop still as the FBI agents and deputies surround the killer with their guns drawn.

Ten seconds of mayhem, then it's over.

27

Agent Hensel and Deputy Filmore drag the broken body of the child murderer off the rocks as the hot glare of the helicopter's spotlight turns night into day. As Darcy huddles with Hunter and Jennifer on the shore, Hensel reads the killer his Miranda rights. It doesn't matter. The murderer is incognizant to Hensel's words, losing blood and minutes from death. A Medevac helicopter sets down in a clearing above the ridgeline, but Darcy knows the killer will die before he reaches the hospital.

Agent Reinhold rides with Darcy, Hunter, and Jennifer on the way to the hospital. Once inside, Jennifer peels off her drenched clothes and changes into the dry replacements Laurie brought. Even after she changes, Jennifer's teeth chatter as if her bones iced over. The doctor, a small man with an overbite, diagnoses Jennifer with a concussion, but Darcy knows the real wounds run deeper. Did her daughter watch Sandy Young and Emily Vogt die?

Darcy requires three stitches for the wound across her forehead. She's lucky. The bullet missed her head by inches.

Hensel ducks his head inside Darcy's room after the nurse clears out.

"How are you holding up?"

"As long as I have my children, nothing else matters. What have you learned about Stetson?"

"No priors. He worked as a private contractor, mostly odd jobs, and led a double life. The house in Scarlet River looks barely lived in."

"So he didn't do eight years of jail time."

"No. He was content holding onto Nina Steyer. Reinhold has two theories. One is Stetson lost interest in Nina after she matured and started kidnapping and murdering teenage girls again. The other is he contacted Michael Rivers and began hunting."

"That would explain why he stalked Laurie."

"Right. He was following orders. No reason to believe he found an interest in women his age. The Rivers connection also explains Stetson's obsession with Jennifer."

"And the private contractor angle makes sense. Stetson had the skills to repair an abandoned house."

Hensel nods, but there's a grim set to his jaw as he closes the door behind him.

"There are things you need to know. Stetson kept the girls in a spare bedroom with the windows boarded over. He chained them so they couldn't escape."

Injury and rage work through Darcy. What sort of animal tortures teenage girls?

"Bruising around the neck indicates Stetson choked Sandy Young. Darcy, we think he made Jennifer watch."

A sob comes out of Darcy's chest. The light in the room seems to fade as she clutches her arms around her chest.

"How does my daughter come to terms with a nightmare like that?"

Hensel falls into a chair beside Darcy's cot and uncertainly places a hand on her arm.

"I don't know, but that girl of yours shows more fight than most of the agents I know. If it wasn't for her, I wouldn't have gotten a clear shot at Stetson. The newspapers will say the FBI and sheriff's department saved Jennifer Gellar, but she saved herself."

"But he murdered a girl in front of her. That's not an image she'll ever escape."

"You'll get her help, Darcy. And if she's anything like her mother, she'll survive and become a stronger person."

"Like me?" Darcy's laugh doesn't meet her eyes. "I'm afraid to walk into a dark room alone, and my cousin needs to count my anxiety meds so I don't overdose. Face it. I'm the last person my daughter should use as an example."

"And yet you were dead on about Stetson using the stream to travel between his home and Cass Park, and if it wasn't for you, Cherise Steyer would fall asleep tonight wondering if her daughter is still alive and if she'll ever see her again. Your instincts remain sharp. You're still the best profiler I ever worked beside."

She expects he'll make another pitch for Darcy to come back to the BAU, but he doesn't. Maybe that train left the station, or he doesn't trust her to stay clean. She's known Hensel long enough to recognize when something is on his mind. He has more to tell her, and she can tell by the way he works the words over in his head that it's not good news.

"Just say it, Eric."

It's late, well after midnight, though she's lost track of time. Hensel sits back and moves his eyes to the window. Lights flood the parking lot with harsh brightness. The moon is on the other side of the hospital, but she knows it's there. It will follow Darcy to her grave.

"Tipton didn't make it," Hensel says, rubbing his eyes with his thumb and forefinger. "The sheriff never regained consciousness. He passed before they got him onto the operating table. I realize you thought highly of him."

Darcy lets her head fall back against the pillow and closes her eyes. The last week feels like a blur, none of it real. Tipton didn't take Laurie's stalker seriously, and in a panicked state he pressed Darcy and Hensel, the two strangers in town, after Sandy Young's abduction. He'd overstepped his bounds, but Tipton wanted nothing more than to solve the ten-year-old cold cases and prevent another nightmare.

"He was a good man," Darcy says, turning away from Hensel to stare out the window. "All he wanted was to protect those girls and bring peace to their families. If there's a heaven, he's smiling at what you accomplished tonight, Eric, and he's shaking his head that Nina Steyer, the girl he searched for, pointed the FBI to the killer. Besides Cherise Steyer, who would have believed Nina was still alive?"

"You did, Darcy, and you had as much to do with catching Eric Stetson as any of us."

"This county won't be the same without Tipton."

"No, but Deputy Filmore is acting sheriff, and from what I've heard, he's a shoe in to win the next election. Tipton was grooming the kid to take over when he retired, and Filmore was born and raised outside of Millport, so he has an in with the voters."

Hensel notices when Darcy doesn't respond and clears his throat.

"Anyway, Gil Waggoner still has the charges hanging over his head."

"Conspiracy to kidnap?"

"It's questionable if they can make it stick, but Waggoner

ignored Tipton's orders and tried to flee town. State police picked him up outside of Scarlet River."

"I'm worried about Waggoner, Eric."

"You're worried he's a kidnapper in the making."

"Or a rapist. He's working up to it. Waggoner attempting to coax an underage girl into his vehicle is a red flag, and I'm certain he would have attacked Jennifer and me had I not pulled a gun. My guess is he's used chat rooms to proposition teenagers before. I don't buy Waggoner's bullshit story he was only helping Stetson."

Hensel nods before his phone rings. He glances at the screen, intending to ignore the call. Then he raises his eyebrows.

"Problem?"

"It's Quantico. I better take this. We'll discuss Waggoner later."

"Sure," Darcy says, pulling the blanket over her shoulders as the room empties.

Though she's on the third floor, she locks her gaze on the window, afraid if she turns away someone will climb through. The night holds many dangers. Like Richard Chaney, Eric Stetson was another pawn for Michael Rivers to play. His obsession to murder Darcy and her family only grows. There are others, she knows, and they're coming for her soon. She'll deal with the dangers when they present themselves. For now, her only concern is keeping her children safe.

Hensel speaks in the hallway for two minutes, during which Darcy runs scenarios through her head for how best to approach Jennifer about long term psychological counseling. Her daughter is stubborn and too self-conscious of how her friends perceive her. She'll fight Darcy on this, but if her daughter has any hope for a normal adulthood, she needs to talk about what happened.

Darcy loses herself in thought, absently massaging her forehead around the wound, when the door reopens. Immediately, she knows something terrible happened. Hensel's face is drawn, eyes flitting around the room but never meeting hers.

"What is it?" Darcy asks, easing her leg off the cot. "Is it my kids? Talk to me, Eric."

He swipes the hair off his forehead and leans against the door, arms dangling at his sides as if they turned to rubber.

"Eric?"

"That was the Deputy Director. There was an incident at the prison in Buffalo."

Darcy sits up and swings her legs off the cot.

"What kind of incident?"

"They found two of the guards with their throats slashed. Michael Rivers is missing."

"He couldn't have escaped. The prison is locked down twenty-four hours a day."

Hensel taps his finger against his phone, considering.

"New York State Police set up choke points around the prison, and Rivers' photograph is on every news channel in the northeast. They'll catch him, Darcy."

But Darcy knows they won't. This time the Full Moon Killer isn't sending one of his followers to end Darcy's life.

He's coming for her, himself.

And she'll be waiting.

~

Thank you for being a loyal reader!
Ready to read find out what happens next?

Read Whispers in the Dark today

GET A FREE BOOK!

I'm a pretty nice guy once you look past the grisly images in my head. Most of all, I love connecting with awesome readers like you.

Join my VIP Reader Group and get a FREE serial killer thriller for your Kindle.

Get My Free Book

www.danpadavona.com/thriller-readers-vip-group/

SHOW YOUR SUPPORT FOR INDIE AUTHORS

Did you enjoy this book? If so, please let other thriller fans know by leaving a short review. Positive reviews help spread the word about independent authors and their novels. Thank you.

Copyright Information

Published by Dan Padavona

Visit my website at www.danpadavona.com

Copyright © 2020 by Dan Padavona

Artwork copyright © 2020 by Dan Padavona

Cover Design by Caroline Teagle Johnson

All Rights Reserved

Although some of the locations in this book are actual places, the characters and setting are wholly of the author's imagination. Any resemblance between the people in this book and people in the real world is purely coincidental and unintended.

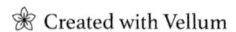

❀ Created with Vellum

ABOUT THE AUTHOR

Dan Padavona is the author of the The Darkwater Cove series, The Scarlett Bell thriller series, *Her Shallow Grave*, The Dark Vanishings series, *Camp Slasher, Quilt, Crawlspace, The Face of Midnight, Storberry, Shadow Witch*, and the horror anthology, *The Island*. He lives in upstate New York with his beautiful wife, Terri, and their children, Joe, and Julia. Dan is a meteorologist with NOAA's National Weather Service. Besides writing, he enjoys visiting amusement parks, beach vacations, Renaissance fairs, gardening, playing with the family dogs, and eating too much ice cream.

Visit Dan at: www.danpadavona.com

Printed in Great Britain
by Amazon